THE
BUSINESS
OF
Death

LEIGH TEALE

 *Midnight Starling Press*

THE BUSINESS OF DEATH © 2014 by Leigh Teale

This book is a work of fiction. Characters, businesses, organizations, places, events, and incidents either are the product of the author's imagination or are used fictitiously. Any resemblance to actual persons, living or dead, events, or locales is entirely coincidental.

Midnight Starling Press
www.MidnightStarling.com

ISBN: 978-0-692-26965-7

First Edition: August 2014
Printed in the United States of America

10 9 8 7 6 5 4 3 2 1

With all my love to

Mom & Dad

for encouraging me to write
and listening to my stories.

*"The thing always happens that you really believe in,
and the belief in a thing makes it happen."*
Frank Lloyd Wright

And to

Chapter Eight

and all the wonderful times
we never had.

Prologue

MALLORY watched the pretty colors swirl. The scattered pills looked like candy littering the carpet. Her vision tumbled and twirled, the lack of focus hypnotizing. With a laugh, she stretched out her hand and brushed her fingers through the air. Mahogany strands tickled the sides of her face as she tried a pirouette. Stumbling, she grabbed the edge of the threadbare couch. A giggle escaped as her mind wove through jagged, crystalline thoughts. Who knew revenge could be so beautiful?

Revenge. Beautiful revenge. Sweet, like the antifreeze cocktail she'd used to wash down the pretty candy-pills. Satisfying, like the knowledge she'd finally won. Yes, she, Mallory Devlin, had won at last. Twenty-five years of torment and disdain, bad luck and broken dreams, and she had won. Perfect Miss Jackie wouldn't be so perfect anymore. Now, she would have to survive on her own. Now, she couldn't steal Mal's world. She couldn't break her. Jack couldn't feed her perfect life with her sister's ruins anymore.

Three times Mallory'd tried to confront her, tried to bring her down. Each time ended worse than the last. She'd never even left the ground, the planes outside the terminal mocking her, their pointed faces looking down on her, always looking down like everyone else. Deriding her. Stopping her. Fourth time's a charm, though, she thought. All she'd needed was a change in tactics.

If Jackie wouldn't let her be, then she'd find another way out. A back door, an escape, a release from the plague of problems that had followed her since birth.

It was all so perfect. What would Jackie do now? Nothing. Nothing, nothing, nothing. She'd be helpless without Mallory. Jackie was a vampire, sucking the life out of her twin by inches, taking Mal's luck and dreams to make herself whole. What would she—what could she do when the food ran out, though? Mallory smiled again, wobbling a little.

Suddenly, the arms gripping the couch grew weak. Mallory collapsed on the cushions, pulling her limbs in close with a shiver.

Her eyes grew heavy as the pain rolled in. It was new and unexpected. Her skin began to crawl as her stomach coiled. She moaned, then sighed as it passed, then moaned again. Weighty with drugs and delusions, her head lolled back on an old embroidered pillow. With limbs suddenly leaden, Mallory found she could no longer sit up. She struggled for a moment before letting the current sweep her out once more. The pain spread, but it was a distant sort of fire.

Through the haze, a woman approached. Mallory tried to call out, tried to ask what the hell the stranger was doing in her house, but her tongue was swollen and numb. Mal's eyes fluttered once, then twice, as she struggled to focus on the wavering woman. As she fought against it, her throat convulsed. Burning liquid surged from between her gasping lips only to be breathed back in again. Surrendering to what she couldn't control, her chest shuddered. It made a deep, rattling, moist sound, like tumbled pebbles in the surf. Then it was over.

The woman held out a hand and Mallory took it, sitting and then standing with surprising ease. Disappointment seethed through every pore like the sheen of sweat on her skin. Wistfully, she looked down at the couch, expecting to see the mess of medications and vomit. Instead, Mal's own body, pale and grotesquely skewed in its death throes, stared back at her. The stranger's face remained unmoved by the spectacle.

"Come along. It's time."

Mallory's lips curled in a new smile, sharp and hungry with possibility.

It was indeed time.

THE BUSINESS OF DEATH

Chapter
One

DEATH stared out at the lowering day as he nursed two fingers of scotch. From an expansive pane, he peered at the busy waters of the Loire River and the imposing Château des Ducs de Bretagne beside it. His eyes flickered over the scene. When he'd first picked it as his eternal view, he thought he'd be pleased to be "back" in Nantes. But the city had changed so much in the last eight hundred years that even his fuzzy memories couldn't find a home here.

The sky mirrored his mood. It didn't rain often, but the area always seemed to have a saturated cast of wetness, even when the sun shone. Outside the trees bent nearly double by the spring wind. The boats of the Loire continued to chug along against the gale, and the black and white flag atop the next building snapped proudly at attention.

He tossed back the last of his drink and walked away.

A vacation, he decided. That's what he needed. A nice, long vacation. They'd grown fewer and farther between since he'd taken over as Head of Human Demise. So many minor military disputes found ways to bleed into major wars, and with seven billion souls in the world, sometimes the job became unwieldy.

But where to go that was fresh?

China had been quite the learning experience in the mid-fourteenth century. He winced at the memory of Yangzhou before locking it down until only the whisper of a name remained.

Katerina.

He considered pouring himself another drink, not that it helped. He tried to refocus his train of thought. The last few decades had seen his fill of Africa. The U.S. perhaps? It was an interesting country, though it lacked much of the history that the rest of the world bandied about like currency. A road trip would be different. Cliché, but different. Yes, a road trip through the U.S. might be a nice way to escape the business of death.

In the meantime, there was a departmental meeting to attend. Checking his watch, he strode out of his office, through the reception area, and around an endless supply of corridors.

Five divisions fell under the heading of the Department of Death and Demise, and each acted with autonomy. Sure, war had to be sanctioned, and plague needed the assistance of his Charonites, but the day-to-day running of things did not require meetings. When the Director wanted to make a department-wide change, however, everyone had to be present.

Yawning, Death took the nearest seat and listened to Henrikson and Kali discuss where the lines separating destruction and famine should be drawn. Rohitashva and Leukippos wandered in as the debate escalated, murmuring a quick "Arthur" to him as they sat. He greeted the latter with as much civility as possible. Human Demise had not played well with Pestilence since the black plague; too much personal history simmered between them. Finally, after several minutes dripped by, the Director of the DoDD waddled in to begin the proceedings.

Across the table, Death saw Kali wince at the garish blue of the director's ill-fitting suit and mismatched tie. Santana Nickleby was a corpulent soul, with dark hair flipped up on either side like unkempt horns, and an oiliness that pervaded his mannerisms. The latter was only faintly masked by the air of power he created around himself like a bubble.

Nickleby settled into a chair at the head of the table and spread out a sheaf of papers with practiced care. For several long minutes he forced each of them to recount their department's latest actions, whittling away the time until he could spring his newest idea. Finally, after Death was ready to hang himself from boredom, the director cleared his throat.

"As I'm sure a few of you have heard, I've been looking into a new matter. Rohitashva, you've done a fine job coordinating, strategizing, and implementing the current civil unrest. And, Arthur, your Charonites have been a great help with the cleanup. However, we all know it just isn't enough to keep up with such an explosive population. If we don't get this under control, everyone," he glanced at each of the unmentioned three in turn, "will have to speed up their present plans. And, frankly, it's only going to cause more work for Human Demise."

He paused and gave Death a pointed look, daring him to dissent.

"Therefore, I propose we create a new division solely for the oversight of HOHs. Not just to escort the souls to Purgatory, as the Charonites already do, but to intercede as necessary."

"Intercede?" Death interrupted. "You mean instigate."

Nickleby chuckled in the pompous, condescending way that never failed to tread on Death's last nerve.

"A whisper in the ear, a slight spiritual nudge. 'Instigate' is such a terrible word. We're not the ones pulling the trigger. Besides, think of all the good it would do. A reduced population would ease the strain on the entire planet. Not to mention, if we created a new division, some of the burden would be lifted from your people." The slick sound of his logic caressed the other four, Death could see it in their faces and the slump of their shoulders, but he sat resolute.

"Human-on-Human deaths are precisely that for a reason," he shot back, his voice steely and even. "They are mortal actions stemming from mortal choices. The things you're suggesting have to be sanctioned to prevent abuse. Creating a whole division dedicated to the stimulation of HOHs is a strict violation of the Basic Tenets of the Beyond. Humans have no purpose without free will, and I can't imagine the other Powers That Be would take it in stride."

Nickleby's upturned jowls grew predatory.

"Arthur, I'm warning you. I've taken your lip too many times over the last few centuries. This measure is for the good of not just the Beyond, but the human race. Think of how much better off the populace would be if it were smaller, not only for the living generation, but the generations to come. They are destroying the planet simply by reproducing. It would be a simple matter to take in hand." His face slid back into geniality, encouraging and coaxing.

"Come now, let's vote, shall we? Those in favor?"

Nickleby lifted a pudgy hand into the air, light glinting off the six rings crammed onto four fingers. With only the slightest of hesitations, Kali, Rohitashva, and Leukippos raised their hands in affirmation. Henrikson's eyes darted back and forth between Death and the Director. His hand twitched. Death saved him the trouble and stood.

"You only called us in here because you know you won't be able to get a majority vote from the other Powers That Be. Well, I cannot in good conscience give you the unanimous approval you need from us to counter that. If you'll excuse me, I have legitimate marks to claim."

Nickleby's face turned apoplectic with rage as Death straightened his tie and swept from the room with goading serenity. On his way out, he passed a young girl with her fist raised to knock on the conference room door. She tilted her head at him, curious, but he breezed past her. No time like the present, he thought as he made his way through the narrow hallways and cramped corridors of the Beyond toward what amounted to their HR department.

If Nickleby thought he could get away with the creation of an HOH division, he had more chutzpa than Death gave him credit for. There were many and varied rules to being dead, but the over-arching theme was a reverence for free will. The only department exempt was that of Fate, and even they tried to leave as much wiggle room for mortals as possible.

When the Basic Tenets were violated, often it was the Fates who stepped in to "fix" things. They were the shadows that lurked in the lower floors of the Beyond. Their agents roamed the Earth, correcting issues and gathering data, while the three Heads of Fate sent out missives to the other six departments. Everything from who was scheduled to die to who was flagged for what job in Purgatory somehow started in their department.

Nona, Verðandi, and Atropos weren't the only things to fear, though. The Powers That Be had their own way of dealing with wayward immortals. Death thought back to the little girl at the door of the conference room and shuddered. Some things were worse than an angry Fate and an inquiry—though an inquiry in and of itself often meant the end of your career.

As he pondered, he took an elevator, then a few more corridors and a flight of stairs, before arriving outside a suite labeled "Immortal Resources." Breezing through the entrance, he found a young man in Victorian spats and braces sorting through folders.

"Thom, I need to speak with Amraphel. Is he available?"

A moment later a middle-aged man in rabbinical dress appeared. The yellow and red of his ephod stood starkly against the white of his robes. Amraphel stepped forward and shook

Death's hand before ushering him into the inner office.

"What can I do for you?" he asked once they were comfortably seated. Death steepled his fingers.

"I'm tired, Amraphel. The machinations are getting old, the battles are unpleasantly predictable, the bureaucracy is tedious to say the least. Simply put," he released and spread his hands like a magician, "I need a vacation."

"A what?"

"A vacation. You know, a bottle of bourbon in one hand, a bottle of suntan lotion in the other."

Amraphel fidgeted with his already straight yarmulke. "My good man, you are death personified. Death does not simply take a holiday."

"But, it could. I have. Others have taken on high-residual cases before, and there are plenty of Charonites who can handle the rest of the duties for a few days. They might even be able to survive without me for as much as two weeks."

The other man's eyes sprang wide. "Two weeks!?"

"Maximum," Death replied.

"Two weeks is a bit much, don't you think?" Recovering his composure, Amraphel stood and walked toward a large calendar graffitied with color-coded notations. "Maybe one week. Maybe. One of the Middle Eastern wars is winding down, and I know a few people who can step up for a time." His gaze turned thoughtful. "Check back toward the end of the year. I'll consult with Nickleby, and we'll make a decision by then."

End of the year? Death knew changes took time in the Beyond, but it was only the beginning of April. Death gave a quick bow of acknowledgment before leaving to return to his duties. His fingers itched to slam the door, but he refrained. Calm. He'd allowed himself to be worked up by Nickleby. It was unfortunate; it seemed like no matter how hard he'd tried to control his emotions, after eight hundred years things still slipped inside. Death let out a slow, sigh-like breath as he walked back to his office.

While two weeks was a long shot, he had hoped they wouldn't drag Old Nick into the equation. He would never consent to give his least-loved employee a break. Things had been fine between the two of them for a few centuries until Death had ascended to his current position. But once he became Head of Human Demise, Death saw his superior for what he really was.

Over the last six hundred years their working relationship had become strained. While Nickleby couldn't fire him—Death had never overstepped company policy—he could make the afterlife very uncomfortable. In the last century alone, Death's role had been expanded far beyond acting leader of the Charonites. While this sounded nice, the truth was that it chained him to a filing cabinet with only a small number of hands-on cases per day. What was the point in being Grim Reaper if you were rubber-stamping forms behind a desk?

Shaking off his gloomy thoughts, Death reached into his pocket and withdrew an inch-long scroll. As he unrolled it, the vellum grew until it reached the size of a regular sheet of paper. Across the page flowed glowing gold calligraphy in a classical hand. Each line held only a name, leaving the timing and method up to him. Unlike his predecessor, he had a penchant for the uncanny or dramatic and had garnered quite the reputation for creativity. Few people died of old age or mundane health problems when they were on his list.

Other lists existed, of course. The simple cases, the older marks, and even the very young were farmed out to the Charonites. However, the "high residual" cases—those whose demise would have unforeseen, yet far-reaching impact—were his. Rarely famous, most of the time they were average people who never saw it coming. Through their deaths, however, they acted as the first domino in the intricate pattern of a living universe.

All but one name on the day's list had been crossed out. He'd finished most of his rounds earlier in case the meeting took longer than scheduled. Focusing on the final line, he flipped through the associated file in his mind.

Jaime Farris was a good guy, a little high stress perhaps and without any real hobbies, married six months and up for a promotion. Such a pity to kill him. Well, it would be a pity, if he let such things get to him. It had been a long, long time since he'd felt sorry for a mark. Death was inevitable, after all. The one constant in an ever-changing world.

Collapsing the parchment and returning it to his pocket, he strode down the hall and emerged on the greens of Fort Tryon Park, New York. Projecting, which caused new immortals no end of frustration, came as easily to him as breathing used to. It was a perk of the job, being able to quickly travel from one place to another, and he never grew tired of it. Death simply focused on his destination as he walked, and within seconds, he emerged just outside his intended end point.

Cars rushed past him on a nearby road, ruffling his titian hair and flapping the edges of his suit. With eyes like blue ice, he waited. Not blinking, not breathing, just calculating. Angles, velocity, probability all flashed through his mind faster than the blonde in the pink shorts could jog. She didn't spare him a first glance.

A sudden gust of wind swirled around an aging oak. There was an earsplitting creak, followed by a series of staccato snaps. The great tree tipped precariously before toppling onto a passing car. Screams rang out as Death walked to the wreckage and helped the driver out of the carnage. Witnesses ran over manning cell phones like life preservers, some calling for emergency services while gawkers took photographs.

"Oh, God! I can't believe that just happened!" Jaime ran his hands down his rumpled clothes and through his hair. "I've got to call my wife. Has anybody seen my phone?" He rushed about like a mad man, turning out his pockets and accosting people nearby. "Hey, mister, can I borrow your cell?" he asked a middle-aged man who was gaping at the wreck. "Mister?"

Abruptly, Death's victim froze as if realizing only one person in the crowd was paying the least bit of attention to him. Death stood watching him with a neutral expression. The sounds of the world faded as the young man turned in place. Belatedly, he seemed to notice where the tree had fallen.

"Oh," he repeated, this time with several shades more disappointment. Death laid a pale, freckled hand on the younger man's shoulder as Jaime let out a final sigh. All around him, Death knew, the world began to drain of color as it faded to light.

When the young man was gone, Death scanned the faces of the crowd before departing. It interested him to observe the living in a crisis. Their emotions ran wild from curious and gossip-hungry to distraught and panicked. He made a step forward to return home, then stopped.

There, on the sidewalk, stood a leggy brunette loaded down with equipment bags. She was pretty enough, he supposed, the fan of her hair and slant of her mouth tugging at his memory. But what really grabbed his attention were her eyes. Though their hazel-brown was obscured behind oblong frames, for just one second she had looked at him. Not past him, not through him, but *at* him.

The moment their eyes met she glanced away to find a cab, but he knew and was unnerved by it. Death took a few surreptitious steps forward, focusing on her life aura. Blacker than oil it shone in a body-hugging ribbon. He relaxed. Often those about to die could see him. In all likelihood, she was on one of the other rosters for later in the day.

No sense in waiting. Flipping backward through her record, he searched for an allergy or other useful information. Then, he stopped and stared, all pretense of composure deflating. A faint shimmer surrounded the black like a shield of gold.

Impossible! Stunned, he marched forward until he disappeared. Moments later, he continued pacing the checkered tile in his flat.

Black gold!

For years he'd theorized and mused. He'd turned and toyed with the idea, but that's all it was: an idea, a mental exercise. Years and years ago he thought he'd seen it, but he'd been mistaken. Besides the memories best left undisturbed, deep down he couldn't help but take it as a personal affront. It was as if she'd walked right up to him and dared him to off her.

Disgusted, he threw himself into an overstuffed chair. For several minutes he brooded. It wasn't possible. If he'd never seen black gold in eight centuries with the Department, why would he now? He gave himself a mental dressing down, more upset over his reaction than at the supposed slight. Leaning forward, he poured himself a drink from an elegant carafe on the table.

Studying the amber liquid through his crystal tumbler, he considered all the possible explanations. The most credible answer would be wayward lights or an aura ripple. Maybe she was a sunny yellow and his eyes had been playing tricks on him. Not that that was much better, but it was a far easier explanation. A fellow didn't get to the position of Grim Reaper by way of a short fuse. Methodical, logical, calm: those were the keys to the game.

There was no such thing as black gold.

Jack stared at the place where the stranger had stood. She'd emerged through the park trees only to be arrested by the sight of twisted metal pushing up around a rotten trunk like a lover. In the middle of the panic, a solitary man calmly surveyed the scene. He stood out, not just as a pillar of calm within panic, but for his looks. He was tall and lanky, his parchment-like skin clinging to the angles of his face and hands. The dark blue material of his suit was well tailored, but only served to make him stand out more in the crowd of business casuals.

As his gaze swept the crowd, it connected with hers, and a knife-like sense of déjà vu threatened to overtake her. Tearing her eyes away, she raised a hand to hail a cab. When she looked back over her shoulder a moment later, he was gone.

A shiver ran up her spine as she climbed onto the cracked leather seat with all her equipment. Before the car drove off, she double-checked her lot. Reflector. Light box. Francesco. She ran a loving hand across the camera case as she gave the driver her address. As soon as they pulled up outside the apartment complex, a frazzled blonde burst from the lobby.

"Where have you been?" Her tone was accusatory and Jack couldn't really blame her. It was already mid-afternoon, and she'd promised weeks ago to help her friend pack.

"I'm sorry, Lindy. The shoot took longer than I thought."

"The shoot? You said you had the day off. You said you took the day off weeks ago, specifically to help."

"I know, I know. I did. But Louis called and…"

"Louis!" Lindy nearly spat the name as she helped Jack lug her equipment inside. "Girl, if you're going to jump every time he says go, at least get a ring." Heat from Jack's cheeks battled the cool press of her glasses.

"It's not like that," she mumbled as Lindy dragged them into the elevator and hit the button for the fourth floor.

"Honestly, Jack, you need to learn to say no more often."

Jack closed her eyes and took a deep breath. The irony of the statement wasn't lost on her, but to keep the peace she made light of it. "I said no last week when everyone wanted to go to a bar."

"You're allergic to alcohol. What were you supposed to do, drink water for five hours before calling a cab?" Lindy unlocked the door and maneuvered the reflector down the hall and into the living room. Jack groaned inwardly as she spotted the single brown box in the foyer. She put Francesco on the couch before storing the other equipment in the closet. Then, she counted to ten before walking into the far bedroom.

It was a disaster area.

Lindy had taken all the clothes from her wardrobe and piled them on the bed. In another corner, she'd begun stacking books and papers and picture frames. Unassembled cardboard boxes lined the floor. To top it off, the owner of the mess was nowhere to be seen, though Jack could hear her speaking to someone on the balcony. Jack popped open a box with a shake of her head and got to work.

Several closed lids later, Lindy waltzed in, her sour mood from earlier transformed.

"Oh! I can't believe this is really happening. You know, my aunt once told me that New York City was where dreams went to die, but just look at us. You're a famous photographer, Veronica is a fabulous pastry chef, Patrice is doing... Whatever she's into this week. And I'm getting married!"

Jack didn't have the heart to remind her friend that she was far from famous, Veronica hated her job—or more specifically, her boss—and Patrice had just been let go from yet another temp agency. The packing tape made a shrill shriiiip-ing sound as Jack sealed off her sixth box of knick-knacks.

"Do you think you could move some of these boxes into the hallway?" Jack asked. Lindy's face fell, but she complied. Jack looked at the clock and realized with shock how late it had become. If she'd just kept the one promise instead of trying to please two people, all of this would be done by now.

Leaving a note this morning saying she'd be back soon had seemed like a good idea, but clearly Lindy had taken it as an excuse to delay the process. Jack may have issues saying 'no' but at least she didn't have dependency problems. Todd, the cause of the cardboard boxes, was in for a reality check once the honeymoon ended. Shaking her head, Jack ran a marker across the top to indicate what was inside before moving on to the next pile.

"Next."

The line – one of many that spiraled in all directions – shuffled forward. At first Mallory found the stark whiteness of the unending room nearly blinding after the dimness she'd kept her house in. Now, though, it was as if she'd always been here.

How long had it been? One day? Two? Maybe even a week. Time seemed to run both fast and slow here; fast enough to convince her it would all be over soon and slow enough to feel like eternity. At least it gave her time, though. Time to think. Time to formulate a new plan. Death had not been the escape she'd looked for. Obviously, it was something much better. If she could ever get out of this damn line.

Pressure rose in her chest, the need to set her plan in motion stirring violently within her chest. It made her fingers tingle and curl, her shoulders roll uncomfortably, and her feet tap to the annoyance of those around her.

"Next."

With a jolt, Mallory realized she was being

called. She practically ran from the front of the queue to the desk a few yards away.

"Name."

"Mallory."

The dumpy little man behind the counter looked over his spectacles at her.

"Full name."

"Mallory Isabelle Devlin."

He shuffled through a stack of files until he found hers. She noticed a red sticky-flag hanging out the side and leaned closer to read it. The man snapped the folder shut beneath her nose and gave her a much harder look than before. Mallory settled back with pursed lips.

"So, what now? You just check me in and then I can go back?"

"Go back?" He sounded confounded, as if no one had ever made that presumption before.

"Yeah, you know, haunt people. Be a ghost. Whatever."

"My dear, this is the Beyond. You are dead. There is no going back."

Now her agitation boiled to the surface. She'd waited, she'd kept her cool all this time in that stupid line, and he was going to tell her she couldn't go back? That she couldn't enact her new plan?

"That's impossible! I have things to do. You can't keep me here!"

His stony look transitioned back to boredom,

as if he'd heard it a million times before. "Miss Devlin, you have been tagged by the Fates as a possible recruit. You have three choices. You can either accept their offer and become an agent of destiny, you can move along to your predetermined afterlife, or you can stand over there," he pointed at an even longer and more snarled line than the one she'd just left, "and file a complaint."

Mallory's thoughts raced. An afterlife was out, plain and simple. There was nothing she could do from either Heaven or Hell. Clearly filing a complaint was useless in this place. That only left the Fates. Her eyes narrowed.

"What does a Fate do?"

He laughed. The sound made her blood sing in her ears and brought whispered images of strangling him into her brain. She struggled to hold it in, to remain calm and make a new plan.

"You won't be a Fate. Those three keep everything running smoothly, like an IT department or the CIA. No, you'll be one of their agents."

"Like a secret agent?" she asked, catching the mention of the CIA.

"Hardly. You'll investigate when things go awry with destiny and report back. If you stick it out long enough, you might be invested with the power to fix problems. Unless you plan to hang on for at least a millennium, however, you'll never make it to be a Fate. As you can imagine, retirement doesn't happen very often in the Beyond, and the Fates already have a replacement lined up for when the next one goes."

"If I work for the Fates, can I go back? Is there a way? For destiny, of course." She added the last with a nervous emphasis as his gaze sharpened.

"I've half a mind to request a redirection for you." He opened her file once more and began flipping pages. "With your attitude and," he raked his gaze over her, "assets, I think you'd be much more suited to the DoDD. You're exactly Santana Nickleby's type, attractive and teetering on the edge."

Mallory's anger surged like acid, boiling away at her insides. The last thing she expected to carry over from life was a reputation for being crazy. She opened her mouth to yell at him, to tell him where he could go and what he could do with his opinions, but he cut her off with a practiced air.

"You've obviously got some unfinished business that's driving you. If you really want to do anything about it, the only person that will help you is Old Nick."

He stamped several of her pages and slipped a new one in from another pile. Then, he slid the folder to her. "Report to the Fates for now. Go through that door at the back and give this folder to Nona. Good luck. Next!"

Mallory picked up the file and looked around

for the door. It was barely visible in the distance, a white door against a white wall. She walked to it and tugged it open. Inside lay a black hole. Not an imploded star and not a hole in the floor, but utter blackness on every surface. It was so dark she couldn't even tell if there was a surface. Certainly there was no "Nona." With a tentative step, she pushed herself into the void.

She shut her eyes tight, afraid of the dark for the first time in two decades, and took another step. Mallory choked down a breath and took a few more. Then, the color behind her eyelids began to lighten. Peeking through her lashes, she found a dimly lit office with a woman staring at her. Without a word, Mallory handed her the file.

"Ah, Miss Devlin. We've been wondering when you'd arrive."

"They should really do something about how long those lines are. It's ridiculous!"

"What, in Purgatory? No, my dear, I meant when you would cross over. You've been tagged for quite a while now."

"What? Why?"

"Existence, both above and below, is about balance. You have none. We needed the help, and you are the most likely candidate to learn a lesson in balance while maintaining enough of your faculties to get the job done."

"God, I can't even escape the shrinks by dying. I should have picked the afterlife."

The woman gave her a paper-thin smile.

"Go see my sister Verðandi down the stairs and to the left. She'll show you around and give you your first assignment."

THE BUSINESS OF DEATH

Chapter Two

MALLORY slunk through the dimly lit corridors toward what she hoped was an elevator with a directory. A chair squeaked in an office behind her, and she whipped around in paranoia seconds before slamming into something solid.

She reeled back, pressing herself against the wall and eying the woman she had nearly trampled. The young woman's crushed linen shift was partially covered by a twisted wrap of black Spanish lace, which wound around her arms and flowed down like sleeves. Her wavy brown hair reminded Mallory strongly of herself when she got out of bed in the morning, and her hazel eyes were a dead match for Jackie's. Mallory straightened like a ramrod, the memory of her sister bringing to the fore why she had to get out.

"And who are you?" she asked with renewed

aplomb.

"They call me l'Tradita." The woman drew herself to her full height, suddenly imposing and a little bit regal. "You must be Miss Devlin. We've been expecting you."

Mallory waved the last comment away, trying to keep the conversation off herself. "'They call me?' Nobody talks like that. What's your real name?"

"I chose to lose my own name long ago. Seven centuries is a long time to dwell in the dark, and some things are best left in the antemortem."

"Antee-more-tehm? What's that?"

"Life. Or Hell, I suppose, depending on your perspective."

"Oh. So there isn't a real Hell, then? They mentioned an afterlife when I first got here."

"Yes, well, the people in Purgatory would know more about it than I. I wouldn't know, never having had an afterlife myself. If you'll excuse me." L'Tradita resumed her path down the hall, and Mallory swelled at the idea she hadn't been questioned, that she might make it where she needed to go without any unnecessary explanations. Then she realized she had no idea how to get where she was going. Maybe it would be worth it to ask; surely her luck would hold out for one more question.

"Hey, drama queen, do you know how to get to the DoD?"

"The DoDD, you mean? Whatever do you need with Nickleby's department?"

"I can't discuss that right now," Mallory replied with a feigned air of importance.

L'Tradita narrowed her eyes and titled her head ever so slightly. Silence reigned between the two of them for longer than was comfortable. Finally, she set her garnet lips and pointed a long, elegant finger in the direction Mallory had been heading.

"It would be wiser to keep your distance from those who deal in death. However, if you choose not to take my advice, then take the stairs at the end of the hall. Go up one flight, then left. Ride Elevator B to Floor 15 where there's a directory that will provide further assistance."

With that she walked away. It was all Mallory could do to keep from high-fiving herself. She was getting out of this God-forsaken basement, getting to where she needed to go, and getting the job done. There was so much more scope for revenge in death than there'd ever been in life. This new plan would work for sure, and then Jack would pay for everything.

In the distance she heard the grandmotherly tones of Nona, pitched high at l'Tradita's entrance. "Ah, Katerina my darling, you're back! Have you met our new recruit?" Mallory rolled her eyes and started down the hallway.

Up one flight.

Left.
Up fifteen floors.
Right.
Right.
Down one flight.
Left.
Up two floors.
Switch elevators.
Down four floors.
Right.
Left.
Down one flight.

If she wasn't dead, she would have been worn out by the time she reached the section of the Beyond ostentatiously labeled the Department of Death and Demise. Impressive lettering hung above the entrance to a cavernous reception area lorded over by a tiny woman with explosively red hair. Soon Mallory found herself seated in a very rich, very masculine office, feeling her way along with her feminine wiles.

Mallory crossed her legs in a demure fashion, even as she tilted the rest of her body in a much more inviting manner. It was the little things, she'd learned in life, that could get you what you wanted. Certain people needed to see certain things. Her eyes remained downcast as she gave the Director a cat-in-the-cream smile. Every bit of her exuded innocence and vulnerability, but the invitation was there. As expected, her prey practically salivated on his tie.

"What can I do for you, young lady?"

"Well, you see, sir," she began, lifting her eyes but leaving her lashes lowered for effect, "I was told you could help me. I have unfinished business, and I'd do anything to be allowed to take care of it."

"Anything, hm?" He pulled at the collar of his shirt. "Well, well, what kind of unfinished business are we talking about?"

"It's my sister. She made my life a living hell. She drove me to death, and before that she spent twenty-five years stealing everything I ever wanted, ever needed. I just want to return the favor."

He eyed her shrewdly.

"Were you a killer in life," he paused to look at the file before him, "Miss Devlin?" All the gruesome thoughts she'd had through the years, all the impulses she'd never acted upon—though just barely—reared their head in her mind's eye. Swallowing hard, she stood and closed the gap between them with a slinky gait. Mallory leaned a hip casually against the side of the big desk.

"Does it matter? I was told you could fix any problem. Someone with that kind of reputation must be pretty powerful. Maybe the most powerful person in the Beyond." She trailed the fingers of one hand down his arm. Her voice took on a low, smoky timbre. "Like God." His pupils dilated at her words.

"And, what exactly would you have God do?" He closed in on her now. The heat from his breath brushed her arm. Mallory raised herself slightly and sat precariously on the edge of the desk, her legs dangling mere inches from his. Her eyes remained hooded, inviting, while her trailing hand worked its way down his chest.

"Whatever he wants. Forever's an awfully long time to sit behind a desk."

She made what she hoped was a noise of disappointment as he pulled away. Rolling his chair over to a bookshelf, he removed a slender volume. The cover was faded and worn, but she could just make out gold etching where the title should have been. It was unreadable now, but the book seemed to radiate a power that demanded reverence. He laid the book on the desktop and flipped to a blank page.

"This is the Book of Mortal Correction. If something changes, if an unscheduled death is specially sanctioned, or if a human is missed, it's written in this book and will appear on the appropriate list for immediate demise. Now, let's see." He took out a fountain pen and scrawled the date across the top of the blank page. Then, he handed it to her. "Just there, on the top line. Make sure you write the full name, and as you do so, focus on your intended."

Mallory looped her sister's name onto the page

while concentrating as hard as possible on the last time she'd seen her. Her smile held the ferocity of a lioness on the hunt. She couldn't wait to see dear Jackie again.

The noise of the cafe swirled around her. Normally Jack enjoyed setting up camp here, liked the music, liked the smells, liked the quiet. Quiet was something entirely different from her current surroundings. True, she usually came in the early evening, after the office had closed, but before she inevitably trudged home to Lindy and Todd making out on the couch.

For lack of anything more enticing to do, like sleep, Jack was now being serenaded by the cacophony of the early morning coffee shop. Easily three times as many patrons wove in and out, each entrant ringing the little bell, each table holding conversations, each cup being called aloud as the cashier flirted with the customers.

"Will that be all for you today, Mr. Denevieve?" the girl at the register asked coyly as she leaned forward on the counter. The guy in the EMT jacket murmured a response and then moved off to the barista's everlasting disappointment.

"What can I get you today?" she asked the next man with a much more porcelain smile.

"LAURA!?" called the man behind the

espresso machine.

"And then I said, 'Stacy you can't just leave him. Think about all that money!' And she said— can you believe what she said? Just imagine! She said, 'But, Terri, I don't love him.'"

"Soy non-fat latte with an extra pump of chocolate-hazelnut and a scoop of toffee crunch. Don't forget the whipped cream."

"NATE!?"

Pursing her lips, Jack snapped the screen of her laptop shut and stuffed it into her bag. She'd get more work done at the circus. She glanced at her watch. It was close enough to opening that security would let her in the office building.

Grabbing her gear, she swung out of her chair and towards the door, nearly colliding with someone else who was leaving. The EMT from earlier tried to apologize and opened the door. Flustered, Jack ducked her head, murmured a reciprocal apology, and hurried out toward the nearest subway.

Half an hour later, she adjusted her glasses and squinted at her desktop computer. The headache threatening behind her eyes reminded her she needed to make another optometrist appointment. She clicked through the photographs from the night before.

Layout and Design only needed four or five pictures, but she always gave them an abundance of options. Each one she selected had to be scrutinized and touched up within an inch of its life. Jack dragged the stylus with care along another area, sharpening the edge of the Atlantic sea scallop. She was so intent on her task that she didn't hear the footsteps approaching her cubicle.

"Those frown lines are going to become permanent."

She jumped at the sound of Louis' voice, knocking over her pencil cup and sending the contents flying. Her upturned face flushed as he watched with mild amusement. He leaned his arms against the top of the barrier and gave her a blinding smile that stretched his thin, dark face.

"I'm sorry. Did I frighten you?" He swooped inside the five-by-five box and knelt to help her pick up the rogue items. "How're the pictures coming?"

"They're great. They just need a little bit more work."

"Jack, honey," he stopped and put a hand on her shoulder, "how many hours have you already put into these?"

She shrugged. "A few. It's not a big deal; it's my job. I'll have a folio sent to L&D by this afternoon."

"When you say a folio, you mean you're sending them at least twice as many as they asked for, don't you?"

"It's always best to have choices," she replied, putting the ceramic mug and its collected contents back on the counter.

"This is why I call you my rising star. You're dedicated. You're relentless. You're a perfectionist. You're amazing. But I have to wonder, do you ever take a break? In four years, I've never seen you so much as enter the break room. Even yesterday, your day off, you still went on assignment for me."

"What would you have done if I'd said, 'Sorry, Louis. I'm busy hauling off yet another roommate. You'll have to do it yourself.' Besides, I take breaks. Twice a week I go down to the bagel shop for lunch."

"Because I used to send you as an intern. And you still bring one back for me. Do you see where I'm going with this? I worry about you. The last thing I want is for my rising star to burn out."

Jack pressed her lips into an appreciative look. Louis was more than just her boss. He'd been her mentor since college and within the last year he'd also become her friend. His large brown hand drifted from her shoulder to squeeze her knee, but there was nothing sexual in the gesture. Her therapist had once asked if she fancied Louis, and she'd had to laugh. The thought of ending up in bed with the lanky, gay man had been the highlight of a particularly depressing session.

"Thanks, Louis, but I'm fine. Really. I just need to finish these up." She spied the folder tucked beneath his arm. "You came down here with another assignment, didn't you?" Now it was his turn to show mild embarrassment.

"There's a fashion shoot down on First and Lexington later this afternoon. Becca's still out with the flu, so I thought you might be up to it. I didn't see anything else on your roster that couldn't wait until tomorrow." Jack slipped the file out from his well-manicured hand and flipped through it.

"No problem, Louis. Just let me send these off and I'll head down."

"Thanks, darling. I knew I could count on you."

"Always." He left her with the file and turned to walk away. However, fishing in his pocket, he returned and held a note out to her.

"Oh, Rochelle asked me to bring this to you. She said some woman called looking for you, but that she couldn't get through to your line." He peered over at the large gray desk phone. Aggravation suddenly overtook Louis' otherwise friendly voice.

"We've talked about this, Jack. This is a business. You can't just unplug the phone. What if L&D had a problem on their way to proof? What if Angie called? She's my boss! How am I supposed to explain why you're unreachable? I mean it this time. Keep it plugged in or you'll leave me no choice."

He shook his head before continuing in a

calmer tone.

"It's bad enough you rarely charge your cell. What if there was a family emergency and someone needed to reach you?"

"What family?" she responded, her voice quiet and laced with sadness. "I'm sorry, Louis. I'll keep it plugged in." She took the note from him, before reaching over to snap the line back into the wall and turning back to her computer.

Death sat in the back most booth of a New Mexico diner. The chrome and Formica décor screamed 1960s Americana the way little else could, but the framed periodicals and little green tchotchkes made sure you knew where you were. In the corner lounged a wizened old trucker whose auras glowed soft gray and forest green. Passing on from him, a young couple sat in deep discussion. The woman kept vacillating from off-white to charcoal, signifying she was making a life changing decision. Her luck aura, however, held steady on a very telling magenta. Noting her, Death moved on to the middle-aged lady walking through the door. Her peach polyester suit clung to her curvy frame in the oppressive heat. Huge glass pearls choked at her neck and her overstuffed purse thwapped softly at her side. A thick swath of midnight enveloped her, highlighted by a thin line of sapphire blue.

Death's lips twitched in approval. Blue was the color of those that made their own luck. True, hers was about to run out, but she'd fought her own battles and won her fair share of them, he'd wager. He himself had been a blue once. Of course, he'd also been a hard drinking, masochistic son-of-a-bitch, but he liked to think people could change.

Something dignified for Miss Gladys Fanton, he decided. Seven times out of ten he would have her choke on a sandwich or maybe have an allergic reaction to lettuce. Not for a hardworking blue, though. A simple heart attack, perhaps. He didn't often do simple, but then, he didn't often do blue.

As he fixed it in his mind, she rubbed her arm and ordered an unsweetened tea from the counter. Knowing it might take a while depending on her tenacity, he slipped into the men's restroom to corporealize before resuming his seat. The smell of the food set off an echo of hunger in him that, while unnecessary, would be a pleasure to fulfill.

Startled, but less so than she would have been if he'd simply appeared in the booth, a waitress sallied over. Sixteen going on sixty, she had a platinum ponytail and stage makeup that cracked in the dry desert air. Snapping on bubblegum the color of her lipstick, she gave him an I-hate-my-job smile.

"What can I get you?"

He spread a napkin in his lap as he contemplated. Eggs and soldiers, he thought. There was something rustic yet satisfying about cheesy scrambled eggs and a pile of shiny sausages. Of course, he'd prefer to wash it down with something a bit more stalwart than coffee, but these kinds of establishments tended to frown on that.

Favoring her with a placid look, he placed his order and turned to check on his mark. The woman was still seated at the bar, ignoring her symptoms in favor of some paperwork. He was impressed and flicked through her file. She was tenacious, all right. At heart, she was an entrepreneur and just successful enough to push herself even harder. This time, though, it would serve to make things worse.

Sighing, he dialed up the pressure and turned his attention to the plate Brynda-with-a-Y placed before him. By the time he finished eating, the job was done. He threw a few bills on the table, decorporealized in the ensuing hubbub, and led a protesting Miss Fanton to her postmortem. Playing escort to the unwilling was not his favorite way to wrap up a job, and he was glad when he could move on to the next soul.

If the air had been Saharan in New Mexico, it was a veritable oasis in Cuba. Death walked out onto the streets of Old Havana and almost admired the glitter of wet asphalt. Checking his watch, he headed south and east, winding his way through both wide thoroughfares and tight alleyways until he reached a small cobbled square.

People milled around the enclosure in various acts of preparing for a party. Women set up wooden booths and decorated them with fabric and cut paper. Another collection arranged flowers in various pots and vases. Behind them, along an ancient brick facing, a young man braced a ladder against an archway, and atop the rungs stood a little old man stringing colorful lanterns.

As Death watched, the old man twisted around and told his spotter to fetch some more hooks. At first, the younger man protested and started to call another man over, but after a sharp command he left his post to follow directions. The older gentleman shook his head and turned back to his task. As he reached high to place another fixture, his boot slipped on a well-worn step. He scrambled to regain his footing, but the damage was done. The ladder wobbled, and he grabbed the lantern string for the little stability it offered. Instead of supporting him, however, the weight of his struggling body twisted the wire, garroting him. As he struggled, the ladder fell with a splintering clatter to the ground. Pop, pop, pop went the hooks holding the lights in place. In a puff of grey-brown dust, the lifeless body hit the cobblestones.

Death strode over and dusted off the soul that

clamored to its feet. Señor Torres' brown leather face was lined with deep sadness. The old man ran a gentle, invisible hand over the black hair of his granddaughter who knelt wailing beside his body. With an instinct born of faith, he seemed to know what had happened and who the Englishman in the suit was. He closed his eyes and took a last, deep breath before fading away to his final destination.

When his mark was properly queued in Purgatory, Death pulled out his list again.

There weren't that many today, an oddity in itself. Wednesdays were the Mondays of the Beyond. No one quite knew why, but as far back as his memory stretched the workload always hit its peak on Wednesdays. Tuesday, by comparison, had been busy as he tried to cram everything around that blasted meeting and a backlog of paperwork. Today's abbreviated list was just one of many things that had seemed off since yesterday. Dismissing his thoughts, he turned back to the roll and browsed the names that had not yet crossed themselves off. Then, in a week already filled with more turmoil than he'd dealt with in a long time, he frowned.

Chapter Three

IGNORING the elevators, Death took the stairs two at a time, weaving down hallways and cutting through offices to reach his own. Striding into the room with practiced silence, he perched on the edge of his secretary's desk and waited for her to surface from her current pile of paperwork.

When she noticed him a less-than-prim squeak of surprise leapt from her lips.

Like most secretaries, Gina Valenka was a reflection of her boss. She wore neatly starched collars with conservative skirts; her taste in jewelry was old-fashioned and impeccable, and though thinning, she kept her black hair swept up in a way that proclaimed her as the one in charge. Perhaps she smoked too many cigarettes, which annoyed her employer, but she often said the same thing about his drinking habits. Single, meticulous, and at the peak of their professions, they made a perfect match.

"Gina," he said her name in an even tone, picking at a wayward piece of lint on his suit sleeve. "Did you make my schedule for today?"

A single line of annoyance furrowed her brows. "Of course, sir. Yesterday."

"And has anything unexpected come up since then?" With the offending lint gone, he leveled his gaze with hers and tilted his head a fraction. The air grew electric, dangerous and cold despite his neutrality. The look of professional annoyance slid off her face as her hands began to flutter.

"No, sir. Of course not." It had been close to a century since the last incident. The nightmare of paperwork that had followed had been enough to make anyone check their work twice. His already thin lips narrowed as he leaned close to her.

"And the only way my list can be altered is through you, correct?"

"To the best of my knowledge, sir. That's protocol."

"Allow me to rephrase, then, Gina. Does anyone else have access to the master list?"

"You know that's against the rules, sir. There are regulations, checks and balances." She unlocked her desk drawer with a trembling hand and slid out a slim ledger. In silence, she flipped to the entry for April 5th. Then, her hands froze. Her wide gaze shot to his.

"That wasn't there this morning."

Once more, they looked down at the name under Gina's French manicure. Jacquelyn Katerina Devlin. The script was wide and rounded. Unlike Gina's handwriting, which prided itself on beautiful efficiency, this had too many curls and stood too upright.

"No, Ms. Valenka," he replied, frost edging his voice. "It wasn't." In a swirl of dark blue silk and confirmed suspicions, he was gone.

Death strode down the passageway to the Director's office. After a few moments, the passage flared into a semicircular reception area with two monstrous desks flanking the sides like guard dogs. A young woman sat by the entrance flipping through a magazine, but her place in his mind was fleeting.

Like a hawk waiting to strike, another woman perched behind one of the two large counters. She eyed him as he approached the large, wooden door centered on the back wall. Sweeping across the frosted glass pane in thick black letters were the words:

Santana Nickleby

DIRECTOR

Death didn't bother with the pretense of knocking as he blew straight past the protesting secretary and ignored the askance look from the waiting soul. Opening the door, he walked up to the big desk. Death stopped inches from the man behind it and stared him down until he hung up the phone.

"Ah, there you are. I've been expecting you. Anything interesting happening in the world of the living?"

Death fought to keep his face impassive. "Define interesting." He took a seat with more care than necessary. A chuckle sounded from behind the over-sized heartwood desk.

"Oh, come, now. Something must have happened for the great and powerful Grim Reaper to storm back to his flat in a huff yesterday."

"With all due respect, I don't take kindly to spying. You should remind your minions of that."

"Not going to talk about it, eh? What could have been so infuriating as to break that icy façade? All the people you hate are dead, and you'd need a heart for love. Death has no natural enemies. Tell me," Nickleby inquired, leaning forward, "what makes a man like you tick?"

"Nothing," Death lied, unable to iron out all the terseness before it escaped. "But, that's not why I'm here, and you know it." He leveled his steel-like gaze on his superior and churched his fingers. A signet ring, quartered with lions passant and fleur de lis, flashed in the florescent lighting.

"Do I?" Nickleby gave his visitor a grin reminiscent of a bulldog, his jowls lifting a fraction before falling back down with a weighted jiggle.

There was danger in Death's narrowed eyes.

"The name. Where did it come from?"

"I'm sure I have no idea what you're talking about." Nickleby examined his fingernails, not bothering to hide the lie from his tone of voice.

Death stood and slapped his hands on the desk, leaning forward. "There are channels. There are protocols. There's goddamned paperwork! You don't just add a name to my list and expect me to swing a scythe."

The air tightened, and a bulb flickered overhead. The man in the chair maintained his placid look.

"Again, I have no idea what you're talking about. And, even if a name did get added to your list, I'm sure there's perfectly sound reasoning behind it."

"Who is she?"

"Why don't you go find out for yourself? I have more important work to do than curate a dossier for you." With that, Nickleby turned back to his work, dismissing his incensed employee.

Back to New York, Death thought grimly. Despite the population density, it was unusual to find himself in New York City. To him it was crowded, noisy, and just plain unpalatable. Charonites handled a lot of the marks in such conditions. Imagine if everyone who shuffled the coil in the five Burroughs died of an "act of God" or an ironic accident. No, most passed on in the usual way. Health problems made up the bulk of it, though until a few years ago there had been a steady rise in HOHs.

Human-On-Human deaths were not something his division had a hand in. True, someone had to be there to make sure the transition went smoothly, but associates were never to cause one human to end another with malice unless cleared by a higher authority. As he'd tried to remind Nickelby, HOHs were a mortal choice resulting from mortal issues. In general, only the most novice of Charonites received those lists with exact times and places at which to be present. These deaths introduced them to the business and acted as a quick way to harden them to their duties. There was no room for runaway emotions.

Finding Jacquelyn, like most of his marks, required a process. Projecting was a skill honed through time and technique. First, he focused on the name, allowing it to drag his consciousness through her typical routine. As he narrowed in, the patterns became more specific.

On Mondays she skipped lunch and picked up Friday's dry cleaning. On Tuesdays and Thursdays she took an extended morning break for coffee and returned home by six. Wednesdays she holed up in the office and disconnected herself from the world. Something was different today, though.

He could almost see her, a dark shape making

her way through a blur of city sidewalks. As his body followed his mind, the image became clearer and clearer until he pushed past to stand just a few blocks ahead. When the scenery cleared, Death looked around for a means of demise.

A large geranium rested a little too close to the edge of an overhead balcony. Not quite spectacular enough for someone who was going to hogtie him with red tape. A name appearing from out of nowhere was bound to come with at least an inch of paperwork. The rusted grating over a manhole looked promising in its fragility. Then, he spotted another woman on the opposite side of the street. She rocked a stroller as she looked back and forth for an opportunity to cross. Examining the pair closer, he saw a cream aura encircling the baby, accented by a thin stripe of red.

Death smiled.

The mother began to cross the street as a taxi came roaring over a large hump in the road. She would have made the opposite sidewalk—close but without incident—except that one of her stroller wheels loosened and turned crosswise. To avoid her, the taxi swerved into the path of an oncoming Lincoln, which in turn swerved onto the roadside as Jacquelyn passed. As she lifted her foot to step into its path, her cell phone rang.

The bright sound of Mozart's Violin Concerto in A blaring from the pocket of her sweater made her hesitate, and the corner of the sedan grazed the edge of her arm instead of slamming into her body.

Death stared at her with incredulity. He knew now why somebody wanted her dead, and he couldn't blame them. He wasn't crazy, and he definitely hadn't imagined things. She existed and the wrongness of her existence boiled beneath his skin. As she looked around in shock at the scene that had just unfolded, she caught his eyes for the second time in as many days.

Marked for death, but too lucky to die.

Black gold.

With barely a stride, he was back where he began. The look of surprise at his quick return slowly dissolved from Nickleby's face as Death paced and ranted with barely a breath between.

"For centuries I've made inquiries. Not one person in this whole Godforsaken place has ever had the decency to take my theories seriously! A few have even laughed at me. But now that one's turned up, everyone is more than willing to let me deal with her."

"Slow down. What on Earth are you talking about?"

"Black gold."

Nickleby screwed the cap back on his fountain pin and carefully set it to the side. In the pervading silence a typewriter could be heard from farther down the hall. Tap, tap, tap, ping! The Director cleared his throat.

"Black gold? You expect me to believe this mysterious new mark of yours is black gold?"

"She is."

"A myth you've toyed with for nearly a millennium suddenly proves itself to be real, and you don't even bring her back with you as proof?"

"And how was I supposed to do that? Her luck is perfect in every way. It's like a slap in the face. She's supposed to be dead, only I can't lay a finger on her."

"So you didn't kill her, then?"

"Of course not! Fulfilling such a mark will take thought, finesse... Time."

"I see." With that, Nickleby went back to filling out forms, stamping files, and signing contracts. Frustrated, Death began to ramble off different ideas for dealing with her. Occasionally, the Director looked up at his irate visitor, but he said nothing.

"... I could trap her in a room. A dark, impenetrable room where she'll never escape. Three or four days and no amount of luck will save her. Not elegant, certainly, but it could work. I could orchestrate an explosion. With a close enough proximity, she'd have no chance of escape. Perhaps there is someone close to her that's unlucky enough to cause a dip in that sparkling gold shield. Once they're together I might have the opening I need. No, that's no good. It'd be faster to just appear, tell her the problem, and ask her to off herself."

Death shook his head as he wound down. It was obvious his boss had lost interest long ago. He doubted Nickleby could repeat a single word back to him. Death leaned over the desk with both hands braced, staring the Director full in the face.

"Well?" Death asked with a hint of desperation. Despite their rocky relationship, there was no one else he could go to in such a situation. Mirroring Death's actions from just a few short hours ago, he templed his fingers and tapped his full lips with the steeple.

"I think you're absolutely right."

Death's shoulder's slumped as he propped himself against the arm of a chair. His eyes still reflected an inner maelstrom, but relief relaxed the taut muscles of his face. "You do? Which part?"

"You need a vacation, and a vacation you shall have." Death opened his mouth to protest, to explain how important this girl was, but Nickleby held up a hand while passing a folder across with the other. "Amraphel already talked to me, and it's done: Administrative leave at its finest. Take as long as you need. One week, two weeks, just go. Oh, and try to remember that your time among the mortals, however temporary, comes with restrictions. If you forget, we'll have to remind you."

The last statement lit up his eyes with a look of malicious pleasure. Once the folder left Nickleby's hand, he turned his attention back to the scatter of papers in front of him, a smile lingering on his face.

"See Ms. Fezwick on your way out. She'll give you anything else you may require."

Seething from the tone of dismissal, Death straightened with reluctance and returned to the reception area. While it was true he'd asked for a vacation, what he wanted now was answers. As he approached the mountainous counter to his right, Ms. Fezwick held out her hand for the file.

Luneil Fezwick's diminutive form sat atop a stool that leveled her with Death's six-foot-three. Hair the color of burnished copper was pulled back tightly from her pixie face only to explode into a halo of fiery corkscrews. Blue almonds peered from behind half-moon spectacles and were accented by a thick circle of kohl, and her pouty lips dazzled in Hollywood red. Her skirts were high and her necklines low, and she could tell you to go to Hell in six different languages without raising her voice or lowering her words-per-minute. She would have been incredible if it weren't for her sullen frown.

"You will be provided with papers should you choose to travel, and anything you are currently owed for paid time off will be deposited into an account. You are forbidden to act in the capacity of a reaper while on leave. All job-dependent powers such as projection are hereby revoked for the duration of leave. Please minimize all other power usage, particularly, but not limited to, when in the presence of mortals. If you have any questions or concerns, voice them with Immortal Resources before you depart." She stamped the papers in triplicate and handed them back.

"Have a nice day." Her sarcasm practically dripped onto his Italian leather shoes.

With measured steps, he returned to his own office. He'd wanted a vacation, but this was unlike any other he'd taken. Something wasn't right. It felt tantamount to being canned. Death stopped in front of Gina's desk and handed her one of the stamped triplicates.

"Ms. Valenka," he began slowly, weighing every word, "I'm going to be absent for a week or two. Nickleby will probably send over someone to lord over everything, but I'm depending on you to keep everyone in line. If you need help, take on a temporary undersecretary like we discussed last week."

So saying, he closeted himself in the office behind her. On his desk inside the black plastic bin labeled "IN" rested a stack of manila packets, waiting for him. Ripping them open one by one, he retrieved a fresh checkbook along with a wallet and a travel visa. He then turned to a cramped alcove behind the door and rummaged through the bowels of an aging filing cabinet. Pulling out a few old notebooks, he stuffed everything in the largest of the envelopes and walked the few yards to a hidden closet.

At first, he simply threw clothes into a duffel bag, but after a few moments he stopped, poured himself a drink, and began to repack everything into a real suitcase with his customary care. Soon the only thing left to do was settle on a mode of departure.

While he had many supernatural abilities on his own, projecting wasn't one of them. Now that he had been taken off the job, he would only be able to fast travel between the mortal realm and the office, nowhere else, and even leaving would be tricky. He looked at his visa once more. It listed him as French, triggering a quick internal rant about how he was not now, nor had he ever been, a citizen of France. In his day Brittany had been British. In his mind it still should be.

As he gazed at the view from his office, a small part of him supposed it was a good thing. He could use the scenery to aid in a final projection out of the Beyond. A taxi to the airport from there was obvious, but then what? He thought back to his American road trip idea.

America was a large country, he mused. It spanned an average of 3,000 miles across forty-eight contiguous states. Two weeks should be long enough to chart a leisurely course, spending a fair amount of time at each stop, while still staying on the move. His mind flickered briefly to the reason his vacation had been pushed through so quickly.

A rising sense of wrong pricked at the back of his mind. *Black gold.* Had Nickleby known? It all seemed just a bit too convenient for him to be put on "vacation" just as Nickleby wanted to create a division for HoH's. And that name appearing from nowhere. That name. The image of her rang more alarm bells in his mind than anything. A vacation was exactly what he needed.

California, then. That was far enough away from New York and the girl to keep his mind off things. Once there he could try to figure things out at his leisure and maybe have enough time to actually relax. He mulled over the possibilities of the third largest state in the Union.

"Well, that was disappointing."

Santana looked up at Mallory as she closed the door and slunk against it.

"Disappointing, yes, but more so unexpected. He should never have been the one to receive that name. Now we have a new problem."

She raised an eyebrow at him. "Well, what're you going to do now?" she asked.

He laughed and wagged a finger at her. "It's not what I'm going to do at all, my dear. It's what you're going to do."

Mallory gave him a startled, curious look.

Standing tall, she strode over to the big desk and sat on the edge. She wrapped the fingers of one hand around his far cheek and let her thumb stroke along a fold of skin. Gritting her teeth, she curled her lips in what she hoped was a seductive smile. Patience was not her strong suit, but she was beginning to learn it wouldn't take him long to get where he was going. He looked far too pleased with himself.

"And just what is that?"

"I can't fire him, at least not yet. He may be a pain in my ass, but Arthur's done nothing wrong with the exception of failing to kill a mark. That'll require an inquiry, though, which will reflect badly on me. I doubt he'll let it go, and he may yet do something to oust himself. Trying to take out a mark while off the job would certainly do it. That, of course, depends on his tenacity. Amraphel said he wanted that vacation pretty badly. In the meantime, you're going to prove your worth. You have two weeks, Ms. Devlin. I'm promoting you to be his 'temporary' replacement. If you want to keep your position, I encourage you to tie up both our loose ends."

"And if I fail?"

His eyes turned sharp, like pin-pricks of luminous coal. The frown lines around his face deepened. The breath in her chest grew painful to hold. Ice trembled along her arms, though she tried to remain poised and confident. Power was all about confidence, after all.

"I'll have to reinstate him, of course, and find another way to be rid of his meddling. And you — you will cease to exist."

"What, you'll send me to Hell?" She lifted her chin defiantly, even as she stuck out her bottom lip in a half-pout. He laughed again. Far from jovial, now it had a malicious ring, edgy and cold.

"Oh, no. No-no-no, my pet. There are far worse things in the Beyond than Hell."

Alacrity

Pas-de-Calais, France — April 1218 AD

ARTHUR, Duke of Brittany, leaned heavily against the table. The hard edge of the wood pressed into his arms as he studied the map before him. He drained the flagon at hand and called for another. When it didn't come, he banged the cup against the tabletop and called again, his eyes never leaving the parchment.

"Ah, quit yer bellyaching!" a rough voice exclaimed as a young man burst through the doorway. Arthur turned to see a face that wavered on the edges of familiarity. After a moment, it clicked and he grinned.

"By God! Gilbert, is that you?"

"I should be the one surprised. You're supposed to be dead these past fifteen years! The butcher whispers to the baker that John murdered you with his own hands, and the king does nothing to deny it. When you disappeared from that God-forsaken prison, well, what were we to think?"

Arthur grimaced and slapped his visitor on the shoulder.

"My guards thought sneaking me out would save the country. Dear Uncle John had other plans." Bitterness laced his voice. John had always been a bastard; usurping the throne and nearly killing his own nephew was only one of his crimes. "I heard about Runnymede and your Great Charter."

"Someone had to do something. John was out of control."

"Yes, and now he's dead, leaving a child-king in his place. Tell me truthfully, Gil. Had I been in his position, would you have done it?"

Gilbert de Clare, Earl of Gloucester, scratched at the blond scruff along his jaw.

"Maybe not. There's a reason Richard appointed you his successor. Eventually, though, the barons would have acted. This is the thirteenth century. In another generation or so, we'll have no need for kings and tyrants."

"How did you find me?"

"Your men are very effective. They've been sniffing around me for some time, testing to see if I'd be loyal."

"And will you?"

Several long minutes passed as Gilbert looked down at the map his one-time friend had been studying. Arthur didn't fear his disloyalty; more, he needed the help. Finally, with drawn out words, the earl spoke again.

"I've got a new wife and a baby on the way. Did anyone tell you?" When Arthur didn't reply, he carried on. "It's a tough choice to desert your king, even if he's new and a bit too young for his whiskers. Years ago, I threw myself into the fighting and the bloodshed, but now I have to think about Isabel."

"You're deserting the son of a pretender. I'm Richard's heir and the lawful King of England. Your family will be safer under my rule than they ever were under John's—than they will be under Henry's. I've been working on this campaign for years. There's no way we can fail."

Gilbert nodded, his look absently flitting across the ground.

"We were boys together once," Arthur reminded him, his voice slick and prodding. "Remember the summer you came to Nantes and we played at soldiers?"

"You were a brilliant general."

Arthur pointed out clusters of objects on the map, making sweeping motions to convey plans of attack. "My troops are ready. It will take time to mobilize them, but I only need a few men like you to help me lead them. England can be ours once more."

Gilbert's muddy eyes lifted to the slightly older man's steel-gray gaze.

"Join me."

After only a moment's hesitation, Gilbert gripped Arthur's hand. His mouth was set in a grim line, but the handshake was resolute. "My Liege."

Again, Arthur called out for more drink, demanding a second flagon for his guest as he stabbed a dagger into the table and leaned against it. With the Earl of Gloucester on board, they were mere steps away from wresting the throne from little Henry. As it happened, Gilbert's father-in-law was the new king's regent. The whole kingdom knew there was no love lost between the two, but it could provide Arthur with an easier flow of courtly information.

As they talked strategy and intrigue, his mind wandered to what else Gilbert could bring to the table. More than just tidbits on Henry's policies, he was sure. A longing for more personal information stirred within him.

"Have you any news about sweet Alix? Last I'd heard, the King of France married her off to a cousin."

"Aye, Peter of Dreux. She's had a child, too; a boy she named John."

Revulsion turned Arthur's stomach.

"Of course she did. What, with Eleanor being held captive all these long years, she'd be a fool to risk the duchy." My duchy, he thought. With their older sister held as a political prisoner, their mother abdicating in favor of him, and now he being believed dead, little Alix was considered Duchess of Brittany. Of course, that didn't leave much for her younger twin Kate.

"It's not so bad, Arthur. Perhaps she'll name the next one after you."

"God willing, by then she won't have to worry about appeasing a false king."

He forced a smile and called for yet another round of drink as they turned back to the map. It wouldn't be long now.

Chapter Four

AS the amber glow of the lights flickered to life, Mallory stopped the swaying motion of her chair. The older woman who walked in wore a pressed blouse and tweed skirt, and Mallory wriggled a bit in her own more fashionable attire, glad to have found the closet in the office beyond. Her office. A smile curled her lips, even as a noise of surprise escaped the secretary's lips.

"Good morning," Mallory said, standing with a stretch and crossing the sparse office. She held out a hand, her newly manicured nails a vibrant red.

"Who are you?"

The hand dropped, and her ruby smile faded. "I'm the new Head of Human Demise."

"Ma'am?" Shock was evident on the older woman's face, as was a slight hint of revulsion.

Mallory felt a sudden surge of temper coursing just below her surface.

"Your boss," she supplied bluntly. "And you must be Gina."

"Yes, ma'am."

Was she imagining it, or was there mutiny in those eyes? Mallory took a steadying breath. "Well, what do you do around here? What do you do for me?"

Gina walked around her and seated herself in the now-empty chair. With a practiced hand, she unlocked the top drawer and began sifting through the detritus. In stark contrast with her starched demeanor, the inside of the desk held crumpled packs of cigarettes, half-sharpened pencils, and scattered paper clips in a cacophony of colors. Finally, she pulled out a tiny roll of paper and handed it to her new employer.

"I make the lists."

Confused, Mallory fiddled with the little scroll. She turned it first one way and then another, before finally tugging the ends in opposite directions. Mallory jumped when it started to grow as the parchment unrolled. Soon it was as big as a regular sheet of paper, and a list of names flowed across it in gold ink.

"What the hell is this?"

Gina's puckered lips twitched. "Your marks for the day, ma'am."

"How am I supposed to go after them? I can't

leave, I'm dead."

A look of horror crossed the secretary's face, and a ball of dread curled in Mallory's stomach. She hated being wrong. The feeling of stupidity turned the dread to solid ice and within seconds she could feel panic creeping up her spine. Of course there was a way to leave. How else could the Grim Reaper do a job? In a flash the panic morphed into anger. Anger with herself, with Gina, with Santana Nickleby for setting her up to look like a fool. That's all anyone ever did. Why should she expect the afterlife to be any different?

"You project. Just... focus on your intended and make your way there." Gina's mouth hung open slightly and trembled, as if she were searching for better words. It was clear, however, that she couldn't explain it any simpler. That didn't make it sound less like gibberish, though.

Frustrated, Mallory snapped the scroll closed and shoved it back into Gina's hands. Her heels made a satisfying clicking sound on the cold tile as she walked away.

"Keep your list," she called over her shoulder, her voice higher than she'd intended. "Assign it to someone else, do it yourself, I don't care. I have more important things to do."

With that, she slammed the office door behind her.

A few twisted corridors later, Mallory poked her head around a door innocuously labeled E-4.

Inside, several Charonites mingled around couches and counters. Nickelby had been kind enough to give her a brief rundown of the chain of command, and now she intended to put it to work. Pulling herself up confidently, she rounded the corner and cleared her throat. Every voice stopped and every eye turned at her entrance.

"You're all my new little helpers, I take it." A few gazes turned from curious to offended, but she didn't care. "Which one of you has been here the longest?"

A weathered, old man stepped from the crowd. The corner of his mouth twisted up as he chewed on the inside of his cheek before speaking.

"And just who are you?" The words flowed out soft but craggy as he eyed her with suspicion.

Mallory flashed him her biggest, least sincere grin.

"I'm your new boss. Things are going to be changing around here, and I'm going to need everyone to step up."

"Everything runs just fine the way it is. Nothing's changed in the four hundred years I've been here, and I wouldn't believe you if you told me it'd been any different a thousand years before that. What happened to Arthur?"

"He's gone. I'm the Head of Human Demise now." She could hear her voice pitching, feel the cracks in her façade forming. A sharp tongue darted out to moisten her stretched lips. "You are all my employees now, not his. Do I make myself clear?"

"Well, what happened to him?" a female voice from the back asked.

"It doesn't matter!" She tried not to shriek. "I'm going to need someone to show me around, give me a hand. You," she said, pointing at the old man. "As the oldest, you must be pretty well versed in this place."

"Yes, ma'am, I am. But, showing you around is really more of Ms. Valenka's job. She is your secretary, after all."

"When I give you an order, you'll obey it. This is a new regime. The rest of you, get back to work." When no one moved, she finally snapped. "OUT!" One by one they filed out, casting her dirty looks until only she and the old man were left. Sighing with relief at the emptiness, she threw herself into a chair and looked up with a sullen expression.

"I want you to tell me all about what you do here and how you do it. Start from the beginning. How do you project? What skills do you use to murder your marks?"

"I don't murder anybody. I fulfill their fate by helping them pass on. Once that's done, I escort the unwilling to Purgatory or let the willing go and move on to the next target. It's very peaceful, and I generally evoke very little blood."

"But HOW do you do it. Explain it. Is there a

passage out to the world of the living, or can you just do it from anywhere? HOW do you kill the people on your list? Can you kill someone who's not on a list? Is it possible to take out someone who's already dead?"

Two heart beats passed in silence. Then three. Four.

"I don't think I'm qualified to give you the answers you want, ma'am. Perhaps someone in Immortal Resources or Celestial Intervention could help."

Mallory stared at him in shock. Had he really just said that to her? After he'd made it clear he knew what he was doing. Better than anybody else. The oldest employee! He'd tried to shuffle her off like an inquisitive child.

"If you'll excuse me, ma'am, I have marks to contend with." So saying, he walked out the door. Fury built in Mallory's brain like a noxious cloud. She rocketed from her seat and threw over the nearby table. It clattered to the ground and sent coffee cups against the far wall in a tinkling shower of porcelain and dark stains. Her fists balled so tightly that her nails dug into her palms like claws.

How dare he; how dare they all. She'd show them. She stalked down the hall toward her office, her steps now muffled to angry thuds by the hallway's carpet.

Jack made her way off the plane and into the bustle of San Jose International. Jostled back and forth by the merciless crowd, it took her half an hour to retrieve her hastily packed baggage and make her way toward the wide bank of doors. Just as she was about to exit and look for a cab, however, a hand tugged at her sleeve.

Whirling around, she found herself chin to forehead with a buxom black lady in a flouncy dress and jacket. The woman reeled back a step when her eyes lit on Jack's face, as if she were seeing a ghost. After a moment, she seemed to recover her wits.

"Jacquelyn?"

"Yes."

"I'm Mrs. Careby, your sister's social worker. Sorry I'm late, but the traffic out there is horrible. The car's right this way."

"Thank you," Jack managed as the woman whisked her toward a sedan waiting at the curb. Mrs. Careby had a heavy accent, which reminded Jack strongly of the last time she'd gone to the movies. She was chagrined to note it had been more than ten years since *Sweet Home Alabama* released. Of course, the memory of Mal's reaction to the movie made Jack wonder just how she'd treated her displaced Southern social worker.

They loaded up her sparse luggage and

pointed their way toward Sunnyvale without a word. Several minutes ticked by before Mrs. Careby spoke.

"Mallory never said she was a twin."

Jack swallowed. "I don't think she wanted to be one."

The silence that descended weighed heavy in Jack's chest, making it hard for her to breathe, hard to block out the memories. For eight years she'd been gone, and despite her own early attempts to stay in touch, Mallory had cut off all contact with her sister.

Jack heard a few things from others back home. Mal spent a short time in women's lockup, for which Jack had sent part of the bail; she'd also done a small stint in mental rehab, but she'd left voluntarily and was reportedly doing better. After a while, the updates and messages dropped off. Until the phone call yesterday, Jack hadn't even known Mal had a social worker.

The guilt she felt over leaving Mal behind, the memories of Mal she desperately tried to repress—those were the real reason Jack routinely visited a therapist. Her shrink called the nightmares, the social withdrawal, and the constant need to please "survivor's guilt." Even though Mallory hadn't been dead at the time, for all intents and purposes she was. And now she really, really was. Jack's breath caught in her throat.

They pulled up outside the little bungalow and old memories washed over her. Even though she appeared calm, inside she shrank back. It was as though she reverted into the tender seventeen-year-old looking for a way out. Mrs. Careby parked in front of the red brick walk, and they approached the house.

Spindly columns held up the tiny porch and heavy curtains hung at two huge picture windows. The McKinley Avenue house had seen better days. As part of the historic district, it had to maintain a certain standard, but even that hovered dangerously low. Weeds towered high, and the pale siding desperately needed to be pressure washed. Jack allowed the older woman to go ahead of her into the house. As she lingered on the concrete stoop, the long-forgotten scent of Nana Holley rushed out the door and over Jack's senses.

She and Mal had spent six years cooped inside the tiny two-bedroom house with Nana Holley. As their last living relative, she had been reluctant to take them on, but she had succumbed to her sense of duty, despite her feelings about her dearly departed son and his wife. Even twelve-year-olds knew when they weren't wanted, however. Now she was gone, too. She'd died soon after Jack left for New York. Everyone and everything was gone except the memories.

Bracing herself, Jack walked in the door. She wasn't sure what she expected, but nothing had changed apart from an additional layer to the clutter. Boxes and papers were littered everywhere, and cobwebs hung from every corner. Jack cringed at the quilt of dust clinging to the edges of the ceiling fan. Hearing the social worker in the next room, Jack made her way back, trying not to focus too much on the things around her.

Mrs. Careby was bustling about the postage stamp kitchen making Earl Grey and humming to herself. Jack took the purse off her shoulder and sat down at the little wooden table. A moment later a mug magically appeared before her, and the other woman nestled herself down in an opposite seat.

"Jacquelyn, baby, what do you know about your sister's disease?"

Jack startled at the no-nonsense opening, but recovered quickly.

"As a teenager, she did some drugs and drank a lot. I know she struggled with depression. When we were fourteen, she spent six months cutting on herself. Never enough to harm, just enough for other people to notice. I also know she took up shoplifting at one point, which combined with minor possession, landed her in jail for a bit. That's really it, though." That, she thought, and the memories.

"I did what I could for her, but she's the toughest case I've ever worked. From the start, I could see she traveled a path of self-destruction, but I never really thought it would lead to this. Your sister's chief problem seemed to be that she was able to internalize the, forgive me, crazy. Unless you really made her mad, or you saw her every day for longer than a week, you had no way of knowing what dwelled beneath the surface. She was in and out of rehab three times—twice completely voluntary—but they always sent her home or let her walk out. She wasn't there long enough for them to see what needed fixing."

Jack looked at Mrs. Careby, her hazel eyes meeting the social worker's chocolate brown. "Have you called a priest, yet?"

"No, honey. I didn't know exactly what needed to be done on that front. I'm a Methodist. I did set everything up with the funeral home like you asked. Even picked a real pretty dress out of the closet for her and had it taken down."

"Thank you," Jack said quietly. The older woman patted her hand.

"Not a problem, sugar. Now, I have to get back to the office, but you call me if you need anything. And let me know about the rest of the arrangements." Jack nodded silently as Mrs. Careby finished her tea and let herself out. Taking out her cell phone, she began calling every Catholic church in a thirty mile radius, starting with their old parish.

Chapter Five

JACK shook hands and accepted air kisses intermittently for two hours. Her black linen suit did little to protect her from the freezing blasts of the funeral home's air conditioner. She was glad she'd kept her long hair down. Not only did it provide warmth for her face, but the dark curtain of hair surrounded her petite wire frames and acted as a blessed disguise. When people she'd never met gave her startled looks of familiarity, she was grateful they were less so than they could have been.

Behind her lay a practically unrecognizable young woman, with chestnut hair lightly curled and a look of contentment. Mallory had been made up in a floral peasant dress with a crocheted lace collar, an outfit Jack still couldn't believe had been found in their old closet. A row of variegated gold studs ran along each ear, however, showing a little of Mallory's true spirit. Blushing carnations and sunny roses covered the casket, with sprigs of baby's breath woven in a base of ferns. Her sister had never looked more peaceful, Jack thought, glancing at the pearl rosary folded gently in the pale hands. Perhaps because life had never given Mal any peace.

As children they'd been inseparable: Mal and Jack, always looking for the next big adventure and finding tragedy in the most unexpected places. The universe enjoyed toying with them, but for more than a decade the accidents only made their bond stronger. However, that was more than half a life ago. Just after their twelfth birthday, Poppa Pete had a heart attack and they left the familiarity of the Salinas Valley for the unknown of Sunnyvale and their estranged Nana Holley. It was in Sunnyvale that the change really began.

They had reached the age when they were starting to make separate friends and enjoy different hobbies. Jack discovered band and photography, while Mal found boys and the heady drug of popularity. Then, one day, another girl pointed out that only Mallory seemed to suffer the consequences of the twins' predicaments.

From that moment on, the notion lodged itself in Mal's mind that Jack was to blame. Every science fair fire, every peanut butter food poisoning, every wobbly ladder, and every broken mirror led back to Jack. After all, these things only happened when she was around. Never mind that as twins in an incredibly small space, it was impossible to be far from one another. The idea began to spiral in Mal's imagination and form an unbreachable schism between them.

Hurt and alone, Jack left town at the first opportunity. As soon as she escaped Sunnyvale, things changed. The close calls and late night trips to the ER dropped at a staggering pace. Her first choice school accepted her, even offering scholarships. She won a coveted internship for photography majors, which eventually landed her a steady job. Even her housing fell into her lap when she needed it most. Her dreams were coming true. The only mar on everything was the lack of contact with Mal. Mallory burned that bridge as soon as her sister reached the other side and never looked back.

Jack looked down at the face that mirrored her own and felt a void in her chest. Everyone was gone now. Their parents, Poppa Pete and Grandma Charlotte, Nana Holley, even Maggie the collie, and now Mal had joined them. The survivor's guilt that had landed her in therapy swelled within her chest. The visitation room was empty now, and the gentlemen from the funeral home busied themselves with rearranging flowers and closing the casket for transport to the cathedral. She'd never felt so utterly alone.

The following Mass was short, and the proceeding graveside service even shorter. She couldn't complain since she was grateful to have found a priest in the first place. While official doctrine had changed over the centuries, many remained hesitant to provide services for the self-interred. Even after everything she'd been through the last few days, Jack couldn't bring herself to think of the appropriate term.

As she trudged back to Mal's old jalopy, which she'd temporarily appropriated, she thought of the affairs left to settle. The car needed to be sold and the accounts balanced. And then there was all that stuff Mallory'd left piled everywhere. Just thinking about the boxes made Jack tired.

Pulling up to the house, she frowned at a dark SUV crouched in the drive. It reminded her of a panther waiting to strike, and for good reason. As she got out of the car, a middle-aged man exited the Escalade. He was balding and paunchy, with a too-tight suit and a boldly striped tie. She stood near the front door and stared at him as he approached with a million-dollar grin.

"You must be Mallory's sister. I'm Tom. Tom Belvedere. I'm so sorry for your loss."

She nodded and shook the proffered hand lightly. "Thank you, Mr. Belvedere."

He reached into his inner pocket and pulled out a card. "Please, it's Tom. If you need anything, anything at all, you just call me." Jack looked down at the card. Belvedere and Associates, Real Estate Dreams and Rock Bottom Prices. She stiffened.

"My sister is barely in the ground and you're digging for a business opportunity?" Her voiced cracked, and Tom backed up a step with a calming spread of his hands.

"I'm just trying to help. Many times those left behind aren't sure who to turn to for help with taking care of these little matters. That's all."

She crumpled his business card in her fist. "Get off my property, Mr. Belvedere. I won't be requiring your sympathies today." Turning, she stormed into the house and let the door slam shut behind her. The nerve of some people, she thought, preying on grieving families. What kind of a person reads the obituaries for targets?

Fuming, she started a pot of coffee and whipped off her jacket. The old clock on the wall read four in the afternoon, but she needed the energy. The place looked like it hadn't been properly cleaned in years, and the boxes she'd noticed the day before were overflowing with papers and folders and notebooks. It was more like the apartment of a graduate research assistant than the suburban home of a welfare-dependent manic-depressive.

The first thing to do would be clear out the clutter. Scouring the rooms, she built a fort around the couch with the all the paper material she could find. It took more than half an hour to locate everything, which was saying something in such a small house. Settling down, she began to read.

Hours later, Jack had shoveled through enough papers to blanket lower Manhattan. Box after box contained medical files and psychologist's reports and, as she moved on from the records and clippings and into a series of journals, a picture emerged.

It wasn't about the childish disagreements and petty fights of two young women forced to share everything. It wasn't about cries for attention and living dangerously. Mallory had really and truly hated her—she blamed every unfortunate happenstance on Jack. It started with the prepubescent realization she was the only one ever injured in their frequent accidents. From that point, it spiraled into an incoherent blame game of epic proportions. Near the end of high school, it had become more than accusations and depression. Mal seemed to have snapped.

And, now, these scattered pieces of her broken life were like the ultimate suicide note. A final middle finger to a scorned sister. True or not, Jack couldn't help but think the vast collection of mental paraphernalia was intentionally left for her benefit. Rubbing her burning eyes, Jack looked around. The fort was all but demolished and the sun was beginning to peek through the front curtains.

Why? Why did Mallory let such coincidences consume her? She let such a little detail of their lives swallow her whole until nothing was left to be saved. And now her soul would pay the ultimate price. Jack fingered the simple cross she kept tucked in her shirt, but the action was more out of guilt than hope. Deep down she began to blame herself as much as Mallory had.

Sighing, Jack slumped against the couch's back and closed her eyes. The caffeine had long since run out, leaving her an empty shell. She couldn't continue. Jack rose and staggered to Nana Holley's old bedroom to fall backward on the sagging mattress. Within moments, she was asleep.

Despite fitful dreams, she didn't awake until afternoon. Exhaustion, both physical and mental, dragged at her, but she couldn't stay in bed. There was work to be done and only two weeks off to do it. Of course, there was also the little matter of answers. She needed to understand where everything went wrong, how it all happened, if she could have prevented the terrible ending.

After throwing on some clean clothes, Jack approached the shut door at the end of the hallway. The old room smelled stiflingly of violets and heather, and Jack let out a cough at the must. A white wicker bed replaced the bunks the twins had shared throughout their teens, but it rested against the same wall, covered in the same fading pink comforter. On the far side, a packed curio cabinet flanked the one window with a modest bookcase. The fauxriental rug on the floor showed years of teenage pacing, and dust bunnies colonized the ancient radiator cover. It was the pictures, however, which really grabbed Jack's attention. Her eyes held wide as she spun in a slow circle, taking in the sight.

All four walls were plastered in what Jack at first assumed were pictures of both of them. Squinting closer, she realized with horror that they were only of herself. Not just photographs either, but newspaper clippings, gallery announcements, and magazine pages Jack had contributed to. She was certain that if she spun fast enough they would come to life like a home movie. Obsession steeped the potpourri-filled air. Horrified but unable to turn away, Jack stepped toward one of the collections.

The collage hung over a narrow desk overflowing with more papers. As she drew closer, a neatly aligned row of journals appeared beyond the mess. Jack picked up the last one and opened to a random page. A small plastic card fell from between the leaves, and as she bent to pick it up, she caught part of a neatly scripted entry.

I feel free when I'm here. It's like nowhere else in the world. Outside is angry, confusing. Here, there's peace. My social worker says it's good for me. If a few times a week helps me keep a job, the membership is worth it. But, it's more than that. I can almost see the hate, like another me. She sits on the other side of the path, looking. But here, she is not me. Not me. Not Jack. Someone else I can send away. Sometimes, she stays away. But, not for long. That's why I have to come back. Always, I have to come back.

Jack looked at the pass in her hand. Hakone Gardens. Her brow creased, and she turned a few pages. The flowing, loopy script slowly devolved back into the more usual, cramped scrawl.

This is so stupid. I don't want to go to some crazy Jap-crap garden. I'm not crazy, that bitch that calls herself a social worker is. I've had years to think about everything, to work it all out. I know. Sitting in a flowerbed drinking tea isn't going to do anything. I know now. There is no escape. There are breaks, but then the world breaks again and again and it's time for it to stop. She knew that. That's why she left. She left me broken. She left me to break. She left me so she could stay perfect, just like always. Perfect Miss Jackie. Perfect, perfect, perfect. She did this. No matter how far, I can feel her breaking me. Always breaking. Breaking me to stay perfect. But I'll show her. She doesn't know that I know, but I do and I'll show her. Now I'll be perfect. Now I'll be free.

Slamming the book shut, Jack gripped it in

shaking hands and looked down at the card once more. She'd held it so tightly a small cut arced across her finger. A dotted, red line welled through the split skin. Hakone Gardens, she thought numbly, sucking on the wound. She had to see them. Had to walk them. Had to understand. Even if there wasn't anything to understand at all.

Her sister's madness ate away at her insides, making her question everything. Was she really the cause of all of Mal's misfortune? Mallory seemed convinced so. Something had certainly pushed her down the crazy path. Jack noticed for the first time she was shaking and unbidden moisture had gathered in the corners of her eyes.

Putting off the inevitable for just a bit longer, she ran from the room and shut the door hard behind her. Jack grabbed her purse and the set of keys from the kitchen counter. Mal's old Yugo, once voted the thirty-ninth worst car of all time, would have to do for the time being. With a dash at her nose and a bout of heavy blinking to clear her vision, she threw herself behind the wheel and headed to Saratoga.

"And that, ladies and gentlemen, concludes our tour. Feel free to roam the gardens and the gift shop. If you would like to go through again, the next tour starts in half an hour."

In a much better mood after a twelve-hour delay, an eleven-hour flight, and a lost reservation, Death stepped off the porch and into the afternoon sunshine. The Winchester Mansion had not been quite what he'd expected. While it was much more than a rambling Queen Anne, and he'd caught glimpses of the otherworldly in a few of its corners, the place was quite airy. Instead of dark damask and heavy wood paneling, many of the rooms and hallways were painted cream, and the interior trim was a wide range of bright colors. The exterior was just as cheery with daffodil siding and crimson roofing. Most of his fellow explorers seemed impressed with the ambiance, however. One even claimed to have heard her name whispered in her ear.

As they tromped toward the parking lot, he overheard two women in front of him. One of them was rifling through her bulging fanny pack for an itinerary while the other looked at a compact map.

"I'm telling you, Laney, we don't have time. We have a schedule to keep if we're going to make it to the next stop by dinner."

"Oh, please, Theresa? An hour won't push us back too far. It's just a few miles away, and they say there's a ward on the place that'll cleanse any who meditate there. It's supposed to be filled with good spirits, like a heaven for the Zen."

Death almost laughed out loud. The idea of a

tourist attraction being heaven for the Zen was absurd. But unlike the two biddies in front of him, he had no set plans. He called out to them and quickened his step. Catching up, he lacquered on his most charming face.

"Excuse me, ladies. I'm sorry, but I couldn't help overhearing. Laney, was it? Where is this meditation point you were talking about?" She flustered in a way that nearly flattered him as she dug out a brochure and handed it to him. He read aloud, "The Western Hemisphere's Oldest Asian Estate and Gardens. That sounds absolutely perfect. Do either of you know how to get there from here?"

"Oh, sure. Just go down to I-280 North and take the Saratoga exit. Turn back south and it'll take you to Big Basin Way. It's on the left. You can't miss it."

Theresa gave her companion a look that made plain she'd spent far too much time planning this unnecessary sidestep. Death thanked them again and wandered back to the rental he'd picked up at the airport. At the time he'd assumed the black Corvette convertible would blend with ease into the American landscape, but it attracted far more attention than a car had a right. Sliding behind the wheel, he pressed on to his next adventure.

Chapter Six

JACK deposited her token and passed through the turnstile onto the first pathway. After a short distance, she reached an open pavilion where she was granted a majestic view of much of the gardens. Just below flowed a large koi pond with a steep moon bridge arcing across. As she wandered past, she looked at a map she'd grabbed from the office. Cross-referencing it with notes she'd made from the last journal, she headed counterclockwise through the maze of paths.

First, she climbed uphill toward the Moon Viewing House. Built without the intrusion of a single nail, it acted as a tea pavilion for those who wished to participate. Bowing her head, she continued through a wisteria tunnel. The dripping purple blooms above and the rustic cobblestones below gave a magical sense that anything could happen.

As the lane led in a gradual incline up the mountain, she could almost picture good spirits dancing in the blossoms and protecting those who traveled there. She wove through looping footpaths and bursting beds until she found what she was looking for. Next to a fenced-in shrine sat a small stone pagoda. A dirt trail lead from there up to a door and beyond that, she hoped, answers.

If she were honest with herself, Jack didn't know why she was here. When she'd found that little card and the subsequent diary entries, she'd felt an all-consuming need to come. Now that she was here, she wasn't so sure. This wasn't a movie. Answers didn't just stroll up and hand you their card. Still, perhaps a modicum of peace could be found, if only for the afternoon.

Stepping through a little doorway, Jack felt transported to another world. Whereas the previous gardens had been floral and traditional, with a clean and well-ordered oriental bent, this was a forest. The bamboo garden was a grove of green shoots and tan pipes. They swayed and creaked in a gentle breeze that she'd been unaware of until she'd entered. It was like music for the soul. A stone bench called to her and she replied without hesitation. Holding the journal in her lap, she could almost feel her sister. Not the angry, hurt, confused sister of her memory, but the lucid and meditative sister who had penned thoughtful missives under the protection of this organic fortress. In the silence of the garden, a single tear slid down her cheek.

She stayed like that for some time, trying hard to remember the good times, trying harder not to be consumed by the bad. After several minutes, she sensed someone watching her, their gaze resting heavy on her skin. Raising her eyes, Jack stared. It was the man from New York—three thousand miles away and looking more dangerous than ever.

His anger burned into her, radiating like a heat wave in the cool shade of the garden. With slow, excruciating steps, he approached. Setting her jaw and lifting her face, she stared him down. The wind picked up and began to howl as fast-gathering clouds sucked at the light. A small hand grasped the cross that had fallen from inside her shirt. Either this was a hallucination or he was the embodiment of her sister's madness.

"Who are you?" she asked in a hoarse whisper as he came closer. "What do you want?"

"What do I want?" he repeated incredulously. His voice, even and soft, with a bit of an English lilt, seemed much older than his body. "What I want, Miss Devlin, is to be left in peace. What I want is for the world to make sense. Once upon a time there were rules. There were standards. There was order. And now there is nothing because you shouldn't exist. So, now, you won't."

With a snap of his fingers, a seven-foot scythe appeared in his hand. A simple black affair with knots and gnarls spaced in uneven breadths along the length of the handle, the blade shone in its decorative cast, like a piece of deadly lace.

"So, it's true." Her words were unexpectedly naïve, and his step forward faltered. "There's something wrong with me. She saw it, didn't she? My sister. She knew. That's what drove her crazy. I really am the cause of all the problems. It was me all along. But I have to know, what did I do? Why shouldn't I exist? What is so wrong with me that it hurts everyone around me?"

With his mouth set in a silent, grim line, he raised the scythe like a Louisville slugger and prepared to strike. Suddenly, rain began to fall. The wind that had been pushing and pulling at their clothes became an insistent gale, and the bamboo swayed and creaked around them. As Jack braced for the impact, the weapon glowed as if hot in his hands. A second later, the heat forced him to drop it; before touching the grass, the blade vanished in a twist of smoke. Confusion and a flicker of anger crossed her would-be attacker's face. Then, he stalked from the enclosure so fast she barely noticed him leave.

Immediately, the air cleared and the noise subsided. Only a light mist continued to fall, glimmering in the bright sunshine as the clouds moved along. Jack sat on the bench for several minutes, unable to grasp what had happened. She'd recognized him, of course. He was the man from New York, the man from the accidents, and he'd been carrying a scythe. Not only that, but he'd intended to use it on her. Then, as sure and sudden as he'd been in front of her, he was gone. Now, she wondered if he'd been there at all.

Shaking, she rose to her feet and exited the garden. As she neared the door, a broken knob of bamboo lying in the verdant grass caught her eye. She picked up the stub and turned the wood in her hands. The little pipe was about three inches long with an immature yet hollow diameter. Something about it seemed to call to her. Slipping it into her pocket, she left the estate and made her way back to the highway.

Even with the A/C running full blast, her clothes were still soaked when she got home. After the twenty-minute drive with nothing but her thoughts and a broken radio, it became clear to Jack she'd been hallucinating. Of course, she wasn't sure if she liked that explanation any more. No one could blame her for imagining things in light of a family history of mental illness, but that did nothing to ease her mind. What if she too were within inches of spiraling down the same path as her sister? Jack worked to control her breathing and her thoughts as she changed clothes for the second time.

Moving around the house, she assembled all

the journals and organized them by date. When done, she ensconced herself on the still surrounded couch and cracked open the oldest diary. The entries began when they were kids and Mal had been laid up in the hospital yet again. Jack remembered the book well—a gift from a friend of the family. The glossy cover showed off the Ballerina Bunnies and their other Lisa Frank pals, and it sported a little metal ring on the side where a lock used to hang. Everything about the diary, from cover to entries, was typical of a ten- and then eleven-year-old. Typical, that was, until Poppa Pete passed away.

Jack and Mal had gone to live with their maternal grandparents before either of them could remember. As toddlers, they'd been in a terrible car wreck with their parents and were lucky to survive. Adding to a soon-to-be string of misfortunes, their grandmother Charlotte died within a few short years. Then, not many years later, Poppa Pete had a heart attack. That was when things changed for real. Mallory had been alone with him when it happened and, according to the journals, she blamed herself. She'd hidden the depression well. Even Jack hadn't known anything was wrong at first. It wasn't until after they'd gone to live with Nana Holley that the problems became apparent.

Mal realized that of the two of them, only she ever got hurt. From then on, diary entries became more analyzing and depreciating. With rapid succession, the author's eye returned to each downfall to find Jack's role. What had she done? What hadn't she done? By fifteen, it was all over.

She talks about leaving like it's an option. I wish she would. If she were gone things would be okay. I'm clumsy enough, but things are only really bad when we're together. And I'm the one paying for it! It's always ME. My blood and my bones and what does she get? A few stitches. A band-aid. Whatever. She's taking it from me; I know it. Somehow I get extra damaged so that she won't be. Like a vampire, drinking my blood so she can live.

But, despite everything, the fact remained Jack had only seen the vitriol she was reading later in their life together. To see it appearing in their early and mid-teens made her sick to her stomach. Again, the so-called survivor's guilt reared its ugly head. Perhaps if she'd been more observant, she would have caught onto her sister's spiraling mental situation. Maybe she could have done something to fix the rift between them.

Jack put down journal number five and rubbed her arms. Chill bumps covered her flesh, and she shivered. Night had fallen as she read, and through the open curtains, the city lights sparkled in the distance. She'd missed the sunset, but the California night compared nicely in terms of beauty. She stood with a stretch and crossed the carpet to look out the window. In most places, the night sky was black with pinpricks of white, but here the sky sang. It was like a quilt of blue velvet studded with precious jewels. Many were diamonds, but scattered around were rubies and emeralds and sapphires. It was unlike anywhere else she'd ever been.

Seeing the beauty of God's creation led her thoughts back to Mal. Easter was tomorrow. Perhaps seeking out the counsel of a priest would help Jack work through her feelings of guilt and blame. Maybe he could help her understand what would become of Mallory and if any hope for her soul existed. She shivered again and closed the curtains before returning to Nana Holley's room and preparing for bed. Jack couldn't bring herself to sleep in their old room just yet. Crawling under the musty coverlet, she clasped her hands and closed her eyes, praying for protection and peace.

"Saint Michael the Archangel, defend us in battle. Be our protection against the wickedness and snares of the devil. May God rebuke him, we humbly pray, and do thou, O Prince of the heavenly host, by the power of God, thrust into hell Satan, and all the evil spirits who prowl about the world seeking the ruin of souls. Amen."

Then, though she tried to focus her thoughts on the celestial defender, she found herself slipping gently into sleep.

Of course, Death thought wearily. Between her luck and their surroundings, fortune must have smiled on him to get as close as he had. Bamboo was well known to be more than just a lucky charm. The Asian cane was one of the few natural wards against evil and, though he didn't consider himself as such, his intentions had been less than impartial. Furious with both himself and his circumstances, he hurried from the wooded alcove and back to the car. He needed another plan of attack. Some time to pull out his old notes and formulate new theories would make all the difference.

He pointed the car southeast and followed the flow of traffic. He let his mind wander on the problem at hand without much heed to his surroundings besides staying in his own lane. Of course, one of the problems with not needing to eat, sleep, or urinate was the lack of temporal awareness. Seven hours later he entered Las Vegas—five hundred miles from where he needed to be.

Cursing, he parked outside the Mandalay Bay hotel. Now what? With a sigh, he walked the strip. It was true he'd wanted a vacation, just as it was true this would be the perfect place to pick back up. But what about her?

He couldn't let this continue. Something was

seriously wrong if he ran into her three times in as many days and she still lived. And why so far apart?

Twice she'd been in New York and now California. There were so many pieces to the puzzle. There was the name, the appearances, her auras, and his sudden "vacation." Even that stupid look on Nickleby's face when he dismissed Death from his office was wrong. Something was off and she was the key.

Or maybe he really did need a vacation. It was all so tangled.

As he walked, Death tried not to focus too hard on the people he passed. The myriad of dark specters around every corner were difficult to ignore, to say the least. Las Vegas might be the live entertainment capital of the world, but it was also where people came to die. Statistically speaking, visitors were more than twice as likely to commit suicide in Glitter Gulch, and residents were forty percent less likely to do so if they left the city and never came back. Put that together with the high murder and accident rates, plus the everyday deaths of a city that crammed 4,300 people into every square mile, and it added up to be a lot of work for both the city morgues and his Charonites.

Instead of the people, Death tried to turn his attention to the lights. Everywhere he looked both modern and vintage signs proclaimed the audacity of Vegas nightlife. Neon headlines boasted luxury and vice. Billboards spread rumors of wealth and happiness. For over an hour, he wound his way down the vast sidewalk taking in the surroundings. He didn't need to gamble or otherwise pay for pleasure; he just needed to take his mind off things for a little while. The distraction wasn't working, though. With a sigh, he admitted defeat and picked up his pace.

Coming full circle to his starting point, he checked into the hotel and entered one of the exclusive elevators toward the back. The button for the thirty-sixth floor lit up at his touch, and without a sound, the car lifted into the air. His suite was modest but impressive and, to his mind, well worth the money. Here the word opulence was no longer necessary. Now, the prevailing themes were sleek yet plush. From the marble bathroom and polished wood to the down comforter and deep-soaker tub, he wasn't sure that one night would be enough. Maybe all he really needed was some time to relax.

He poured himself a beverage from the mini-bar and savored it as he sifted through his bag. Under the clothes and other accoutrements, his hands found the old notebooks he'd sequestered from his office. Drawing them out, he took them to the living area and spread them across the coffee table.

The original Immortals were those whose pure

white life aura bore a brightly gilded band. Even babies weren't born with sparkling white life auras, and the color deepened depending on how close you were to death. Immortals, though—those who the ancients often called demigods or heavenly host—never faltered. They were twice blessed with infinite good luck and infinite life, and often, the otherworldly had to intervene before their egos erupted into something messy and hard to clean up. Now, almost anything that couldn't die or came of supernatural origins was called an immortal, but at one time it had been special.

The same essential principal held true for weeping roses. Their curse of infinite life came with an unusually hefty price tag. A ring of crimson bound them to their unending life force, like a magnet for the undesirable. Terrible accidents and life-altering incidents followed weeping roses like a noonday shadow. Often the bad luck spilled onto loved ones. Only the most stalwart of roses could stay sane. Like with Immortals, if there was no intervention, things had the potential to spiral out of control. More often than not, though, roses cleaned up their own messes.

Then there were the cursed. Only by the grace of slipping through the cracks did they make it far in life. A life aura of jet black wrapped in a blood-red luck aura was too tragic to dwell on, even for death personified. Fated to die and saddled with the worst imaginable luck, most didn't make it out of the womb.

While he'd seen his fair share of the other three, black gold had never come up. As far as he knew, no one before him had seen it either. Black gold was an idea, a probability, a myth. If extremes existed at either end of the spectrums, then it was a given that all such extremes must be possible. The theories he'd spun bridged the bulk of the notebooks spread before him. He'd even been amused at the irony of someone so lucky and yet fated to die. That amusement had been at the theory, however. The question now was what to do with her.

Killing her was obvious. Screw the vacation. He would take her out, and then return to the Beyond to untangle whatever web Nickleby was weaving. He would need to track the girl down again, of course, and that would require help. He needed an innate tracker—someone off the radar, but still vested in their abilities. As he ran through the possibilities and contacts in his mind, his mood improved.

Given a few days, he could finish the job properly and put this whole ugly business behind him. Maybe he would get a promotion for all the thought he'd put into this. Grim Reaper was a good gig, but with an eternity stretched before him, there were other considerations.

Ailment

IT had been raining for two weeks straight. The smell of cold mud and horse shit leaked in beneath the tavern windows. Downstairs, the sounds were muted. There was no drunken revelry, no loud debauchery—just men holding their breath and drinking their beer. Even the whores were silent and pouting, their pockets empty for the first time in months.

Upstairs the mood was even worse. Arthur sank his face into his hands, the rough bristles scratching at his calloused palms. The sound of the rain hammered into his head, and he ran his fingers up to rub at his temples. Spread across the desk before him were diagrams and letters, all splotched with rain and ale. With bleary eyes, he reread the latest news. Little Henry's soldiers had rounded up a troop of his own. He'd sent them ahead to make preparations, but instead they'd been met with a coup.

Someone was playing both sides.

Seventeen years of work, and it was unraveling faster than a poorly spun tunic.

Someone would pay.

The cold pressed in on him from all sides, even as the heat of anger coursed through him. Shivering, Arthur pulled his woolen cloak closer and poured more ale into the pint at his side. It splashed out, causing the ink on a map to run in rivulets of red and black. He cursed and mopped up what he could with the edge of his sleeve.

All these years, all this planning. The spying, the secrecy, the lies, the labor. Skulking in darkened rooms and fetid inns, meeting traitors by candlelight. Everything. And now it was all going up in smoke.

He tried to take a deep, steadying breath, but instead wet coughs wracked his body. As they cleared, he drained his newly filled flagon. Without a second thought, he backhanded the earthenware tankard and listened to the satisfying smash of pottery against stone. The violence nearly made up for his sequestration, though he would have to call for another if he wanted more drink.

No, he didn't want to see anyone—couldn't trust anyone—not even the serving wench.

Rising from his stool, he stumbled to the window to gaze at the town below. The air was stifling, like a heavy compress on his chest. The weight of the world held in such a tiny room. He threw open the casement and let the rancid smells and freezing wind roll in. The latter cooled his feverish cheeks, even as he pulled his cloak tighter. Arthur turned and paced the room as best he could.

Gilbert's messages had become less frequent of late, and rumors swirled through the scattered encampments of betrayal. It was a possibility Arthur didn't want to face, but it was a possibility nonetheless. There were others, of course. Percy had yet to return from his scouting mission months ago, and Arthur had always had his suspicions about Hertford. However, his oldest friend remained the most likely suspect.

Another series of coughs overtook him, moist and burbling in his chest. He leaned against the wash basin for support, and when it passed, was not surprised to see the all-too-familiar hemoptysis. The sputum bled into the water, causing little swirls of scarlet as the color dissolved. He wiped his mouth, smearing the remaining droplets of blood, and caught his reflection in the tiny mirror.

He was nearly unrecognizable from the man of just a few years before. His health was rapidly declining in the way of most desperate young men, but he was no longer as young as he acted. The bruised circles under his eyes hung in ever-deepening folds, while the few freckles across his nose stood in sharp relief against his parchment-paper skin. He hadn't bothered to shave in weeks, but instead of a beard, his face was swathed in patchy scruff. Thirty-three was too far from death to look this much like Hell.

The shadows whispered all around him as he stumbled to the bed. It sagged beneath his slight weight, his muscles having withered and his bulk long since gone. He struggled to catch his breath, couldn't concentrate. He needed to set out a new plan of attack. They were so close—everything was so very close. But all he could think about was one more drink to burn away the mucus closing his throat.

Suddenly desperate, Arthur tried to call out for a serving wench, or an inn keeper, or even one of his own men, but sound wouldn't come. He tried to rise and do it himself, but his limbs felt heavier than any battle armor. With a small exhale, he lay back on the bed, allowing gravity to be his manservant. His mind whirled as his body shuddered under more choking and chills.

After what seemed like hours, some of the shadows peeled away from the walls. An old man in a dark robe made his way forward and looked down at Arthur. Reaching out, he laid a hand on the trembling chest. For a moment, it felt like drowning. Then, comfort spread.

The man beckoned Arthur to follow, and the would-be-king was amazed that he could so easily swing up and out of the bed. Once he was on his feet, he faced the intruder.

"Are you a physician? Did one of my men send for you?"

"No."

"Well, who in God's name are you, then? These are private quarters."

"You'll have to learn to control that temper of yours. There's no room for that in the business of death."

"I do not often repeat myself, sir. I say, who are you?"

The old man swept a wrinkled hand at the bed, and Arthur turned. Below his body lay twisted in the threadbare sheet, his mouth open and eyes glazed. Confusion overtook him as he whirled back to the man. Resignation clear on the man's face, he answered in a practiced speech.

"I am not the Devil, nor am I an angel. I am merely here to escort you to the Beyond. Now come. It is time."

Chapter

Seven

MALLORY stalked from the hallway and into Gina's line of sight. The older woman stopped her work and watched as her new boss paced the room. Mallory could see the questions and indignation that flickered across the secretary's face, but the other wisely reined them in. Instead, she shut her eyes, took a deep breath, and cleared her throat.

"Ma'am, I was wondering if you had considered the proposal on your desk yet."

"What proposal?"

The corner of Gina's eye twitched, and Mallory narrowed her gaze in suspicion. They were all turning against her, one by one, she was sure of it. They'd never let go of the old regime, not as long as the last Grim Reaper lived. She felt the pressure building.

"About hiring an undersecretary to help with the increasing workload. The last Head—"

"I don't care what the last head said!" Mallory shouted, releasing the pressure before it destroyed her. "I am the Grim Reaper now, and you'd do well to remember it. Go, do whatever. Just don't bother me anymore today. And don't try to give me another one of those stupid lists tomorrow. I have far more important things to take care of."

With that, she gathered herself up, tossed her hair over her shoulder, and stalked out of the room. In some ways, death was more maddening than life. She'd bullied a Charonite into spying on her sister; not a simple task, she'd been informed—something about luck and shielding. She'd sat through an entire Celestial Intervention lecture on Sheol, aka The Great Nothingness, and how immortal troublemakers were dealt with in the Beyond. She even had a new, new plan on just how to pull everything off with a beautiful bang. But no matter how hard she tried, one thing was still in her way.

Projection.

Everyone she talked to said it was the simplest, most basic power. Sure, not all dead were vested with it, but those that were assured her it was easy peasy. So why couldn't she do it? She couldn't even manage to project from one end of a hall to the other.

Something was wrong. It must be Nickleby. He

gave her the job and set her up with the powers. Perhaps he hadn't given her quite enough. Maybe he was holding back. But why?

He wanted the old Head gone just as much as she wanted her sister dead. And he'd put her under a deadline to boot! Maybe a little extra persuasion would grant her the power boost she so desperately needed. Mallory sidled up to the humongous counter to the left of Nickleby's door and gave Luneil a winning smile.

"Is he in?"

Without replying, the hawk-like secretary reached out a bony finger and pressed the buzzer on the intercom.

"Human Demise to see you, sir."

Moments later, a crackled reply came back.

"Send her in."

Luneil gave Mallory a curt look full of boredom. She sniffed, then returned to her work as Mallory waltzed past her and through the big wooden door.

"Ah, there you are. I wondered if I would be seeing you today. How goes the search?" Santana Nickleby stood from his desk and approached her as she leaned against the back of the door. She'd never been afraid to use her body to meet her ends, though this particular mark made her stomach roil. Usually, they were much nicer looking; even the losers didn't have the face of an obese bulldog. She clenched her jaw in distaste, but stuck out the pad of her lower lip in a sultry pout.

"I have everything I need except the power. I need more. They're running around the living world, and I'm stuck here. If I just had a little more power I'm sure I could break through and tear their little worlds apart. Just think," she continued, dialing up the sex appeal, "if he was gone, I could agree to anything you want."

"Mmm, anything?" He wrapped a strand of her hair around his finger. Mallory slanted a look at him through fluttering eyelashes. Without warning, he gave a tug that brought tears to her eyes. She snapped her lids open and stared at him, picking her words up with a slight stutter.

"A-anything. You said there needs to be changes in the department. I can help you. Isn't that why you chose me? You knew I could help you bring about great things." She reached out and ran her hands over his chest, toying with his lapel and tie. He dropped her hair, and she let out a small sigh of relief. "All I need is a little push. Once they're gone, death will be so much easier for both of us."

Nickleby put his large, ham hock-like hands on her shoulders. He ran them down her body as sensually as she supposed he could, though Mallory felt more like she was being pawed at than seduced. There was a lecherous gleam in his eye, and a smile played at the corners of his mouth.

"It takes focus, my pet. You're new at this. You

need to channel all your passion into the singular purpose of finding your mark." He closed the small space between them, pressing her tighter against the door. "I don't think you're quite passionate enough. But we can fix that."

Nickleby toyed with the hem of her skirt, and a shudder racked her body. It was a reaction of revulsion, but he took it as a tremor of desire. Mallory closed her eyes so that he couldn't see her pupils contract in disgust.

Then, as he eased the material up over her hips, she suddenly reopened them and locked her determined hazel gaze with his. She could play this game. If there was one thing she'd learned from all those nerdy kids her sister hung out with, it's that sometimes the piece with the least going for it could win the match.

"And then I'll have the power? Then I'll be able to destroy them?"

"With my help, you can be unstoppable."

It was an hour north from Las Vegas to Angels' Peak. Nestled into the side of the mountain was a small town, which played host to less than a thousand people. Much like the Nile Delta, its growth sprang from a nearby tributary, and the fertile banks provided a welcome spot of cool green in the arid Nevada desert.

Death registered only mild surprise at how young and vital most of the population seemed. He noted the plethora of cream or soft gray auras, an overwhelming majority with luck ranging from joyful yellow to steady blue. In a way, it was refreshing after the mortality shakedown that was Vegas, but it was also a little odd. The last time he'd been here, it was little more than a ramshackle farmers' collective. Now there were multiple playgrounds and a nearby state park, and the wide sidewalks were ideal for the many people he passed walking dogs or riding bikes. Angels' Peak was a healthy little community, to be sure, but he knew there was more to the middling auras than just exercise.

With that in mind, he drove around with an eye out for the man he needed. After only a few minutes, he'd found him. A lawn filled with long tables and colorful awnings bustled with people sniffing fruit and weighing vegetables. Several young people worked the stands, exchanging cash and checks for brown-bagged goods. But behind it all, a lone man sat on the back of a pickup, with a big straw hat and a smile.

"Hello, Clarence."

The man's emerald green eyes flew wide, his breath hesitating for just a moment. Clearly, he wasn't expecting anyone to find him on the top of a mountain. When he saw who was speaking, however, his face crinkled into a myriad of laugh lines.

"How's it going, old boy? Haven't seen you in an age."

"I wonder why."

"Oh, now. It's not like I'm doing anything against the rules. A bit off-grid, maybe, but perfectly legal."

"You're successfully sustaining a population through metaphysical means. Entire auras are shifting because of your meddling. How is that legal?"

Clarence's grin grew wider in laid-back self-defense. "I'm just growing grub. If they choose to pair my offerings with a more active lifestyle, it's none of my doing." Death quirked an eyebrow at him and pursed his lips, waiting. "And, well, if because of their vitality some of them choose to leave town for a big adventure in an elsewhere that does not have access to my bountiful produce, then I reckon the scales stay balanced."

"What's your angle, Clarence? What do you get out of all of this? It seems like a waste of time if the scales stay balanced, as you say."

"Boy, I have all the time in the world. Sometimes a man just wants to do something different. As for an angle, I haven't figured that out yet. But don't you worry. I'm sure I'll come up with something in a decade or two."

Death shrugged his shoulders and changed the topic.

"I need a favor."

"You know, the angels have a saying: when Death asks a favor, hide your wings."

"That doesn't even make sense."

"It may have been mangled from the original Arabic. And, anyway, we all know what it means."

"I need you to help me track a girl. A woman, really. She's proving to be an elusive mark."

The celestial's eyes narrowed. "You, the Grim Reaper, need my help tracking a mark. Why?"

Death considered telling him everything. He was sure Clarence would be able to help him see through the cloud of coincidences and get to the heart of what felt so wrong. But if the rogue angel knew Death was on the bad side of a Power That Be, he might not be as encouraged to help. Piqueing his interest a bit might, though. Death took a deep breath. "Black gold."

"Bullshit. I've been around the block a few thousand times, my boy. There is no such thing as black gold."

Death stared at Clarence for a moment as though he'd been slapped. That had been the exact opposite of the response he'd hoped for. Recovering quickly, Death bulled ahead. "Listen to me. She's real. I've seen her. I've tried to kill her twice. And now I've lost her. You're the only one I can turn to."

"Why don't you just project? Focus on her. As

determined as you seem, I'm sure you'll land right on her doorstep."

Now he was irritated. Of course another immortal would see projection as the obvious solution. He would have to tell him a little more, after all.

"Yes, that would be lovely, wouldn't it? Unfortunately, I'm on vacation. No projection, no tracking, just basic functionality. A few parlor tricks, some standard physical manipulation—in other words, useless. So, are you going to help me or not?"

Clarence leaned back, scratching his chin, and watched a puff of cotton roll across the cornflower sky. "Don't you have better things to do than be out here pestering a man doing God's work? Relax, get a tan." Clarence poked him in the ribs. "Eat something."

Death cut him a look. "I don't suppose the Seraphim would bother to look for a missing low-rank hundreds of miles in the middle of nowhere."

The geniality on Clarence's face dimmed fractionally, and his emerald eyes became as flat as green glass. "Are you threatening me, boy? It's unwise for a creature of the underworld to mess with an agent of God."

"I'm no more creature than you are agent. We're both dead men with goals that don't always line up with our superiors. Now I'll ask you again;

are you going to help me or not?"

"Why is she so important to you? Let her go. I'm sure one of your minions will run across her and take her out. Everyone dies eventually. Oh." Suddenly, Clarence cocked his head in understanding. His gaze softened, and he reached out a hand. "You think it's her, don't you?"

Death shrugged off the touch. "Of course not. I have no reason to believe in reincarnation. A Charonite facilitates your demise and, if needed, escorts your soul to Purgatory. From there you either get a job or an afterlife. The lucky few who retire on good standing return to Earth as an Immortal. That's it, and there's no proof otherwise."

Clarence gave his visitor a sympathetic look, his interest shifting. "Where do you think she is?"

Death chose to ignore the ambiguity of the question and focus on the present. "The last time I tried to kill her, she was in San Jose, California, but the time before that she was in New York City. Her name is Jacquelyn Katerina Devlin."

At the name, Clarence cut him another knowing glance but said nothing. With a soft sigh, he went back to cloud gazing. For several minutes, they sat in silence as the crowds of people ebbed and flowed around them. Finally, the angel spoke again.

"I can see her, but I can't pinpoint an exact location. Something's blocking me. She's definitely in California, and the emotional vibes coming off her indicate she has a lot to take care of. A large weight is keeping her in place. She'll be there for a while."

"Where?"

Clarence's face twisted in discomfort, as if searching for the information somehow tugged at his soul.

"Sunnyville. Sunnydale. Something sunny at any rate. She's moving around a lot so that's the best you're going to get. Sorry, old boy."

Death hung his head before nodding in acknowledgment. "Say, Clarence, hypothetically speaking, how would you penetrate a shield of perfect luck?"

"Well, you could always get the CI involved, but from that sour look on your face, I'm sure you'd rather not. The way I figure it, there are only two ways to go. You could fight fire with fire, that is, find yourself something luckier than luck. Or, you could go the opposite route and get your hands on a cursed object to plant in her possession. That'd bring her luck down a notch. I'd try doing the job myself a few times before taking such drastic measures, though. Messing with something as elemental as luck can have unforeseen consequences."

"Thanks. For everything."

"No problem. Now I respectfully suggest you either get back to work or get the hell out of

Nevada."

Death stood from his perch on the back of the pick-up and stretched. "See you around, Clarence." With that, he ambled back to his car and the awaiting interstate.

The Yugo's clock blinked the wrong time, but the buttons to fix it were either broken or their labels had long since worn off. Older than Jack, the car was in relatively good condition for a death trap. Sure, rust pockmarked the pale yellow paint, reminding her of a splotchy fourteen-year-old, and maybe the seat belts were fraying, and the brakes pumped a bit slow, but at least it ran. Jack looked at her watch as the bells began to ring for evening vespers.

As she entered the Cathedral of the Madeleine, the church seemed much smaller than she remembered. The Aztec gold walls played off the pine floors and honeyed benches and warmed the chill the April breeze had left on her arms. Passing down the wide central isle, she gazed at the dusty-red pilasters capped with minty buttresses, which always gave the nave an air of perpetual Christmas.

It was the apse that drew her eye the most. From a distance, it reminded her of Van Gogh's *Starry Night*. Approaching the marble altar, she gazed at the details of the stars, multihued with stylistic circles and dots draping elegantly over a depiction of the crucifixion. Everywhere she looked were gilded angels, and the swelling organ music impressed upon her the presence of God.

Jack knelt through the two hours of evensong, benediction and mass. With each rising litany, her mental and spiritual burdens diminished as if the resurrection of the Christ eased them off her shoulders. Her faith brought comfort like little else. After the last hymn was sung and the last of the clergy exited the nave, she made her way through the crowd toward the car. As she was leaving, though, a hand touched her shoulder.

"Sister. You must be new." Turning, Jack found herself face to face with one of the deacons. Not surprisingly, she didn't recognize him. He wasn't much older than her, and anyway, she'd been gone for nearly eight years. Jack bowed her head in deference.

"Actually, I grew up here. I haven't been home in some time, though."

"Oh? Where do you live now?"

"New York."

"So far? What brought you back?"

"My sister's funeral." The sound of the words leaving her lips triggered the weight of her guilt, settling it firmly on her shoulders once more. Glancing away from his open, empathetic face, she glimpsed the petite woman to his left. Her blonde hair hung to her shoulders, sweeping a blue knitted cardigan, and she placed a hand on his arm in an unconscious gesture of possession. Light glanced off the woman's wedding band and though she had a warm smile, Jack's own loneliness made her turn her head.

"Excuse me. I'd better go find dinner. I appreciated the service."

She stepped to the side and began to walk off when the woman called out to her. "Aren't you spending Easter with your family?"

Jack stopped and turned with measured care. "I don't have any family. Not anymore."

The deacon and his wife exchanged glances before he replied. "Why don't you have dinner with us? Janice put on a pot roast before we left. We're fairly new to the area and we'd love some company."

Every instinct as a New Yorker told her not to accept such an invitation from complete strangers, but twenty-five years as a staunch Catholic won out. Half an hour later, Jack had to admit she'd missed home cooking. Janice's pot roast reminded her of Nana Holley's and made her a little sad that she'd never learned to cook more than boxed spaghetti.

Over dinner, they'd made polite conversation. Deacon Franz remained contemplative throughout most of the meal, interjecting with a lone question or insight here and there. Janice wanted to know all about life in New York, and Jack had been interested to learn about Salt Lake City where they'd moved from. By meal's end, Jack was glad she had accepted their offer. After lunch, Jack insisted on helping with the dishes and Janice handed her a towel.

"What was your sister like?" she asked as Jack dried the silverware.

"I don't know." An awkward pause punctuated the conversation before she continued. "I mean, I thought I knew her. She was everything to me when we were kids. As we grew up, she went her own way, did her own thing. She got into some trouble and didn't play well with others. But I always thought it was just a phase. Part of me believed that maybe if I left she'd work things out."

"Why would leaving help?"

"She blamed me for a lot of things. I got too much attention, my grades were too good, my hair was too perfect, I made friends too easily. If I could do something she couldn't, if anything blew up in her face, it was my fault. That's one of the reasons I moved to New York. If she had time alone, maybe she could figure it out. She could claw her way out of the dark and make something of herself. I guess she couldn't."

"I'm really sorry, Jack. It must have been very difficult." With the dishes done, Janice led her into the living room and onto the couch. Deacon Franz sat in a nearby chair reading his Bible. He gave his wife a look and, after giving Jack a hug, she excused herself. Marking his place, he set the book aside with extreme care before scooting to the edge of his seat.

"Did you hold a proper Mass for your sister, Jack?" he asked. She was a little bit taken aback at first, having never mentioned how Mallory had died. Then Jack bowed her head, realizing how obvious it was every time she mentioned her.

"Yes, thankfully, though it felt rushed. I've never been to a funeral that was held the same day as the vigil, but the priest insisted."

"I'm sorry that our rector didn't see fit to perform the service, especially as the Madeleine is your home church. Some are less open to the idea of mitigating circumstances. I'm going to pray for your sister, that her soul might be delivered into Heaven. From what I heard you telling Janice, she seemed like she was a disturbed young woman. I'm sure the Lord will have mercy upon her. But, you need to stop blaming yourself. I can hear it in your voice and see it in your face every time you speak her name. It is not, and never was, your fault."

"Wasn't it? I'm the one who left. I should have stayed. Maybe I could have helped her. Maybe I could have done something, anything except walk away." Her words echoed every condemning thought she'd had over the last several years.

Everything her therapist had tried to reconcile but couldn't, summed up in those last six words.

"Jack, listen to me." He laid his hands on the clenched fists at her knees. "Satan is powerful, and if you'd stayed he would have dragged you both down. God gave you gifts along a different path. Perhaps acceptance into NYU was God's way of getting you out of an impossible situation.

"I'm not saying you should forget your sister. I'm simply saying you should focus on counting the blessings God has given you and thanking him for his timely and enduring deliverance. Always remember the struggles your sister went through and how it tore her away from you. Always remember because it will keep you strong in the face of the Devil's trials. But don't let her memory keep you in a holding pattern of grief and blame.

"What you need to do is let go and let God. It's cliché, but true. The only way you'll feel peace is to turn these matters over to a higher power. Remember what happened, but erase all thoughts of blame. Let go of the pain, and let God give you peace."

Jack nodded as she blinked back the moisture in her eyes. He was right, of course. But the remembering made the letting go nearly impossible. Jack gave the deacon a courageous, but hollow smile. Time would help, she was sure.

In her dreams, Jack paced down the long

corridor with unsure steps. She followed the dizzying pattern in the carpet and listened to the heart-thumping music that poured from behind a far door. A sense of wariness made her hand tremble as she reached for the door's handle. Inside, a ballroom was outfitted like a nightclub. SUNNYVALE SENIOR PROM hung across the stage in giant, glittering letters as girls in evening gowns tried to shake it like strippers.

Wandering the room in a confused but achingly familiar daze, she found a partitioned room near the back. She decided to duck inside and catch her bearings, but ran solidly into another person. Her gaze trailed upward from the peep-toed kitten heels to the red spangled skirt and the sweetheart neckline that now hung just a little askew. Above it all, Mal's catlike smile spread over sharp white teeth.

"What're you doing back here?" Jack asked, startled. In the back of her mind, she already knew the answer. The déjà vu was like a slow and steady suffocation.

"Oh, just enjoying the party." Mal leaned in close, soft lips pressing against Jack's ear in a motion more chillingly seductive than sisterly. "Now you'll know what it's like to have your life stolen." She drew her face away with a look of smug unrepentance and waltzed off. Her gait held a satisfied sway that Jack had come to recognize only too well. Ripping aside the heavy curtain,

Jack stared horrified as her boyfriend struggled to fix his Double Windsor.

"No!" she yelled, but the mimicry of the past was drowned out by the steady beat of the bass. Their eyes locked, and Chase gave her a confused and apologetic look.

"Jackie? I can explain…"

She spun on her heel, knowing what he would say. Jack ran across the dance floor and ducked into the bathroom. There, she sank to the floor and curled into a ball where she remained, sobbing and unnoticed, until she woke a short time later.

With the back of her hand, she dashed the still-fresh wetness from her cheeks. The dream had been accurate in almost every respect. The fact that the memory came back to haunt her years after she'd solidly repressed it disturbed her on a deep, deep level. Maybe some things you couldn't let go of for good. Maybe, even if you thought you'd moved on, something was always waiting to drag you back down. Mal's words echoed in her mind,

"Now you'll know what it's like to have your life stolen."

Unless you counted her obsession, Chase Vandervoort had never been Mal's. She always claimed Jack had stolen him from her, but Jack had never seen Chase show an interest in her deluded twin. For almost a year, Jack had been with him. She'd fantasized about their lives together after high school, dreaming about forever, and it was all destroyed in a single play.

Rolling the resurfaced memories over in her mind, Jack realized she couldn't let it go. Holding on to the past dismissed Deacon Franz and went against everything her therapist had tried to tell her, but she just couldn't. She needed answers like oxygen, had to get a handle on what went on inside her twin's twisted mind. Glancing at the clock, she rose and prepared properly for bed before downing a sleeping pill and succumbing once more to the darkness.

Chapter Nine

WITH an energy born of grief, Jack spent hours cleaning the old house on McKinley Avenue. Now with the exception of the boxes of papers stacked around the couch, the place looked almost good enough to sell. It was something she had thought about off and on since the funeral, and now she knew she couldn't stay. With a little over a week of bereavement leave left, there was just enough time to clear up affairs and put the house in order.

She'd rescued Mr. Belvedere's crumpled business card from the yellow linoleum of the kitchen floor. It now hung at a jaunty angle from a magnetic chip-clip on the refrigerator. He was a slick man, but he just might be the person to discuss her options with. Despite her lingering feelings of hostility toward him, she was beginning to regret how she'd treated him. Maybe he hadn't been as bad as she'd thought. The last thing she wanted was to become like Mallory, taking out her frustrations on people she only imagined deserved it. Taking the card down, she hesitated only a moment before dialing the number.

It proved a less awkward conversation than she'd feared. Jack felt the need to apologize, even though part of her didn't regret the things she'd said. Mr. Belvedere was pleasant, even if his voice sounded slick to her ears, and assured her there were no hard feelings. They decided to meet for lunch at the Sunnyvale Art Gallery, which boasted a full-service restaurant in addition to its showings.

At a quarter to twelve, she freshened her lipstick and kicked her way out of the Yugo's perpetually jamming door. Jack straightened her outfit, which was skewed from the exertion, and made her way into the cafe with as much confidence as she could summon. Mr. Belvedere sat at a white linen table in the middle of the sun-drenched room.

"Well, hello there, young lady." His smile made clear he wished bygones to be bygones, but something nagged at her, refusing to let her forgive him for his earlier feigned friendship. She was beginning to regret having called him at all. Surely there were dozens of other Realtors she could have blindly picked out of the phone book. Too late now.

"Hello, Mr. Belvedere." She shook out her napkin as she took her seat and placed it across her lap. He threw back his coffee as if it were still early morning instead of lunchtime. A waiter hurried over and took her order of ice water and a salmon wrap. Jack folded her hands on the tabletop and waited for him to speak.

"So, you've decided to sell? It's a great little house, though it does need some fixing up. I took the liberty of looking up other comps in the area. Your sister's house will go for quite a nice sum since many of the other houses are duplexes or condos."

"Grandmother. It's our grandmother's house."

"Oh. I'm sorry. Is she deceased as well? I mean, that is to say, you do have the right...?" He looked flustered, her choice of tense setting in motion an instant worry that he might be deprived of his prize.

"Yes, she's gone. They're all gone. I filed the petition with the judge of probate last week, so you have nothing to worry about. What I want to know is what I need to do, how much you think it's worth, and how you plan on selling it."

Mr. Belvedere relaxed a bit. For an hour, they hammered out the details of the sale. Jack would need to complete a few minor improvements, some of which could be done remotely from New York. As far as selling the house, he seemed to have a fairly comprehensive plan, and by the end of the interview, she was satisfied he would do his part.

After he hurried off to another client's open house, Jack wandered over to the exhibition side of the gallery. A banner proclaimed the current show as MORTALITY AND THE BEYOND. As she entered, she was taken in by the dramatic use of lighting and contrast. The space itself, though maze-like due to a series of random partial walls, had been split neatly down the middle in terms of subject matter. All the walls on the left side were painted black while those on the right stood starkly white. Touring the facility, she peered closely at each photograph.

Simple four-by-six glossies rested next to canvas-sized matte prints in a progression of subject. Jack began on the right wall and worked her way around with an attention to detail. The manipulations were quite good, and within a few minutes, she found herself sucked into the images of heavenly beings interceding in the lives of mortals. Light flares and blurs, double exposures and shadows, all fell in just the right places to create believable 'scapes.

When she came to the large artwork at the end of the long room, she saw why the walls were divided by color. A single photograph straddled the line, depicting an old woman asleep beneath a patchwork quilt. At the foot of her bed, two beings struggled. On the right grappled a heavenly host and on the left lurched what could only be described as a demon. Jack stood for several long minutes staring at the picture. Her eyes combed the details, taking them as unbidden as if they'd been words in her ears. She didn't even notice at first when another person approached the display.

"Interesting, aren't they? None of these use any real props, save for a few bed sheets. It's all in how the picture was taken, how the light reflected, how the film developed."

Jack jumped, startled by the intruding sound. Looking toward the voice, she saw a young man not much older than herself. He appeared to be in his late twenties and sported closely trimmed facial hair to go with his military-short haircut. Grinning, he held out his hand.

"I'm Nate by the way."

"Jack," she replied, taking his warm, rough hand in her small, cold one. "Are you a curator here?"

"Me? Nah. I'm in town visiting family. They decided to do some shopping today, so I came down here to look at the exhibition. I do have an art history minor, if you're looking for an expert." He gave her a lopsided grin, and she tried and failed not to laugh.

"Art history, hm? There isn't much historical in this show," she pointed out. His face fell, but she could tell his spirit was far from crushed. "Where are you from?"

"The Big Apple, love. Washington Heights." He said the name with a showman-like flare of his hands, overemphasizing the importance and size of his chosen abode. Jack's brows shot up, her wide eyes full of surprise. "Though I'm originally from Indiana," he said in a more subdued tone.

"You're joking." He looked at her quizzically as she continued. "I work in Washington Heights, just down from Fort Tryon Park. I'm a photographer for one of the magazines downtown and do some freelance stuff on the side. I came west for family, too." She crossed her fingers that her last answer had dodged neatly enough to dissuade further questioning.

"So, I guess you should be my expert, then," he countered. She blushed, but he chuckled. "Why don't we walk together for a bit? Us New Yorkers should stick together. Besides, a pretty girl should never be unaccompanied. There are strange men about. You might need me to protect you."

She was taken aback at his flippant statement, thinking of the otherworldly man she'd encountered three times already, but Nate waved her on to the next part of the exhibit without noticing her hesitation. From the struggling celestials, the mood turned darker. The left side of the gallery teemed with images of unholy creatures playing tricks on mortals. As they progressed back around to the front of the display, they discussed the different techniques employed by the artists to achieve their goals. It was fascinating–more so because for having someone knowledgeable to share it with.

At the end of the exhibit, they took a turn around the adjoining florist shop and art supply store. The little building really was an odd mash-up of businesses. Jack stopped to press her face into a collection of tulips. They had a fresh, clean smell like sunshine after a brief rain.

"I love tulips. Our grandfather grew them in the front garden. I remember they always bloomed right around Easter. He said they stood for devotion and eternal life. A little bit of Heaven on Earth."

"They taste pretty good, too," Nate chimed in. Her brows scrunched together as she turned to look at him. "I was out with some friends and we ordered desert to split. It had crystallized tulip petals and..."

"Caramel ribbons over white chocolate cake? It was far richer than you'd imagined, far cheaper than it should have been, and you were the only one brave enough to eat the petals."

"How did you know all that?"

Jack held up a knowing finger and gave it a little twirl. "Because last spring it was the specialty desert at Second & Nine. My roommate Veronica created it, but when plates kept coming back with the flowers still on them, her boss decided it was too expensive to keep going. I think this year she's doing violet-flavored custard in a phyllo shell."

He shook his head. "In a city of eight million people, you just happen to know the chef behind the dessert I had the one time I had a night off a year ago. That's crazy."

"That's New York."

They passed through a short doorway and into the art supply store. Jack picked up a display camera and played with the settings. "So, you know all about me. What about you? What do you do?"

"I'm an EMT at night and a student during the day. I'm trying to work my way up to Paramedic, but that requires a two-year program. It's easy enough since I already have a health sciences degree, but there's still a lot of work involved."

"Health sciences and art history. What were you planning to do?"

"I honestly have no idea. My parents insisted I go to college, and those were programs I liked. I think a lot of kids these days fall into that trap. It's just expected they'll go to college, and because they don't have to work for it, they don't really think about why they're there until graduation."

Jack nodded. "My grandmother threw a fit when I picked photography as my major with a music minor. She threatened to come to New York and drag me home, but when I pointed out she wasn't paying a dime for anything, she let me be. Nana Holley had a point, though. If things hadn't worked out just right, I would be living here and working at the local quickie-mart."

"That would have been a tragedy."

She set the camera down and gave him a small smile. "I don't know. I mean, at least this part of Sunnyvale feels like a small town. In New York, you pass a hundred thousand people a day and never get to know anyone. Sometimes I feel lost."

"You just need to get to know the right people." They exited the building and wandered back toward the parking lot.

"When do you get back to the city?" Jack asked.

"Probably Friday. I have a few more days off, but I have errands to run and things to take care of. You?"

She thought about it for a minute, calculating the days left. "I'm not sure. I have another week, but if things fall in line I may be back sooner."

"Be careful out there. Don't pick up any hitchhikers or strange men," he said, repeating his earlier sentiment with a grin.

"Like you, you mean?"

A hand flew to his chest in false offense.

"I don't know what you're talking about. We practically live across the street from each other. I'm not a stranger."

"Living on the other side of the park in New York City is like living three towns over in Indiana. It's definitely not just across the street."

"Touché. Maybe you should take my number,

though, in case you get homesick."

He tried so hard to be smooth, but the pick-up line came out adorably contrived. Jack smiled brighter than she had in weeks. Nate scrawled his name and number across the top of a rumpled gallery pamphlet. Nathaniel Denevieve. She raised an eyebrow at him, and he parried it with a laugh. It was a hearty sound, not in the least embarrassed or awkward.

"My mother was fond of vowels. At least, that's what I tell people."

Jack laughed too. It was a nice feeling, one she'd missed. Even in the city, she worked too hard to give much time to laughter. Her roommates had always pestered her about that. Reaching for both the brochure and the pen, she unceremoniously ripped the former in half and scribbled her own information on the bottom. He looked at it, the edges of his eyes crinkling with the excitement of courtship.

"Jacquelyn Devlin," he read dramatically, sweeping her a bow. "Would you like to go out with me next Saturday? We could go to the Met and maybe get a pretzel. My treat. What do you say?" She nodded and he clapped his hands together. "That's great!"

For a moment, they stood at her car not saying anything. She was unsure how to proceed—they'd agreed to go on a date, but they weren't dating. Technically, they were little better than strangers at this point. Her feet shuffled as she looked for the appropriate way to end the conversation and get back on the road. Luckily, he seemed to pick up on her awkward body language.

"Well, I guess I should be heading back to my family. I did travel three thousand miles to see them." He backed up and gave her another silly bow, reaching out to capture and kiss her hand. "It was a pleasure meeting you, Miss Devlin. I look forward to our next encounter." A dimple flashed as she did a slight curtsy before opening the car door. It squeaked in protest as she gave it a vicious tug.

"Me, too."

Chapter Ten

DEATH drove through the city at a slow crawl. It was big, but he was patient. After his chat with Clarence, it was obvious Sunnyvale was the referred to town. Now he just had to find her. Preferably in a setting not surrounded by bamboo.

Suddenly, he saw it. A little yellow car, incredibly distinctive and with a brunette behind the wheel to boot. His engine made a guttural noise of protest as he accelerated. He swerved into the other lane and tried to weave ahead to catch up. Horns blared from behind and more than a few fingers saluted him, but he ignored them.

His attention narrowed until all he could see, all he cared about, was the incrementally vanishing yellow box. Without warning, his car shook violently, fishtailing beneath the sound of crunching metal and shattered glass. Another vehicle had been in his blind spot as he changed lanes for the fifth time. Filled with frustration, his head whipped around in time to glimpse the Yugo vanishing from sight.

The two damaged vehicles navigated their way to the emergency lane. The little blue Chevrolet stayed a good few yards back from his black Corvette, but the young man who got out looked anything but scared. He stooped to look at the smashed front end before straightening to make his way over. Death noted his darkening gray and emerald green auras for future reference.

"Where's the fire?"

Death's eyebrows bunched together. *Fire?* "I don't know what you mean."

"You were weaving through traffic so fast, it's a wonder you didn't hit more than just my headlight. You could have killed someone, maybe even yourself."

"Well, I..." Death's lips compacted as he looked the dark-haired young man over. He'd never been in such a situation before and wasn't sure how to handle it. "You shouldn't have been sitting where I couldn't see you."

"Whatever, man. Do you have insurance?" Death pulled an envelope out from inside his jacket and flipped through the contents. Inside were some forms the rental company had given him. He was sure one of them was the exorbitantly expensive insurance they'd required him to purchase. Finding the paper, he handed it to his victim.

"That's ironic. Our cars are from the same place at the airport. Well, I'm sure that'll make processing the claim easier for them."

"It's not."

"I'm sorry?"

"It's not irony. It's an interesting coincidence."

The young man sighed and shook his head. Without another word, he pulled out his cell phone and dialed the rental company. Death stood around for a moment, unsure of his role. Walking around to the passenger side of his bumper, he examined the damage. It was minor, relatively speaking. A thought occurred to him.

He could manipulate the physical world.

It was part and parcel of his job description. He bent the order of the universe to his will to take down his marks. Usually, that meant causing things to move or breaking something; occasionally he would change the nature of an object altogether, like water into wine. But could he do it in reverse? Could he fix something instead of destroy it?

Checking to make sure that the young man was distracted by his phone call, Death crouched next to the smashed taillight. He hovered his hands a fraction of an inch from the jagged mixture of plastic, glass, and metal. Heat radiated between them as he focused all his will.

Slowly, the concave body returned to its normal form. Glass and plastic melted and spread with a steady wave of his fingers, back into their original shapes. Even the paint rippled and smoothed, thinning itself out to cover the missing flakes. When the job was done, he stood and sauntered around the car.

The young man finished his call and walked back over.

"Well, it's mostly taken care of. They said we need to bring the cars over since they don't need to be towed. If nothing else, we'll need to see about renting new ones."

Death nodded absently. He had no intention of wasting more time at the rental office.

"I tell you what, Mr.—"

"Denevieve. Nate Denevieve."

"—Denevieve, the damage to my car is very little. As a matter of fact, I took a look and there's barely even a scratch. I have an errand that absolutely must be done today. You head down to the airport and file a complaint, and I'll be along later this evening to finish it out."

"Now, wait just a minute! You can't fly off on your oh-so-important errand and not take care of this. That errand is probably what caused this in the first place."

"It is, but I'm afraid it's a matter of..." Death trailed off. For the first time, he noticed a colorful scrap of paper sticking out of Nate's pocket.

Scrawled across the top was her name and a phone number. What's more, the handwriting was eerily similar, almost but not quite entirely unlike the unknown script on his list the day her name had first appeared in his afterlife. He shook his head and raised his eyes back to the young man's. "It's a matter of life and death."

Nate sighed, obviously disgruntled but unable to do anything about it.

"I'm taking your insurance papers with me to show the rental company."

"That's fine. I'll be along as soon as I can, I assure you. Say," he pointed at the flier, "do you know Jacquelyn?"

"Jack?" Nate looked down at the half-brochure sticking out of his pants' pocket, then back up, his blue eyes suddenly less grumpy. "We met today, actually. Why? Is she a friend of yours?"

"Yes, but I had no idea she was in town too." The lie came out smoother than he expected. "Where is she staying?"

"I'm not sure, to be honest. We're both living in New York now, so we said we'd meet up once we returned."

"I see." The frustration and disappointment dripping from the two words was genuine. "I suppose I'll have to find her the old fashioned way."

"If I speak to her before you do, I'll tell her you asked about her. What's your name?"

"Oh, it's not that important. I'll see you at the rental office."

With a shrug, Nate returned to his damaged Chevrolet and pulled back onto the highway, this time heading north toward San Jose and the international airport. Death, too, reseated himself in the Corvette and returned to the road.

Things were getting more interesting by the hour. But why would fate keep him from following her only to have him run into someone who knew her? It was a puzzle, and one he wasn't particularly enjoying.

As he drove in the direction Jacquelyn disappeared, Death picked up a definite pattern to the traffic. It was now edging on evening, but instead of returning to the suburbs, many cars were making their way downtown. Following them, he discovered why.

The historic business district was transformed into a brightly colored outdoor festival. Booths lined the sidewalks, and store windows were festooned within an inch of their lives. Even the restaurants set up outdoor tables for patrons to enjoy the atmosphere. He slowed his car to read a passing sign.

SUNNYVALE SPRING FEST

APRIL 9 - 13

9:00 AM until 10:00 PM

Clarence said something was keeping her here. Maybe it was the festival. No, that was silly. He'd also said it was a "large weight" that kept her here. Still, it was human nature to want to be cheered up. If he were a gambling man—which he had been once—he would bet anything she'd show up.

Of course, it could be wishful thinking. He shook his head. Right now he was relying almost entirely on luck, but the luck was all in her court. If this didn't work, he wasn't entirely sure what to do next. There were a hundred and forty thousand people in Sunnyvale, California. He couldn't beat down every door.

Maybe, just maybe, luck was drawing them together in some twisted way. It's true her aura had protected her from his not-so-pleasant intentions before. However, if it was truly trying to keep them apart, he wouldn't keep spying her, wouldn't run across her name in the pocket of a stranger. Some larger machination had to be at work.

Doubt niggled in the back of his mind. He'd been so hell-bent on killing her, he hadn't stopped to think about the mechanics of the problem before. Her luck had protected her from him until six days ago. What had changed?

Nothing.

Nothing had changed before that first sighting. The day had gone as any other. He shook his head again. Clearly, the chase was getting to him. He was stringing together coincidences like pearls.

Death pulled up to a nearby hotel. There had

to be a way to find her among so many people. With all this technology and human advancement, surely there was something to help you find another person.

Frowning, he checked into the hotel and made his way to the room indicated on the keycard. He was missing something. It came from being out of the world so long. Some Charonites kept up with such things, but he'd barely bothered to learn how to use a computer. That itself had been of a necessity when the department attempted to modernize a decade or so back. Death sat in the little club chair opposite the bed and stared at the wall over his fingertips.

There had to be a way.

Begin with the little things, Nickleby'd said. Try to break something without touching it. Boil some water. Move an object. Once you get started, it's like opening a gate.

Mallory's chin dug into her folded forearms. She stared at the potted plant before her, willing something to happen. At first, she willed the dirt to shift. When that didn't work she tried making the terra cotta explode. What seemed like hours slipped by. A bead of sweat trickled down her spine, sending shivers across her skin.

Inside, something began to twist, like the child-proof lid on a medication bottle finally giving way. She felt the shuttered power on the verge of releasing; the same feeling she got after popping one too many pretty candy pills.

The plant shook.

Mallory snapped back, unsure what she did. Then, a determined smile curved her face. She reached out her hands, cupping the plant without touching it. Her fingers curled toward the vines like claws. Hazel eyes narrowed into slits as she popped the cap and pushed the power out, shaping it with her will.

The plant shook again. A shiver began at the roots, making its way up the stem. The viney branches trembled as she focused on their tightly closed buds. With aching slowness, one pink capsule after another unfurled. Time stretched, moisture beading her upper lip, as one petal after another peeled back to take on their appropriate rosy splendor.

Then, after all the blooms had opened, they began to die. Some withered while others rotted. One at the crest of the plant burst into flames. Mallory's smile became vicious, sharp and calculating.

She upended a nearby glass of water over the plant, extinguishing the flames and sloshing dirt onto the floor. Shoving her chair from the desk, she stood and positioned herself at the far wall of the office. With all her might, she imagined her sister standing on the other side by the door. One foot in front of the other, imagining herself walking to her sister, Mallory closed the distance.

Her surroundings became gray. Color and sound drained as shapes blurred and morphed into new ones. She could almost see it. That hateful house full of those awful memories. Mallory forced herself to keep going, slowly taking one step at a time.

The shapes solidified, and then she was home.

Jack practically danced into the small house. For once, she didn't notice the smell of stale potpourri or the bits of fluff her shoes kicked up from the shedding carpet. In the midst of all the terrible things she'd been through over the last few days, life didn't seem so bad.

Humming to herself, she placed her half of the gallery brochure in the chip clip recently vacated by Mr. Belvedere's card. While her mood continued to dance, she decided to get to work. Quickly, she changed into something more comfortable than her power heels and pressed slacks and grabbed a handful of garbage bags. The only room left that really needed tackling was the twins' old bedroom. All the others would only need minor touch-ups and massive donations to the mission center.

Returning to the musty room, Jack paused to find a beginning. The pictures would have to go first. It was unsettling having herself stare from all four walls as if she were an omnipresent deity lording over the process. With a loud snap, she opened one of the bags and balanced it in the desk chair. Starting with the oldest images, those most crinkled and faded by sun, Jack peeled off the pictures and cutouts. Sometimes a single photo came off. Sometimes the haphazard way Mal had pinned and taped them released entire sections at a time.

As she worked, she could see a definite progression. The collection became less professional the farther along she moved. Toward the end of the second wall were fewer headshots and more casual pictures that left Jack wondering how her sister had gotten a hold of them.

Then, as she untacked articles from around the window on the third wall, she noticed handwriting. Her progress slowed as she took the time to examine each piece. Incoherent diatribes on theft and secrets filled the margins of newspaper clippings. Unflattering doodles covered magazine tear sheets and fliers.

Choking on her dying mood, Jack tried to pick up the pace. However, a new sight made her stop cold. One of the last photos, hung with a series of other eerily similar pictures above the desk, should not have been there. More than all the others, it signaled to Jack just how far her sister had fallen.

The photo, a little overexposed and grainy from a telescopic lens, showed the partially open blinds of Jack's bedroom in New York. There she was—in baggy sweatpants and a bra, clearly unaware how exposed she was. Mallory had taken a red pen to the picture, drawing on it, highlighting the blurred outline of Jack's vulnerable form, scribbling the same words over and over and over around it.

"I want what's mine."

What? What had she supposedly stolen? The confusion and horror made Jack sick to her stomach. She clutched the photo so tight it creased. Her breathing became labored, and her head swam a bit as the implications settled in.

Either Mallory had hired someone or she had come to New York herself and spied on Jack. More than that, the violence of the red pen, scratching into the surface of the image again and again, demanding a price that couldn't be quantified, scared her. Even though her sister was dead, she couldn't ease the pounding fear in her heart. She'd known since finding the journals and medical records that Mallory had been disturbed, but now she knew just how far her sister had fallen before her demise.

Dead or not, for the first time she was genuinely frightened by her sister.

Jack looked up, a feeling of helplessness overwhelming her senses. She was drowning, not just in her loss, but in the decay of everything she thought she knew. There was a horror in it, both in the realizations and the actions themselves. And, then, the horror became real.

Her eyes connected with a flickering image of her sister stalking toward her, like a bad hologram or a ghost without enough energy to properly manifest. Mal looked thinner and more confident than Jack remembered, but her face twisted in rage and her hands curled toward Jack like manicured talons. Jack screamed and stumbled onto the floor, where she backed blindly into a corner. As the apparition drew closer the air turned electric. Jack's breath puffed in translucent clouds as the temperature of the room dropped.

Her back slammed into the wall as her sister's icy hand gripped the side of her face. Then, as suddenly as she had appeared, Mallory seemed to be ripped away. Jack gasped at the sting as one of Mal's nails sliced across her skin in the process.

Shaking, with tears streaming down her face, Jack wrapped her arms around her knees and rocked until she calmed enough to stand. With a trembling hand, she used her sleeve to smear at the bloody line welling along her jaw. Her wide eyes darted around the room, looking for any sign of an intruder or otherworldly presence. Within minutes even that vigilance wasn't good enough.

Scrambling to her feet, Jack gathered her courage, closed her eyes, and ran from the room. Her purse sat by the front door with the Yugo's keys draped over the top. She grabbed them and fled into the night, not bothering to lock the door behind her.

Even though it was late, Jack pounded on Deacon Franz's door. Within a minute, he answered, still wrapping a house robe around himself. Sobbing, Jack tried to explain what happened, but only an incoherent babble emerged. Deacon Franz took her gently by the shoulders and led her to the couch while Janice ran to get their guest a glass of water. With a trembling hand, Jack held out the photograph she had yet to release. He took it from her and examined it for a moment before trying to persuade her to talk. Through bits and pieces, the deacon withdrew the story. When it was over she was exhausted, like a hollow shell, unable even to cry anymore.

"Jack, you've had a trying time. The devil is strong and we must always be on our guard. Don't let him destroy you with these images of your sister. She was unstable, but that's not your fault. Don't let these insecurities and weaknesses lead you down the same paths."

Together they prayed while Janice brought a blanket and some pillows from the hall closet. After everything she'd been through, they weren't about to let her go home for the night. She felt somewhat safer and extremely grateful to be in the clergyman's home, though her mind was still in turmoil. Ensconced as comfortably as she could be physically, Jack succumbed to exhaustion.

Jack stood in the backyard staring up at a tall pine tree. The Salinas Valley sun hung high overhead giving everything an over-saturated and surreal light. At the sound of the back patio door sliding open, she turned to find Mallory emerging from the squat brick house with a pitcher of lemonade and two glasses of ice. Mal wore the rattan wedges and the peasant dress Jack had last seen her in. Colorful bangles jangled up and down her arms hiding scars as she set the tray down and poured them both drinks. Mallory walked with nimble grace over the cracked paving stones, almost as if she were floating, and handed Jack a drink while sipping on her own. Jack twisted her attention back to the tree.

"I don't understand," she said aloud after a minute's reflection. High in the branches nestled a small, perfect tree house. Through its open walls a hammock could be seen swaying in a light breeze. Every now and then a few pine needles fell to the low-pitched roof before sliding to the ground below. "It was destroyed. Damaged beyond repair. It's been gone for years."

"Like us?" Mallory replied with a small smirk. Her teeth seemed sharp somehow, like a human piranha. Jack cocked her head, a feeling of wariness washing over her. A sweet, metallic taste blossomed in the back of her mouth, and she looked at her half-finished glass of lemonade.

"What have you done?"

Mallory's smile grew wider. "Sssssshhhhh. It's okay. It's all going to be over soon. Then we can both be free." Mallory tossed back her lemonade as the landscape began to spin.

"Why?" was all Jack could get out before she tumbled into an abyss and onto the living room floor.

Chapter Eleven

MALLORY slammed her fists against Gina's unusually empty desk and let out a half scream of frustration. She winced as the corner of the day planner burrowed into the side of her hand.

"Why?" she screeched to the room at large. "Why can't I do this? She was so close! I practically wrapped my hands around that perfect little neck. Why couldn't I stay? I could have taken her, shown her what true power is. She thinks she can stop me, but she's wrong. Her paltry tricks will buy her precious little time. She makes me sick. Crying and screaming like she's done nothing wrong, like she doesn't know her own sins. I'll show her!"

Just thinking about the ways Jack had done her wrong over the years left a bad taste in her mouth. Everyone had loved sister her more from beginning to end. Little Miss Jackie had always done everything in her power to show Mal up. Jack had gotten the best grades, the best boyfriend, the best job. All Mallory had ever gotten was a bad reputation and a medical record thicker than a textbook.

Once Jack was out of the picture, she would finally be on top—forever. She would have the best of everything. All of Jack's stupid little mortal achievements would mean nothing. A goody two-shoes like her sister could never amount to anything in the afterlife. The Beyond was for strong souls, willful and farsighted.

Mal scrunched her face up and concentrated harder. She was starting to get the hang of projecting, but for some reason, locking onto her sister was like trying to grab hold of a slippery eel. Vague shadowy shapes would fade into her mind, but as she began to push herself toward them to make them more defined, they faded right back into her current surroundings. Picking up a potted plant from a nearby desk, she hurled it across the room where it shattered against the wall. The miniature roses bobbed as they slid to a sad heap on the floor.

Tapping her foot with impatience, she mulled over other ways to make progress. She was tired of asking for help. She wanted action! But if she couldn't make the projecting stick, then there would be no action. There would be no revenge.

Maybe it was Jack herself. Perfect Miss Jackie, once again coming out on top. As Mal thought about it the idea grew and grew. Yes, it must be Jack somehow keeping her from staying. If she could only project somewhere nearby then her darling sister might not be able to stop her. Or maybe she was tackling this the wrong way.

Nickleby wanted the old Head gone for good. He needed to be eliminated if she was going to secure her position. She could project to him and take him out first. That would be action—infinitely better than sitting around setting potted plants on fire. Of course, a flaming hibiscus was one thing. Taking out the former Grim Reaper was another entirely.

Dark thoughts whirled through her brain. No one in the department besides Nickleby was supposed to be more powerful than her, but what kind of defenses did her mark have while on leave? Could he attack in return? In life all hirings, firings, and vacations went through an HR department. If the Beyond had such a thing, they would know what kind of a threat he posed.

Marching into the inner office, Mallory tore through drawers and shelves, baskets and books, looking for information. Surely there was a guide, or a flowchart, or a directory of some sort. She'd nearly destroyed the entire office when she noticed a rectangular magnet hidden on the side of a filing cabinet.

Peeling it off was no small task. The magnet had clearly been in place for years and years, and the bond had been increased by the glue of age. When it finally popped off, a yellowed rectangle remained behind in the original color of the faded fixture. The crackled face held a tiny printed calendar for 1735 A.D., but above that sat an old-fashioned advertisement.

IMMORTAL RESOURCES
for all your interdepartmental needs
and afterlife quandaries

An office location and extension followed. Mal tilted her head at it and pursed her lips in an almost-smile. Slapping the magnet back on the metal surface, she strode from the little room and made her way toward the part of the complex indicated by the graphic. After what felt like an eternity, she located the correct door. A young man in a flouncy cravat eyed her with speculation when she walked in.

"Can I help you, miss?"

"Is this Immortal Resources?" she asked tentatively.

"Yes, ma'am. To whom may I direct you?"

"I need to know what happens if a Charonite goes on vacation. Do they lose their powers? Are they more vulnerable than normal?" The young man, whose brass desk plate read Thom Q. Baxley, blinked at her.

"More vulnerable than what, miss? You're

already departed. If you wish to go on vacation, all you'll have to worry about is keeping to the rules and returning to your duties in a prompt manner."

"But what kind of abilities do you keep?" she asked, frustration seeping through.

"Most of them. You can't project and you're no longer incorporeal. Reaping a soul while on leave is likely to see you sent to the afterlife, though I've seen worse."

"Sheol," Mallory interrupted. Thom nodded.

"How do you get sent to Sheol?"

The secretary's comfort visibly slipped. He fidgeted with his cravat and looked away. "Generally, miss, that doesn't happen. If you want specifics, I suggest you ask the head of your department—"

"I am the Head of Human Demise!" she shrieked. Breathing hard, her eyes bored into him like twin swords. She spoke through gritted teeth. "Find me someone who will answer my question now!"

He tumbled out of his desk chair, scrambling into one of the many offices located along the three walls behind him, and slamming the door behind himself. She huffed and propped herself against the edge of the vacated desk. Her foot tapped an impatient beat as she examined the long red talons of her right hand.

It was the perfect idea. The old Head couldn't

push her back like her sister. He couldn't project away like a little cockroach, scurrying from the light. She would simply take him out first, sending him to Sheol and securing a permanent place for herself in the Beyond.

Then she would deal with her sister.

After breakfast, Janice insisted Jack do something nice for herself to take her mind off all the stress she'd been under. The historic district downtown was hosting a festival of sorts and she mentioned it might be the perfect way for Jack to relax and have a little fun. Grateful, Jack was only too happy to comply with the suggestion.

Just before lunch, she found a parking place and then wandered the alleys of the fair. She hadn't been walking long when two teenage girls burst out of an alleyway ahead of her. They had their arms around each other and were twittering and giggling. Overhead, on the brick siding, a painted sign swirled and pointed down the side street.

MADAME MERIDIES'
Cards, Crystals & Charms

The logo looped around a crystal ball in a font that reminded Jack of the nineteen seventies. For a moment, she hesitated. The Bible forbade consorting with the black arts, but fortune telling wasn't really about magic or devils. It was all just nonsense to part a fool from his money, wasn't it? Of course, after last night she felt a definite urge to play the fool. Uncertain, she inched toward the steel door set in the timeworn brick.

Unexpectedly, the door swung open. A heavy-set woman stepped out and looked around. She wore a thickly embroidered pashmina around her mass of black curls and squat torso. Bright hoops dangled at her ears and around each thick wrist, giving her a gypsy feel. However, below it all, she wore faded capris and flip-flops. The woman spotted Jack, and for a fleeting second, she frowned. Then her face bloomed into encouragement, and she gestured for Jack to come forward.

Her words prompted Jack as a rebuttal to her unspoken thoughts. "God set the stars in the sky to be read and sent the angels to Earth to whisper in our ears. There is no shame in helping you receive the message. Come. You look like you need all the help you can get."

Jack put one unsure foot in front of the other until she reached the shop. Peering inside, she took in the star-spangled room. Every available surface was covered in scarves and confetti, crystals and Christmas lights. With continuing hesitation, she lowered her slight weight into a chair that creaked when she sat. Madame Meridies reappeared from behind a beaded curtain, shuffling a pack of tarot cards and humming to herself. Her kind black eyes rested on her customer as her brown fingers worked the deck. Lightly for someone with such a large presence, she took the opposite seat and settled in.

"For you, I will do three simple, but powerful readings. Together they will lay the foundation of the past, explore the present, and give a glimpse into the future."

Closing her eyes, she took a deep breath, filling her lungs to capacity and holding it there for three heartbeats before slowly releasing. Her expression emptied into a haunting neutrality. In a blur, she snapped five cards from the deck and laid them in a perfect line between them. Jack peered at the titles across their bottoms. Death. The Moon. The Hermit. The Hierophant. The World.

"You feel trapped by an old conflict between you and someone else, someone close to you. You're letting it haunt your present. You've tried distancing yourself from the problems, and you've also tried turning to God. For a little while, it worked, but now you're back to square one."

She pushed the cards forward and lay down a new set as she let her words sink in. The Tower. The Wheel of Fate. The Three of Swords. The Emperor. Jack noted with interest that the final card, the Seven of Wands, rested upside down.

"You lost the person you were in conflict with, but now you're questioning everything. All the prosperity and peace you've gained is rapidly turning around. There's a man who's influencing this dissonance. You're feeling vulnerable and tired, perhaps even guilty, but you should know that only through grief can you experience closure."

One final time she lay out a set of cards below those she'd finished reading. Jack's head swam, but still she leaned over to read the cards. Judgment. The Hanged Man. Temperance. The Ace of Wands.

There was a pause. She looked up curiously at the woman, who held the deck between her hands, as if waiting for just the right time to draw the final card.

"In your future, I see absolution, the redemption of a new beginning. There will be much sacrifice, though don't confuse it with surrender. When opposites join together, there will come strength and power that will shepherd in harmony. I'm getting an underlying sense of family. All of this has to do with someone close to you, probably the person you lost."

Madame Meridies flipped over the final card at last, and then stared at it for several seconds. Her head tilted to the side in consternation and her brow furrowed.

"The Five of Swords is an interesting draw. While it fits well with your other cards, the insinuations are far beyond anything I have read before. Do you see the clash of dark gray clouds being ripped at by the bright blue sky? Then, there, in front is a man confidently gathering swords from a battlefield, while enemies still remain. You will come out the victor in your current conflict, but the conflict has much higher implications than you realize. I would say... Almost celestial. You are an unwilling participant, and it will take its toll. There will be betrayal and alienation, and if you are not careful it will leave an emptiness inside, which you will never be able to fill."

The woman slumped forward slightly. A faint sheen clung to her upper lip, and she fanned herself though the room felt quite cool. Leaving the cards where they lay, she reached out and patted Jack's clasped hands.

"I've done what I can for you. Knowledge is power, but don't let knowledge of the future hinder your present. Bad luck often follows good, but you are stronger than both."

With a weak, courteous smile Jack acknowledged the end of the session. She tried to get up as cordially as she could, but her mind was swimming. Jack thought of the mysterious man, and her sister, and all the horrible things that had happened in her life. To contrast, she also tried to remember the good things, but they only left her with more questions.

For a brief time in New York, it had seemed like the world was hers. She'd blossomed into her own person in college, found a great job, made new friends. But that was sandwiched between the pain of the past and the horrors of the present. Deep down, she knew that fortune tellers preyed off the ambiguity of their readings and the obvious emotions of the clients, but Madame Meridies had seemed genuinely eager to do what she could.

Jack fumbled for her purse and tried to press some cash into the woman's hands, but Madam Meridies refused to accept.

"Why not? Why would you give me a reading for free?"

"As I said before, you need all the help you can get. I see dark times ahead for you. Very dark. You could change the fate of us all."

"But I don't want to change anybody's fate! I just want to live in peace. I want to go back to the city, and back to my life, and be happy!"

"Sometimes you aren't given a choice where the road will take you, only how you act along the journey."

Every day that passed seemed to make less sense than the day before, and Jack was beginning to feel like Alice drowning in the pool of her own tears. Something would have to be done, whether it was a slew of sessions with her psychiatrist or some quality time with a priest. Perhaps she should start journals of her own.

The midday sun rode high over the buildings,

and her stomach growled. She wandered the lanes of the fair in the direction of some restaurants and tried to focus on her surroundings. It helped to clear her head a little, even if it was temporary.

In a little stall a block from the eateries, Jack stopped to watch a small oriental woman create a necklace for a young girl. With nimble fingers, she wove colored strings together with a scattering of tiny beads. Then, she took a pressed tourists' coin from her patron's outstretched hand and punched a hole in it before threading the trinket onto the braid. Beaming, the girl paid for her purchase and loped off to find her friends.

The woman caught Jack's curious eyes and motioned her forward. "I can make something for you," she said with a coy grin. "I can make anything into beautiful jewelry."

"Anything?"

"Anything."

Jack rummaged in her purse. Tucked in a corner, hidden among pens and chapstick, she found what she sought. She pulled out the break of bamboo she'd found at Hakone, half forgotten since that crazy day in the gardens. The woman's eyes lit up with curiosity.

"You carry bamboo in your purse?"

"I found it. It reminds me of someone I lost."

"Bamboo brings you luck and keeps you safe. I have such blinds in my house. It keeps the spirits out. Would you like this as a necklace?"

"Can you make it into a bracelet?"

"I can do anything," she replied again matter-of-factly. Quickly, she selected colors and beads and set to work. Various colors of green and gold wove together for the braid as she deftly slid sparkling black and jade beads throughout. When she was done with the bracelet, she fit the knotted threads through the hollow core of the nob and tied off the ends to make a clasp.

"Oh, it's beautiful!" the woman exclaimed with pride when she finished. She held it up against her hand, turning the bracelet back and forth so that the jewel-like beads danced in the afternoon sun. Jack paid the woman with a smile and turned to find lunch as she fastened it to her arm.

A commotion from the other side of the street caught her attention as she walked away. Delicate china shattered on a cafe's concrete patio, and a patron shouted, "Watch it!" as a chair scraped back and knocked into him. Her eyes skimmed for the source of the ruckus and lit upon a red-headed man in a silk suit. He stood staring in her direction, the fluid lines of his body poised as if to attack. As her gaze locked with his, she realized that no matter how she tried to rationalize it, the events of Hakone were just as real as the bamboo shoot tied to her wrist.

Without a second thought, she ran.

What am I doing? Death wondered as he chased her through twisted back streets and narrow alleys. There had been shocked cries and startled shouts, but as he ran on, those fell away. It was absurd, absolutely absurd, to be chasing some girl–who, he might add, he no longer had authorization to kill–when he didn't even have a plan.

Rather, he'd had a plan, but it hadn't involved this. He'd decided to find her and follow her, looking for a crack to exploit, the perfect chink in her perfect armor. Once found, he would use any official resources he could muster to break through her barriers, even if it meant going Upstairs to do so. By the time he acted, she would have forgotten him, dismissing him as a figment of her imagination. She would feel secure and off her guard. But now it was all ruined. Now she would know he was after her.

In a way, he was glad to be out of the office. Anyone who caught wind of this would think him mad. Even a Charonite would stare at him as if he'd lost it. Why was she so important? What about her made him lose his cool on sight?

On a superficial level, he could explain it away as the principle of the thing. Her life aura wasn't simply black; it was deeper in a way most beings couldn't readily perceive. That indicated a lock. Much like the pure white of an Immortal or a weeping rose, by nature of being at the furthest peak of the spectrum, the coloring was completely unchangeable; it had been black since birth and in theory would be until her death. Like the cursed, she shouldn't have lived long enough to be a thorn in his psyche. And yet, here she was, taunting him with her inability to fulfill her own demise.

Undoubtedly, her continued existence hinged entirely on her luck. The thin ribbon of gold goaded him. It wasn't just bright and insistent yellow like most lucky people—like Katerina. The aura sparkled and shimmered, creating a magical barrier and daring the universe to take a swing at her. He wondered if that same luck was the reason she hadn't appeared on his list until someone took proactive measures to bring her to his attention.

A much deeper reasoning for his madness was one of pride. For the better part of a thousand years, he'd been at this job, and for at least the first four hundred he had speculated on aural anomalies. No one had ever bothered to take note of the rules before. Everyone accepted that a black aura equaled death and a white aura life. Red meant unlucky and yellow lucky. Shades of blue and gray ranged the middle of the spectrums and encapsulated the majority of humanity. No Immortal had cared to dig farther before he'd come along. Like Clarence, nobody had ever seen black gold, so they assumed it must not exist. After a while, he too had given up. He'd locked his ramblings and research away and had almost forgotten about his theories.

Almost.

Then, there she was, like a lightning bolt on a clear day. She had the ability to see him when he was incorporeal. She seemed to sense something was fundamentally wrong with herself. And, at least in the gardens, she'd seemed prepared for death, as if it was something she'd been waiting for her whole life.

Up ahead, she was losing ground. He forced a fire escape to collapse off the side of a building and directed it to fall straight into her path. Somehow, however, the metal trellis fell sideways and landed parallel with the wall. He growled and pushed himself harder, appreciating his temporarily revoked abilities more than ever.

Something a little more complicated, but far more precise, he thought acridly. The front tire on a semi blew as she emerged from the shadows onto a busy intersection. Careening recklessly, the screeching vehicle slammed into a fire hydrant two feet to her left. Barely hesitating, she wove through the ensuing madhouse with Death hot on her heels. He gritted his teeth in frustration.

As they turned a corner, he sighted a fireworks shop. Death concentrated on visualizing his end result, and as Jack passed by the window, the frontal display exploded in a shower of painted glass and blinding sparks. Rushing through the brightly colored smoke and screaming people, he looked for her. Frantically, he searched the way ahead and to each side, but she was gone. It was as if she had just disappeared.

After several minutes, he slumped against a brick wall. His suit was stained, his shoes were wet, and his hair was a mess. As the adrenaline waned, he also felt like a fool. What did he possibly think he would accomplish by throwing such bombastic obstacles at a gold? He knew how the universe worked. What he needed was more subtlety. If he created a pinprick in her shielding, something small-yet-deadly might slip right through.

Despite the odd looks those nearby shot him, Death wandered into a bar and laid a black American Express card on the counter. He needed to think, and there was no better way to brainstorm than with scotch on the rocks.

THE BUSINESS OF DEATH

Adaptation

Nantes, Brittany — October 21, 1221 AD

SCREAMS echoed off the stones walls, undampened by the wool and silk tapestries. It was a sound of pain and determination, which every woman in the castle recognized and every man closed his ears to. The guttural noises ripped raw at the throat of the young woman making them as she lay abed. Her fair hair plastered to her bright pink face, and her hand gripped the woman next to her.

The other woman stooped to her ear to murmur reassurances and the effect of their faces together was startling. Cornsilk to cornsilk and blue to blue, they matched identically, with the exception that the latter figure had sunken, ashen cheeks to contrast. Another woman at the foot of the bed looked up at the two of them and crossed herself. Twins were an unnatural thing.

"Kate…" came a quiet voice in stark contrast to the hoarse screaming. "Kate, you have to promise to take care of my baby."

"Alix, all will be well," she lied. "You will be holding your child in no time. Six months from now you'll have forgotten all about this as you watch him play with his brother and sister."

"Oh, I hope it's another boy. I love Yolande so, but I wish my little John had a play—" She screamed again, causing her sister to reel backward and knock over a candelabra. Other women rushed forward to stamp out any flames, which might have caught on the scattered rush flooring. Alix began to sob, her great belly shaking beneath the tented covers.

"Almost there," the midwife at the end of the bed called, her voice loud to cover the crying. "Push hard, dear, and 'twill all be over."

Another wail pierced the castle, winding its way through attics and dungeons. Alone within a darkened alcove, Arthur winced. It was unfair, forcing him to witness this. Forcing him to tie up the loose ends. Training, they called it. He wondered if anyone would notice if he let her live, if he simply walked away.

"I wouldn't do that if I were you."

Much like his youngest sister, he jumped at the sound so close to his ear. Spinning, he saw a woman with wavy blond hair and large hazel eyes watching him.

"You can see me?"

"Not just me. I'm willing to warrant the one in

the bed sees you, too, even if she doesn't acknowledge it. The dying often see the dead."

"Who are you?"

"Celestial Intervention. I was in the area for other reasons and curiosity about the young duchess got the better of me. I can only guess why you're here."

"I don't understand why they would send me for this. Murdering my own sister in her childbed seems a bit too cruel, even for the Beyond."

"You haven't been a Charonite for very long, have you? You are being sent on assignments like this because they teach you things important to your continued existence in the Beyond. It isn't murder, it's fate. She will die whether you do it or not. It's only a matter of time before your neglect catches up with you, and the consequences are much worse than you can imagine.

"By assigning you loved ones, you are learning that emotions have no place in the afterlife. That's the advantage we have over mortals. Without emotion everything runs much smoother and immortality is much more palatable."

The whimpering cries of a child filled the room. With a grim look, the midwife cleaned and swaddled the child before passing him to his aunt. Kate rocked the baby gently as she took him around to his mother. Alix lay back, sunken into the bolsters with exhaustion. Still, her feeble arms reached out to take a hold.

"You got your wish, Alix. God be praised, it's a healthy baby boy. What will you name him?"

For a moment, Arthur could swear she looked directly at him before turning her gaze to her squirming son.

"Arthur," she said in a barely audible whisper.

The Celestial Intervention agent he'd been talking to smiled as he peeled himself away from the wall and walked forward from the shadows. Pretty thoughts curved the edges of Alix's mouth as she bent with effort to kiss her newborn's head. The midwife and Kate conversed in furious whispers as he passed them, taking note of the blood-soaked sheets.

Alix settled back into her pillows, cradling the young Arthur, and closed her eyes. She let out a sweet sigh as the reaper placed his hand on her arm before trailing down to her fingers, and pulling her into a sitting position. With ease she joined him and threw her arms around his chest, burying her face in the top of his silken tunic.

"I knew it. A woman knows. But I'm so glad it was you."

Tears sparkled in her eyes as she looked from her sister to her son one last time, then she faded from view.

"Well done," the agent spoke again, coming forward from the alcove. "I'm surprised she went so quietly—new mothers seldom do."

"Why are you still here?"

"Want to be alone, do you? Well, I suppose I can't blame you for that. It won't do, though. You've a whole list of other marks and you've wasted most of the day with this one."

"What is it to you, the business of death?"

"I think you'll find Celestial Intervention has its fingers in all the pies. Don't be so cocksure that no one knows what has, does, and will happen. It's all interconnected." She stuck out a hand. "I'm Athena."

"The goddess?"

She gave a very unladylike snort.

"Something like that."

He grasped her petite hand in his. "Arthur."

"Tell me, Arthur, have you learned prognostication?"

"Fortune telling?"

"The art of seeing into the possibilities of the future. It's a skill used almost exclusively by the Fates, but on occasion other departments find it useful."

"No. And I don't see that I'm likely to. Taking the souls of those most dear to me seems to take up an inordinate amount of my time."

She smiled again, this time showing a row of perfect, pearly teeth.

"We'll see."

Chapter Twelve

MALLORY sat in a chair, tapping her foot. Thom had been gone a long time, much longer than she'd like at any rate. She'd managed to reign in her anger at his ignorance, but only just. Now there was nothing to do but wait. Her chair felt too small, confining in the open expanse of the office. Her fingers curled around the armrests, clinching tight in preparation to launch forward. The muscles along her lower back and thighs tensed as the thought of pacing made its way through her system.

Suddenly, she stopped. A young girl, probably no more than fourteen or fifteen, stood in the doorway. Her head tilted, spilling golden curls onto her shoulder.

"Where's Thom?"

"He's running an errand for me. Who're you?"

She smiled, beautiful white pearls flashing behind candy-pink lips. "Iris. Messenger."

"Do people always give their last names around here? I'm beginning to notice a trend."

"Messenger isn't my last name. It's my job. I came down here with a message for Amraphel, but this is the first time in a century I've seen Thom away from his desk. It must be quite the errand you sent him on."

"Well, as Grim Reaper, I do have a certain amount of sway."

Iris's brows rose so high they nearly disappeared into her hairline. Curiosity lit up her big brown eyes, and her lips parted. "So you're the new Head of Human Demise I've heard so much about. How long were you a Charonite?"

Mallory felt smugness welling up within. The corners of her mouth curved, and she stood a little straighter. "I wasn't."

"Oh? How did you learn to use your newfound gifts so quickly? Projecting isn't an easy task for someone new to the Beyond."

"And just how long have you been dead, little girl?"

Any vestige of geniality slipped from Iris's façade. "Nearly three thousand years have I been the messenger of the Powers That Be. I've honed my craft through millennia of practice."

"The Powers That Be? You mean, like God?"

"If you like. The Beyond prefers a far more

segmented approach to theocracy."

Mallory mulled over this. Did that mean that there wasn't a God, or did it mean that there were more people between her and him than a priest and an archangel? She'd never been as religiously inclined as her sister, but she'd never been an atheist either. Now that she was dead, she supposed she should learn the truth.

"So, is there a God or not?"

It was Iris's turn to sneer. "Truth is revealed to those best positioned to seek it."

"What does that mean?" Mallory screeched, unable to contain her frustration. Iris picked some lint off her dress, crushing it between her fingers, and then rubbing it off a suitable distance from her body.

"You either need to become better at your job, or you need to move on to the afterlife. Being in the in-between will get you nowhere."

"Become better at my job? Just how did you learn your, what did you call them—gifts?"

"I died in an age where people believed anything was possible. They believed if you glued feathers to your arms with wax you could fly. When I died, it was no small leap to think I could project wherever I liked whenever I liked. The rest of the powers came over time with promotion, trust, and instinct."

"I believe in myself just fine."

"No, you don't or you'd be able to. If there's

even the slightest doubt, you'll stay where you are. You may force yourself somewhere, but you'll never remain." Iris's eyes turned sharp. It felt like they were piercing through all the layers down to Mallory's innermost thoughts.

"You don't really doubt your ability to project, though. I can see that. You doubt your ability to live up to expectations. You doubt your ability to pull the whole thing off and show everyone they're wrong about you."

Mallory's face flushed with heat. How dare such a little slip of a girl go mining for her deepest fears. It was inconceivable! She opened her mouth to tell her off, to tell her to go straight to Hell, but stopped.

Iris's head jerked up and away, her eyes unfocused, her lips parted, like she was listening to instructions from an imaginary friend. Suddenly, her arms snapped and swirled as if she was putting on a jacket. As she did so, one appeared, and she buttoned the large buttons of the wool coat with care. The sky blue material flowed to her knees, flaring apart around the skirt of her dress.

"I must go. We'll speak again, though. I'm certain of it."

A look of determination lit Iris's face as she took three steps forward and was gone. Mallory stared at the place where she had been. Her thoughts whirled like dervishes. Was it all a matter of belief? Was she trying so very hard that she'd allowed doubt to creep in? Did it really have nothing to do with Jack?

From the other room Thom murmured to someone else by the adjoining door. A moment later another man came out with the secretary on his coattails. He held out a hand for Mallory.

"I hear you need information on The Great Nothingness."

"Yes," she practically hissed in anticipation.

"It's not something we like to discuss, but as you are new, I suppose someone will have to explain it to you."

"I know what it is. I just want to know how it works. How does someone get sent there? Say that I needed to punish someone for," she thought back to what Thom had said, "taking a life while on leave."

The man rubbed his jaw and shifted his feet.

"You have to have the sanction of this department, as well as that of your director. Then you simply lay hands on the Immortal and will them to their final destination. Most go peacefully. There's been a rumor going around for millenia that after a time in Sheol, you get released into a nice afterlife."

"A rumor?"

He shrugged. "I've never seen it happen, though from this side it would be next to impossible to know. Do you have a Charonite who needs such an action taken against them?"

"Yes, yes I do. And the director is already on board."

Death threw back his sixth drink and watched the mirror over the bar. A teenage girl in a sky blue parka sat at a nearby table. Her large brown eyes stared at him unwaveringly beneath a coiffed crown of golden hair and her sweet, pink mouth formed an innocent and unassuming expression. Patrons of all kinds filled the establishment, though she looked a bit young, and he might not have noticed her at all if she hadn't appeared in her seat so suddenly as to make other patrons gasp. No one approached her, though. Mortals had an impressive ability to rationalize things they couldn't explain.

The girl was there for him, and he knew it the same way he knew why. Setting down the glass, he stood from the counter and held up a hand to the bartender, signaling he would be back. With as much nonchalance as he could muster, Death walked over to the young girl's table.

"What do you want, Iris?" he asked, gripping the back of a chair with feigned casualty. Teenager or not, she was one of the most dangerous Immortals he'd ever met. The messenger of the Powers that Be, she was powerful enough to carry out their whims, not just deliver their missives.

"You know why I'm here." Her voice rang out childish, though her words were full grown. He pulled out the seat he held onto and sat without invitation. The man behind the bar shot him a querying look but said nothing to their unusual pairing.

Death attempted a shrug. "I don't need the warning, thanks."

"Clearly you do." She leaned forward in earnest and spread her small, pale hands on the tabletop. "The Powers that Be are not amused by your attempts to take a soul while on administrative leave. You know the consequences of acting without sanction."

He grimaced. "I hardly think Sheol is an appropriate punishment for something like that."

"It's not for you to decide whether the punishment fits the crime," she replied sharply. "If you step outside the bounds of your office, your authority, you will be terminated."

"Is this it, then? Are you going to try and take me out?"

He thought of the darkness and the solitude that awaited those souls imprisoned in Sheol. Devoid of light, devoid of life, devoid of meaning—a continued yet thoroughly deprived existence. Iris eyed him, as if making up her mind how best to strike. He knew it had been some time since she'd been allowed to exercise the full extent of her powers. The air between them hung thick with danger and indecision. Finally, she spoke.

"No."

Death felt his lungs fill and realized he'd been holding his breath. "You caused no irreparable harm today," she continued. "Remember, though, if you unnecessarily expose the Beyond or take the life of a mortal outside the job, there will be no jury with which to argue your case. These rules must be kept for all, or they can be kept for none. I'm sure you understand."

He nodded, hoping she couldn't pick up on his rising frustration. Though meant as a deterrent, her words more than anything made him determined to find his mark and settle the score. It was true he'd wanted a vacation, and it was also true Jacquelyn was the proof he needed for years of fruitless speculation. But since that day in Fort Tryon Park, she had somehow latched herself onto his psyche and he couldn't rest until he'd dealt with her. Even if he didn't kill her, there had to be a way to break her luck.

Death shook through the haze of his reverie to respond to his judge, jury, and potential executioner, but she was already gone like an elusive rainbow on a summer's day. He returned to his barstool and accepted another drink. His thoughts turned dark as he sipped this one slowly.

He'd find her, oh yes, he'd find her. And he knew just how to do it now.

Iris's visit reminded him of another being who, much like herself, existed outside the structure of the Beyond. Years ago, he'd killed the foremost authority on arcane lore, but the man had been so attached to his books that he refused to move on. It was just as well, Death mused, because he'd become a valuable asset to those who needed obscure information. Honestly, he didn't know why he hadn't thought of it before, especially since it was only an hour's drive north. If there was a way to break Miss Devlin's luck, *he* would know.

Suddenly, another thought occurred to him. Books. In centuries past, anything and everything could be found in a book. Even people, if you looked in the right places. Technology had advanced so far now. Surely, there was a way to look up a person if you knew where they were. And just as then, the best place to start these days was probably the library.

For the first time a real plan, like a neat little map, formed in his brain. He hummed as he paid off his tab and wound his way through downtown and back to his car. Soon it would all be over.

A familiar voice wafted into the hallway as Mallory approached her outer office. The even tones and light accent dragged at her memory until she came up with a picture of the woman from the Department of Fate. What had her name been? L'Tradita? What an absurd name. Who wanted to be called tragedy?

She entered the room to see Gina staring curiously at the woman. Gina's brows knitted together as she stuck a cigarette behind her ear.

"Seven hundred years I've managed to avoid this department and its denizens," l'Tradita said. "Seven. Hundred. And now it's all for naught because your new boss can't keep the threads of fate from snarling."

Mallory cleared her throat. "I'm the new Head of Human Demise."

L'Tradita whirled around, her black lace fluttering like wings. "You? You don't belong in this department any more than I do."

"Things change." Mallory shrugged insolently. "What's your problem?"

"My 'problem' is that someone in your department has been toying with fate. Verðandi and Atropos are concerned that the threads are becoming tangled. When one wrong person dies or one correct person doesn't die, it affects more than just them."

Mallory's lips curled in a sneer. "Keep to your own department. We know what we're doing here."

"No, you don't. Death is not a game. It has serious consequences that can linger on an immortal soul for eternity. Once dead we do not forget how we got here."

"How would you know? I bet you've always been in that dark, dusty little department, creeping around hallways like a spider."

More passion lit l'Tradita's face than Mallory expected. It was like she transformed into a different person, a younger person, who had not been beaten down by the sands of time.

"My own life was ended by a Charonite who chose to ignore fate. He seduced me, and then he betrayed me. While the consequences of his actions were contained to the afterlife, there were knots that took much too long to unravel. If whatever you are doing continues down the path Atropos sees, the consequences will be much further reaching than even my own problems, touching both those living and those dead. You don't want me to have to fix your mistakes."

"Whatever. You can tell the old crones down in the Department of Fate that we got their message. Now leave."

L'Tradita's garnet lips practically disappeared with silent rage, but she turned on her heels and walked away. Mallory smiled at the retreating figure with a sense of victory. She turned to Gina, who still looked like a mouse trying to find the cheese, and held out a sheaf of papers.

"Snap out of it. I need you to stamp these or whatever and make sure they get filed properly."

"What are they?"

"Does it matter? Just do your job, which is doing as I tell you."

With that she went to her own office and closed the door. Taking a deep breath, Mallory found the longest uninterrupted path across the office and slowly put one foot in front of the other.

"Arthur Bretagne," she said out loud, trying to pour all her thoughts on the man she was determined to take out. She had no face to focus on, and the name felt foreign on her tongue. "Arthur," she said again, having made it halfway across the spacious room. Outside the window a storm was brewing. The muscles of her face scrunched together. "Death." Mallory made it to the far wall and spun to stride back the other way. Her heels clacked on the checkered tile. "Death, death death!" she called, her voice rising with each syllable.

Jack! her mind screamed.

And then she was there in the rain.

Chapter Thirteen

JACK hadn't even stopped to cry. Her heart threatened to beat out of her chest and her legs felt like jelly, but she kept running. He'd been following her. How else could he have found her in Sunnyvale of all places? Until now, she'd pushed their last encounter out of her mind. She'd convinced herself that she was hallucinating, that it was just her grief and confusion playing tricks on her. But now she could swear the devil himself was after her. Maybe he'd always been after her. Maybe it explained everything.

Jack took a taxi back to where she'd parked her car. In the chase she'd become lost and didn't want to chance running across her pursuant again. Through the fever of panic, she latched onto what the old jewelry maker had said about bamboo. Turning her car east, she headed for the nearest home improvement store.

While she drove, her mind circulated around the one fact she could grasp onto: She'd seen him before. Not just in New York, not just in Hakone Gardens, but before. He'd seemed familiar each time, but just like the first time she'd locked it away. Now she remembered.

Had he really been plaguing the two of them their whole life? Perhaps he was behind what had happened to Mallory, whispering in her ear until she spiraled out of control. Despite everything she now knew, everything she read and remembered, Jack still refused to believe that her own twin could succumb to such darkness without a hand to push her over the edge.

She spent the next hour driving to every hardware store in the area until she maxed out her credit card on enough bamboo blinds to cover every window of the little house. Paranoid, Jack inspected each face in the crowds. Even as she drove, her eyes remained more on the rear view mirror than on the road ahead. Once home, she quickly unloaded her packages and locked the door behind her.

Jack struggled getting the old blinds down herself. The picture windows on either end of the house were quite large, and she was relatively small. After half an hour of fighting with the metal brackets, she sunk into a chair. They had to go up, but she just didn't see a way to get them all done before nightfall.

With a sigh, she trudged to the kitchen to retrieve a water bottle. As she closed the refrigerator door, the motion ruffled a pamphlet clipped to the outside. Pausing with the half-open beverage, Jack combed the ripped page with her eyes. There at the bottom a name and phone number was scrawled in smudged, black ink.

Nathaniel Denevieve

Nate

If adrenaline hadn't been ferociously pumping through her veins, Jack might have smiled. But, how could she explain why she needed all the blinds changed so desperately? She knew how crazy it would sound, but she also recognized she needed help. Pulling the old phone off the wall, she dialed the number he'd looped across the glossy brochure. Rather than leave a voicemail after the third ring, Jack's thumb hovered over the off button. Mentally chiding herself, she began to hang up just as he answered.

"Hello?"

Her breath caught. What on Earth was she doing?

"Hello??"

"Hi, Nate. It's Jack."

"Oh, hey! I didn't expect to hear from you so soon."

"Me either."

He laughed at her frankness. "Couldn't resist

my charm, huh? Did you want to go do something? My rental's out of commission at the moment, but I'm sure I could wrangle something up."

"Well, actually, I hoped you might want to come over to my place. I don't know anyone else around here and I'm having some hardware problems."

"Ah." He voiced rang of disappointment and Jack took a deep breath before plunging forward.

"If you come help me, I'll make you dinner."

"Oh, well, why didn't you say so?"

"Because I didn't want to inflict my cooking on you."

"A little wine makes everything better. Where are you?"

"264 East McKinley Avenue."

"I think I know where that is."

"Great! I'll see you soon, then."

"See you soon," he agreed. Jack hung up the phone, her heart pounding in her ears. She leaned back against the refrigerator, her head tapping against the magnets.

What had she done? She didn't know how to cook! And she hadn't been grocery shopping since she arrived in California. Turning, she plundered through cabinets to find something passable. Mallory obviously didn't cook any more than she. Some dried spaghetti was probably the best bet, though it took some tunneling to find sauce. Along the way she found canned green beans, dehydrated onions, and a small tin of mushrooms. She checked the dates on the packaging and was relieved that everything was still well within its expiration.

Jack put water on to boil and, once it was there, she scooped out a little to rehydrate a tablespoon of onions. Into the rest of the water she unceremoniously dumped the noodles and gave them a swirl as they softened. Once the onions were plump and fragrant, she mixed them together with the mushrooms and the sauce to be heated in another pot. It was nothing fancy, but she thanked God this was the one kind of meal she'd had occasion to prepare in New York. Finding a pretty bowl, she poured in the beans and heated them as well. Then, she drained the pasta and cleaned the kitchen with furious speed.

On cue, the doorbell rang. Jack peered though the peep hole, making sure it was Nate. Despite her fluster over dinner, she was still terrified of what lay beyond the confines of the house, even more so than the thought that her sister's spirit might appear from within. As if he could sense her on the other side of the door, he leaned in to look back at her through the glass bubble.

It had started misting outside and there were tiny flecks of water glistening in his dark hair. He had on a plain cotton shirt and jeans, but he'd tried to spiff up by throwing an open button-up shirt over his ensemble. She snapped open the locks and hurried him inside, appreciating the vanilla tang of his cologne as it overtook the musty floral smell of the house.

"What's the big rush?" he laughed.

"The food'll get cold," she mumbled. Jack made sure the locks were firmly latched, then turned back to shuffle him into the kitchen. He stood there with a bemused smile on his face and a bottle of wine in his hand. She could feel red heat suddenly shoot across her cheeks.

"Oh, Nate. I should have said so on the phone, but I was just so flustered by the day I've had. I'm really sorry, but I can't drink wine."

"I thought you were Catholic?" he asked, a little confused.

"I'm allergic to ethanol. It's really a pain, too. I have to have a special communion, I can't go out drinking, I can't even use most hand sanitizers." Her eyebrows bunched together and she chewed on her bottom lip. She felt like a fool for not telling him the second he'd mentioned it, but to be honest she hadn't really heard him say it. The thoughts swirling through her head had blocked out almost everything but his agreement to come over.

"Man, that sounds like it really sucks."

"Yeah, that's one thing my sister had going for her. Identical or not, she never had a problem with alcohol. It's a great excuse for when you don't want to go out partying with your roommates, though."

"I'll bet." He swung the bottle up and tucked it under his arm. "I guess I'll give it to my sister as thanks for putting up with me this week. Now, you did promise food."

Jack felt the flush across her face receding as she ushered him back to the small kitchen. She'd set up the tiny table with all the formality that she could recall from her days of Home Ec. It didn't look half bad, if she did say so herself, and even the ridiculously simple meal smelled pretty good.

"That's so perfect," he said with amusement as they entered the tiny room. "My mom always used to make spaghetti on rainy nights." Jack would hardly call the misty drizzle outside rain, but she was glad he seemed satisfied with the fare.

"Well, you're in luck because it's about the only thing I know how to cook."

"Is that right? A talented girl like you should know how to do more than boil water."

"And just how often have you cooked since moving to the City of Dreams?"

"Touché."

Instead of himself, Nate talked about his sister Marnie, who he'd been staying with. They'd never gotten on particularly well, but after the birth of his newest niece she'd begged him to come out and stay with them for a little while. After several months of hemming and hawing, he'd come.

"It's crazy. She's like a completely different person now."

"I've heard motherhood can do that to you. Life isn't about just you anymore; it's about them and what's best for their world. I've always wondered what it would be like. I'm closer to thirty than I am to twenty, now. Maybe I'll never know."

"Miracles of modern medicine. I'm sure you'll be fine. Didn't some 60-year-old woman in New Jersey give birth to twins a few years ago?" he asked.

Jack looked horrified, her nose wrinkling and her mouth falling open. "I can't imagine being eighty when my kids are in college! What about you? Have you ever thought about kids?"

"I love 'em, but I'm stuck in the back of that ambulance all night and during the day I'm in a classroom trying to move up the medical ladder. Saturdays I sleep and Sundays I watch football. That doesn't leave a whole lot of time to find a decent mother."

They'd finished up eating and Jack hurriedly gathered the dishes and hauled them to the sink. Refusing his offer of assistance, she swirled soapy water in the enameled basin and picked up a plate. Suddenly, a flash of lightening arced across the black sky beyond the window, followed by a boom of thunder. It illuminated and distorted her own reflection in the naked glass and the dirty china slid from her sudsy hands. With a loud crash it shattered against the sink divider.

"What's wrong? What happened?"

Jack couldn't reply at first. She stared at the image before her, now once more her own. The skin on her arms crawled and her fingers trembled. Tears gathered in her eyes.

"I thought I saw something. It's nothing." She tried to control her labored breathing and focused on picking up the colorful shards.

Nate took her wet hand in his and turned her to face him. "It's obviously something. Why won't you tell me?"

"You'll think I'm crazy. Hell, even I'm beginning to think I'm crazy."

He led her back over to the table and sat her down in a chair before picking up the pieces of plate himself.

"Try me."

"It's Mallory. I keep seeing her. This time I think it was just my reflection, but yesterday I swear she was in our old room trying to attack me. That's what these stupid bamboo blinds are for." She motioned to the pile of boxes in the far corner. "I had to change them out for the Realtor anyway, and this old woman at the fair told me that..." She shook her head. "It sounds so stupid. She told me bamboo blinds keep out the spirits."

Jack glanced over at him, waiting for a condemning look or a dismissive gesture. Instead, he threw away the last of the porcelain chunks before coming over to crouch in front of her and grab her hands. They'd been furiously working a napkin and now the worn pieces had slipped through her fingers to a snowy mound between their feet.

"I don't think you're crazy. I don't know whether you saw what you think you did or not, but I know you've been through a lot lately. And if putting up a bunch of new window treatments will help you get a decent night's sleep, I'll install every last one of them for you."

"It's not just her. There's so much more. You have no idea."

"Then tell me."

Jack could hear her blood pumping in her ears. The lightening outside the window played more frequently against the pane and she closed her eyes to the brightness. Words came tumbling out like a river, unstoppable and fast.

"I think I'm being stalked. Mal had all these pictures of me. Pictures she shouldn't have had unless she was there in New York. Then, this older man that I've run into before in the city not only found me in San Jose, but chased me through that big fair downtown this morning. I think she may have hired him, or maybe it's something else. Something bigger. I just don't know anymore. Maybe it's the devil himself!"

She pulled a hand out of his and pressed it against her face to stifle a sob. The last thing she wanted to do was break down in front of him. It was all so very, very absurd.

"An older man? What does he look like?"

"Does it matter? He's got kind of reddish-blond hair and he's really skinny; kind of pale and always in a suit. And his eyes! They're so cold."

Nate's jaw clenched, and the steadying hand he'd put on her arm curled so that the fingers bit into her flesh. "Have you gone to the police, yet?"

"Right, because they'll take me seriously. 'Hello, my dead sister has hired someone to stalk me. Can I get a restraining order?' I don't think so. What I need more than anything is to get this house taken care of so I can get back to the safety of New York."

"Now, there's an irony. New York City, safe."

"Anything's better than this godforsaken place. God, I've always hated it here."

Nate stood and hauled Jack to her feet with him. "Come on. The dishes can wait. It shouldn't take too long to throw up those blinds since it looks like you've already torn down the old ones. Then we can talk some more."

"Don't you want to run away? I would."

"Nah. I like you, and besides, it makes life more interesting. I really do think you need to go to the police. But, for now, which window do we start with?"

Rain poured around Mallory, but she didn't feel it. She'd finally managed to project for an extended period of time, but it wasn't quite enough. Her mentality was there, even a wisp of her physicality, but her actual presence was no more than that of a ghost. She couldn't touch anything, nor could she make a sound. Water droplets poured through her as easily as if she weren't there at all.

Beyond the kitchen window, she watched the two of them play house. The good looking young man said something and Jack leaned forward in laughter. It was nauseating to see yet another thing go right for her perfect twin. And yet, something else nagged at her memory. She stared at him, the feeling of déjà vu centering around the outsider. Then, like the lightning flash that lit up the yard behind her, recognition hit.

For the last several months she'd had Jack followed, sure her all-too-silent sister was up to something. Things were going just a bit too well. Mallory had been sure it was a set up and that Jack would be sweeping in at any moment to take it all away. The pictures her contact had sent her were innocuous enough, but the same man had shown up in them time and again.

They were never together, but the coincidence had bothered her. He would be getting off a subway as Jack was getting on. He would be entering a coffee shop as she left. Once he'd been just a few seats away from her at some ridiculous art symposium. The private eye hadn't been able to learn anything about the man without a substantial increase in pay, so Mallory'd let it slide. Maybe that had been a mistake.

She watched their interaction as her sister and the young man worked together to place a new treatment in one of the windows. Seeing them together now launched new questions. Had they been together all along? What was he doing in California? As blinds snapped into place over her line of sight, she reached out a hand. It flickered before her like a bad television signal.

Trying to touch the glass, even force it open if she could, Mallory was greeted with a snarl of electricity arcing off the closed wooden slats. It raced up her incorporeal form, bouncing off raindrops and sending her reeling her backward. Stumbling, she found herself once more in her own office.

There was definitely more going on than she'd ever dreamed. Jackie-dearest was obviously learning how to protect herself from her beloved sister. And that man! Yes, things were much more complicated than she'd bargained for.

Still, every visit to the mortal plane was bringing her just a bit closer to her end goal. So what if she hadn't found Arthur? Soon Jack would be out of the way. Mallory would ditch Santana and find a way to resume life after death. She'd heard rumors of immortals who returned to Earth to live normal lives. Once Jack was dealt with, she would find her way back. Maybe she would pick up where her sister left off with this handsome stranger. The thought brought a genuine smile to her face.

Yes. Soon things would be going her way. Forever.

Chapter Fourteen

"THERE we go. Last one." Nate tightened the final screw and together they lifted up the valance and popped it into place. When he lowered the slats to block the dark of the night, Jack felt an enormous weight fall from her shoulders. No harm could come to her here, tonight.

She smiled down at Nate from the step stool, and he smiled back.

Wrapping his hands around her waist, he lifted her down from her perch. Jack tilted her face up to look at him, butterflies replacing the dread in her stomach. He was quite handsome. Her breath caught in her throat as he suddenly leaned down and kissed her.

It had been a long time since she'd kissed someone. The dates she'd gone on before always remained platonic and she rebuffed any attempts at intimacy. Something was different this time, though.

Jack could feel Nate's scruff tickle her chin as his warm lips pressed against hers. Heat rose to her cheeks as his hand slid along her arm. It felt like a long dormant flower was blooming inside her chest, seeking the rain after a quarter century buried in the desert. Tentatively, she raised a hand to his chest, feeling his heart beat under her fingers.

Shutting down the part of her brain that protested, she sank into the kiss, allowing her lips to part as her head fell back. His other arm encircled her waist and both of hers crept around his neck, holding him to her, reveling in the new feelings. Furtive, teenage petting had never felt like this.

Her lungs couldn't get enough air as Nate backed up onto the couch, pulling her down with him. Jack straddled his lap by necessity, trying to keep her balance while not breaking contact. His hands roamed her back, stroking her shoulders and sides, but always returning to clasp her hips. As if it were something she'd done all her life, she angled her face to perfectly match his, deepening the kiss. Goosebumps chased each other down her arms as she realized what she wanted more than anything else.

To be loved, even if it was just this once, even if it didn't lead to a lifetime. She wanted what everyone else had. She wanted to hope it would mean forever. She wanted to seize the night because tomorrow wasn't promised. Jack heard a noise and was startled to realize it was her own moans against his mouth. He reached a hand up and tugged the scrunchie out of her ponytail, causing her hair to fly around and encapsulate them both.

"You're so amazing," he gasped out as he trailed his mouth down her neck to her exposed collarbone. All playfulness from their former interactions was gone. The husky timbre of his voice told her that she wasn't alone with her shaky heart, as his words thrilled her to rise against him. Amazing. No one had ever called her that before. Strange sensations filled her with each touch, each breath, each whisper. She felt full enough to burst, but also yawning with starvation. Closer, tighter, more, was all she could think, the words repeating over and over in her head. When his calloused hands slipped beneath her shirt, running along her ribs and toying with the clasp of her bra, she didn't protest. Instead, she recaptured his mouth, swirling in her own newly discovered passion.

Twisting, he pushed her down onto the length of the couch and she pulled him after her. As if she were a different person, she found her fingers clawing at the cotton of his shirt, pulling it over his shoulders while her legs wound tightly around his thighs. Holding himself up with one arm, he allowed the other to brush the skin of her stomach, gently trailing upward until she gasped and moved restlessly beneath him.

Her blouse bunched high, Nate dipped his head and found one of her breasts with a gentle scrape of his teeth. Jack's back arched, letting out a little cry of pleasure. For a moment he hesitated, afraid he'd done something wrong, but her hands knotted themselves in his hair, urging him on.

They moved together, exploring, touching, tasting, as if they'd known each other for years instead of days. Jack was overwhelmed by how perfectly their bodies fit together. Only the smallest niggle of doubt stirred in the back of her mind, a half-remembered reprimand from when a nun caught her necking with Chase, but she pushed it away. That was ten years ago. Now, she was a woman and her limits were her own. Still, it was only fair to tell him. As his hands trailed down to the waistband of her jeans, she stopped him.

"Nate, there's something I have to tell you."

A frown creased between his passion-heavy eyes.

"I'm— I've never— "

His face softened in understanding.

"We can stop, if you'd like. I'm a patient guy."

A moment of hesitation shimmered between them before Jack pulled him close again. "No," she breathed. The last week had done nothing if not taught her to seize the day.

The new blinds blocked out prying eyes as clothing slowly peeled away to bare skin. In the weak glow of an ancient lamp, they came together. At first there was pain, but soon the world was forgotten in their sacred embrace. Nate made her come alive in ways she'd never thought possible and she swelled with it. As he stiffened against her, Jack held him tight and breathed in his ear, the sensations overtaking her as well.

"Never let me go."

San Francisco wasn't nearly so crowded at one in the morning. The streets were damp with rain and a faint fog rose to meet Death's steps. Like every major city, the warehouse district seemed made for back alley murders and ghoulish encounters. It was like something out of Hollywood: a cat screeched and ran across his path, a car backfired like a shotgun, and in the distance sirens blared. Even his shoes made an uncomfortable schlepping noise on the moist and gritty concrete.

His destination was difficult to find after all these years, even with his long memory. When he found it, the state of decay wasn't surprising. The aged building should have been torn down years ago, or at the very least gutted, but here it remained. He brushed at the faded paint on the door, removing some of the grime with distaste.

Stanton's Books & Curiosities.

Why, he wondered, would anyone put their shop in such a place? For a short time in the nineteen-tens the shop had been a fashionable, though out of the way, stop for the spiritually in-tune gentry. As the years wore on, it evolved into more of a personal collection for the owner and faded from the memory of all except those who valued such things.

Death grasped the ancient knob and let his mind weave through the tumblers of the lock. Turning the handle with ease, he entered the dilapidated depository and swiped at a cobweb that tried to guillotine him. The dim lighting shone down on dark book stacks, piled everywhere like leather-bound skyscrapers. Pages of open tomes ruffled in the draft as he walked past. Suddenly, a pale figure passed out of a curtained alcove. Death cleared his throat and the apparition jumped in fright.

"What! What? Oh. You." The hollow voice slid from surprise into acidity. A slight man with curly hair and tiny, round spectacles, his silk vest and tweed pants seemed no more out of place in his academic surroundings than the pocket watch he fiddled with.

"Hello," Death replied cordially. A large, open volume near the smaller man's elbow slammed itself shut in a flurry of dust.

"Why are you here? I'm still mad at you."

"Oh, come off it, Edgar. That was nearly a century ago."

"You could have given me warning! I had things to do. I had projects to complete. My library was nearly finished!"

"When it's your time, it's your time. If you hadn't had your nose buried so deep in that book of numerology you might have sidestepped the falling air conditioner."

"You should have had the decency to at least *tell* me I was dead. I was more than halfway home before I realized something was amiss."

"I had other marks to deal with. It was a busy day." Death looked at his fingernails. Edgar ruffled and sputtered.

"A busy d—A busy day? Really! You were in such a rush to what, listen to the Orson Welles Radio Hour?"

"I'll have you know War of the Worlds was an enjoyable program. Besides, I had to deal with the panicked masses." Edgar made a hrrumphing sound that echoed in the cavernous room, neither amused nor mollified by his visitor's explanations. He reached under his glasses and rubbed the bridge of his nose, his voice taking on a wearied tone.

"What do you want? Surely you haven't come to kill me again. Though, I confess, I'd like to see you try."

"Actually, I seem to have found myself temporarily relieved of my duties and in need of information. You are the largest collector of arcane lore in the mortal realm. You see where our paths intersect."

"What kind of information?" Edgar asked warily.

"Let's say I've come across an individual with perfect luck. Now, let's say they need to be removed from the situation, shuffled off the mortal coil so to speak. Is there something that would either increase my luck or diminish hers so it could be achieved?"

"Why would you possibly need to kill off anyone with perfect luck? You can't even touch someone who isn't... Oohh."

For the first time since the whole ordeal began, Death genuinely smiled. His look was eager and boyish, happy someone understood at last. "You see my problem, then. In all these centuries, no one has ever believed me. But, you—you and I are cut from the same cloth. We can't just leave a problem, a possibility, alone. You know what will happen if she's left unchecked."

"Are you sure this isn't a matter of pride?" Edgar's beady, bespeckled eyes studied him with shrewd calculation. "She's like a slap in the face to you, isn't she? Someone walking around clearly dog-eared for demise and there's nothing you can do."

"It's not like that. She's always been there, ready and waiting to die, so why has she been invisible to me? The luck is protecting her, like a dike in a high tide, so why reveal her to me now? Once she's been taken care of, I can start getting to the bottom of all this."

"See, slap in the face, like I said."

"Can you help me or not?"

"I can. But, you're not going to like what I have to say. It's going to involve baubles and spells and all sorts of things that folks like you don't naturally agree with."

"Spells? Edgar, immortals may have extraordinary abilities, but spells and human so-called magic are nothing. Pretty parlor tricks full of flashes and bangs. There's no actual substance to magic as such."

Edgar threw his hands up in annoyance. "Then why are you here? Stop wasting my time. If you're not going to believe, move along. Go ask for help from some heavenly host. If you're interested in what I've got to say, come with me." With that, he retreated to the cordoned room. Death silently followed in his chilly wake.

"It's here somewhere, let me see…" A wave of his hands flipped through multiple books and pages as he gave a quick tour of the room. Books pulled themselves off shelves and settled in the rare empty spots as he rifled through drawers.

"Ah-ha!"

He turned, clasping a handkerchief in nearly translucent hands. Laying it down on a little desk, he unfolded its corners. Inside sat what at first appeared to be a lump of bright blue rock. Approaching with caution, Death picked it up and held it under a light.

The stone was about two inches in length and about an inch in diameter. Upon closer inspection, it appeared the object was made of lapis lazuli and had at one time been covered in brilliant gold leafing. Now, the gold was all but worn off, though glittering remnants remained behind in the faint markings of the piece. Running his fingers over the lines Death wrinkled his brow.

"A scarab?"

"Not just any scarab. This is a sacred scarab of transformation. It's thousands of years old." Death became wary. In general, the word sacred meant devoted or dedicated to a deity, and he didn't want some overbearing Immortal breathing down his neck for misusing their property.

"Sacred to whom?"

"The god of transformations, of course. Who else other than Khepri would prize such a thing?" Death relaxed. Khepri wasn't a god any more than he was. Of course, few outside of the DoDD knew the real story.

Considered by the ancient Egyptians as the god of sunrise and rebirth, over time Khepri morphed into a deity of the underworld and major transformation. The truth was, Khprra, as had been his real name, had been an Immortal from time immemorial. In fact, he was the first Grim Reaper. There had been others before him that laid mortals to their final rest, of course. After the restructuring and organization of the Beyond, however, he had been charged as the first official Head of Human Demise. His story was woven into many early cultures and belief systems, most of which did not survive into the present day. By the time of the worship of Khepri, Khprra was all but out the door: On to bigger and better things, which is to say he fell off the grid entirely in an effort to retire. No one had seen nor heard from him since.

Edgar continued his turn about the room, searching for something more. Pages fluttered and occasionally the lights flickered from his agitation. Finally, he pointed with another, "Ah-ha!" to a passage underlying a rough sketch of a beetle-headed man. Death leaned over the shorter man's shoulder and deciphered the hieroglyphics aloud.

"Kheper-i kheper kheperu, kheper-kuy," he began slowly.

"M kheper n khepri kheperu m sep tepy," finished the ghost.

"I became, and in the becoming became. I became by becoming the form of Khepri, god of transformations, who came into being in the First

Time. Through me all transformations are enacted." The ghostly scholar nodded as Death translated. His Egyptian was rusty from centuries of disuse and his pronunciations were stilted.

"It doesn't make a whole lot of sense, does it? However," Edgar began closing books and cleaning up as best he could, "if anything were able to help you with your situation that would be it."

"What will it do?"

"How should I know? I'm just the academic. I would suppose it calls upon the powers of Khepri to enact a transformation. How you do the calling and what you call for is up to you. Maybe you could make yourself luckier. Maybe you could make your mark less lucky. I don't ask, I don't tell, I just read and watch and listen to the whispers of the otherworld."

Death clasped the scarab in his palm and slid it into the silk lining of his jacket. He tilted his head at the ghost in acknowledgment.

"If this works, I owe you one."

Edgar's pinched face soured further. "Unless you can bring me back, I would respectfully suggest that you owe me more than one."

"Two, then."

With another nod Death turned and left, carefully locking the door behind him.

As he drove back to Sunnyvale, he contemplated the situation. Now that he had the key and he knew how to find her location, how would he do the job? Hard as it was for most people to believe, he was not a cruel man. He had a job to do and, if he got a little enjoyment out of the creative process, who were they to judge? Everyone died sooner or later. Arguing with him or calling him a murder, as happened all too frequently, was like being angry with an author because their book ended at the conclusion of the story. Once dead, few quibbled about the manner thereof. He thought wryly about Edgar. When your time came then it came, and for the most part that was that.

Sure, once or twice he'd made deals with people. Those, however, took place under extenuating circumstances. He could also count on one hand the number of mistakes, whether in prematurity or delay, the Department had made since he'd taken over. Of course, the last one had been very nasty business. The paperwork tied Gina up for weeks and he'd been forced to sit in on exceedingly boring meetings and irritating inquiries for much, much longer. To this day, no one in the Beyond was quite sure what happened, and he'd been lucky to walk away with his job.

For more than two years a particular mark eluded death. Even direct assassination attempts had been unsuccessful because no one from the Department of Death and Demise had been present to make sure the severance was complete.

He'd been gutted and poisoned and stabbed and shot and finally drowned before his soul took flight. The final blow came too late, though. In just eight hundred ninety-nine extra days upon the Earth, he'd started a chain reaction that led to several more deaths within the ensuing years—the toppling of an entire empire. His influence, more so than the tensions of the First World War, were to blame for prominent HOHs that carried on past his finality. Death was glad he'd not had to be present for some of them. Especially the last. After his own antemortem, he hadn't been too keen on dealing with deadly politics and royal families.

He brooded for a few long minutes before shaking off the memory of those dark days. The question for the present was how he would get the little Egyptian trinket into the custody of Miss Devlin. He could disguise the scarab as a present; mortals generally liked those. However, he couldn't guarantee she'd keep it with her. Death also couldn't be sure she'd pick the thing up if it wasn't given directly to her. Perhaps if he slipped it into her purse that would count as possession. Women these days were rarely seen without some sort of satchel. Flipping back through their previous encounters he remembered she'd always had the same small tote thrown over her shoulder or clutched in her hand.

Placing the stone in her bag was a matter of circumstance, but then what would he do? Once her shields lowered enough for a breach, what tactics would be of best employ? Death thought long and hard. There were so many options: something little, perhaps, like an allergic reaction or an accidental poisoning. His only concern with those was if she was rushed to the hospital. They would likely take her bag away in admitting and he wouldn't be able to complete the job.

Something larger, then. A car crash? A collapsing bridge? The crushing, yet incredibly precise blow of a falling satellite? The more bombastic the idea, the more enthusiastic he became. As he drove south, his mind's eye filled with domino-effect buildings and far-reaching destruction. Perhaps there was a way to orchestrate it so the task took out both her and anyone else in the vicinity on his list. The creativity and purpose welling up inside him was like a drug. By the time he reached Sunnyvale, he found himself cheerfully humming and feeling much better than he had all week.

Assignment

Yangzhou Prefecture, China — January 1342 AD

THE streets were noisy, awash with sights and sounds as alien to Arthur as death had once been. Oh, he understood the language. Shuffling around the Asiatic territories for the last 120 years had taught him that. But being in a settled town—a city really—full of bright banners, street vendors, and patronage of the arts, was a new thing. Still, for all the liveliness, he felt a sense of boredom with his current assignment.

They'd told him that death was all about balance. His turbulent, militaristic life would give him the skills he needed to be ruthless as a Charonite, but the job would teach him peace. After training they'd placed him in Ghengis Khan's train, cleaning up not just the souls of the war-slain, but those in the camps as well. As promised, the number he grew to the bloodshed the more peace he supposed he felt. He almost preferred the excitement of war over being stuck in this town, though.

Arthur surveyed the scroll he'd been sent to Yangzhou with. Normally it would contain an ever-changing list of marks, but now it held only instructions. He read through them once more, sparse as they were.

He and another Charonite were entrusted with the deaths in the prefecture. A wave of Pestilence had been approved for the eastern coast of China and it was their job to take anyone whose life aura shone black. He'd asked why those names wouldn't be on a list and had been given a run around about the "unpredictability" of plagues and how their approval didn't necessarily go through the Fates' department and on to Death's division.

Collapsing the scroll, he stuffed his hands in his pockets and strolled down to and along the northern bank of the Yangtze River. Only a few deaths had happened so far and, as it was such a large prefecture, few people had put enough facts together to be scared. He squinted at the distant rooftops and tried to focus on the future. Athena had first mentioned prognostication to him more than a century ago, but despite her continued encouragement, nothing seemed to work.

"Why are you frowning?"

Arthur looked with surprise at the young woman who had apparently been walking the bank in the opposite direction. Her dark brown hair snuck out of her headdress, and her dusky skin shone olive in the sun. When he didn't answer she continued.

"Where are you from? I haven't seen you with the Franciscans, and you are no more Chinese than I."

"Brittany," he replied with difficulty, still staring at her. He could see her aura, black as midnight and surrounded by a thin ribbon of sunny yellow. He'd never seen such a combination: So very lucky, and yet she walked right up to death and chattered to him like they were the best of friends.

"Why, that's even farther than Genoa! Is there an English or French settlement nearby? I'm rarely allowed to leave our little Italian community. What brought you to China? My father and brother are merchants and I confess that after mother died I didn't want to be left alone with a nursemaid or some tottering family member. I am a woman after all, not a child, so why shouldn't I come to China?"

"Wouldn't you have been more comfortable in Genoa?" he was amazed to find himself asking.

"But I would have been ever so much more bored! The sights and the smells and the people are all so different than in Italy. It does get a little lonely sometimes, though."

"Aren't there other gir—women your age?"

"No. There are very few women at all. I didn't

think that part through when I insisted on coming along." She flashed him an impish grin.

They were walking side by side down the riverbed now. A few people cast them strange looks. He knew she must look crazy, as he doubted anyone else could see him. Why could she, though? Was it because she was marked to die? She didn't have the plague. He supposed he should go ahead and escort her off the mortal plane.

As they walked down a pier, Arthur concentrated on the boards before their feet, willing them to rot away at a thousand times their normal rate. All it would take was one misstep and she would go tumbling away into the deep part of the river. Her skirts and puffed sleeves would absorb the water like a sponge and within a minute she would find herself in Purgatory.

Her foot hovered over one of the planks, inches from stepping down. Suddenly, she whirled around and called out, "I'm coming, Papa!" She gave Arthur a brief curtsy and dashed in the opposite direction. A few hundred feet from him she stopped and pivoted again.

"My name's Katerina!" she yelled back. "It was nice to meet you. I hope I see you again."

She waved and picked both her skirts and her pace back up. Arthur stood for a moment on the boardwalk watching her receding figure. How incredibly lucky that her father had called her back at the exact right moment. Just how far would her luck protect her? And, in the meantime, what harm could come of letting her chatter at him like a little Italian squirrel?

He clasped his hands behind his back and strode back toward town and his awaiting victims. Maybe being stuck in a town marked by Pestilence wouldn't be such a chore after all.

Chapter Fifteen

JACK awoke in bed, achy but content. Snatches of the night came back in blurs of touch and sound, and she smiled. The tiny voice from before tried to tell her that what she'd done was wrong, that she should get herself to a confessional, but once more she silenced it. Nate's arm draped heavy and warm over her midsection, reminding her of her words from the night before.

Never let me go.

They were words filled with naïveté and the heat of the moment, but that didn't make them any less true. She felt comfortable with him like no one else. While, two "dates" in she was far from ready to say the L-word, she felt in her bones that he could be someone to fall madly, deeply, impossibly in love with. Maybe.

A soft sigh escaped as she tried to turn in his

sleepy embrace without waking him. Using just the tips of her fingers, she traced his brooding eyebrows, his bristled jawline, his sharp collarbone. He stirred, thick lashes flickering open to gaze at her with sky-blue eyes. She gave him a small, tremulous smile, suddenly worried how things would play out. What was the morning after like? What were you supposed to say?

"Good morning," he offered, as if in response to her unasked question. His untried voice sounded gravelly and a tingle ran up her spine.

"Good morning."

"I had a great time last night."

"Just last night?"

He laughed and pulled her closer. "And this morning," he murmured in her ear. Jack buried her face in the crook of his neck, deep pink creeping into her cheeks. His hands began to roam and she could feel the hammer of her own heart with every touch and taste. She rolled over, dragging him with her, the sheets tangling around their legs. He kissed from the skin behind her ear to her shoulders before making his way lower.

"I should be going soon," Nate said softly against her skin as his lips traveled. Through unsteady breathing she moaned in disappointment.

"Do you have to?"

Nate pulled himself level with her face and brushed an errant strand of hair from her eyes. He stared down at her for a long moment and she met his gaze unflinching. Finally, he stooped his mouth to her ear, the warmth and sound sending delicious shivers down her back.

"Not yet."

Jack wrapped her arms around him, her fingers pressing hard into his back as he slipped inside once more. A feeling of far more than lust was beginning to spread inside her chest. His weight was like a panic blanket, keeping her safe and calm. The sun streamed across the bed in bright, unassuming lines as they took their time. The unruly passion of the night before was replaced with a gentle surety that this was destined to be more than a one night stand.

Afterward, they lay together in the sunlight. Jack listened to the even beat of his heart, the soft rise and fall of his chest. Her hand played along his abdomen in slight possessiveness.

"When will I see you again?"

Nate sighed.

"Marnie's got every minute pretty much planned from now until I leave. I'll try to sneak away and see you before I go, though. Don't stay on the West Coast too long. Someone's got to go with me to that new exhibit at the Met."

"And you really can't get a better pretzel than the ones sold right outside."

"Exactly."

Taking the initiative, she lifted up and kissed

him, pouring into it a soft soliloquy of terror and hope. For a moment, he cupped her face and responded in kind. Then, he extracted himself and began to get dressed. Jack watched the muscles of his back gather and stretch for a moment before joining in the search for a missing sock.

As he left he gave her another dramatic bow, much like he had at the gallery, but as he kissed her hand his eyes locked on hers in a look that spelled out his reluctance to leave.

When he was gone, she sat alone in the kitchen. Everything shone in a spotless glow. The whole house was clean and most of Mallory's problems had been chucked out with the weekly garbage. Now, she only waited on paperwork from Tom's office and for the Goodwill truck to come pick up most of the furniture. There were a few boxes of things she felt sentimental enough about to ship back east, but not much.

Thinking about New York made her smile. What would the girls say when they found out that she had an honest-to-God date? Patrice would probably spout some nonsense about kismet, and Veronica would demand to know where they were going out to eat. At the thought of food, Jack's stomach growled. It was midmorning and she realized for the first time that she hadn't eaten since their early dinner the night before. And, as she had discovered then, there was still no food in the house. Not even leftovers. There was actually less food now than before.

With trepidation, Jack realized she would have to leave the safety of the house and do some light grocery shopping. If she was going to be holed up for a few more days, she'd need sustenance. Grabbing her purse, she peeked out the door, sweeping the streets for signs of trouble. Then, she clambered into the Yugo and rattled down to the nearest store, determined to only be gone as long as necessary

It was a long shot, but Death was running out of options. As he flipped through the last week's worth of newspapers at the Sunnyvale Public Library, he scanned the obituaries just as carefully as the other articles. She was here for a reason. It had to be something big enough to drag her across the country at the drop of a hat, and something personal enough that it was keeping her here for more than just a day or two. A death in the family fit the bill nicely, but he kept an eye out for other announcements just in case.

After an hour, he had moved from the regional paper to the county paper, and finally he began flipping through the local edition. Within a single issue he hit pay dirt. Toward the end of the death notices was a tiny paragraph for a Mallory Isabelle Devlin. The careful wording left much to the imagination, but the dates lined up nicely with the timeline he'd established for Jacquelyn. Wedged between platitudes and Mass times, a single line confirmed his suspicions.

Survived by one sister, Jacquelyn Devlin of New York City.

He flagged down a passing librarian.

"If I have a name and a city, how would I look up where someone lives?" She gave him a wary look, and he smoothly supplied a story to fit his means. "An old friend of mine passed away and I'd like to send his daughter my condolences." The woman's demeanor softened and she beckoned him to a nearby computer.

"You can use the white pages to look up an address. Just type in the name here and the city here, then hit enter."

She wandered off and he typed in Mallory's name and last known location. His fingers felt awkward on the keyboard. While he knew the principles behind using much of modern technology, he had very little experience with it.

When the address popped up he was surprised by the other information offered as well. Did people know how vulnerable they were? Birth, marriage, divorce, arrest, and death records. Phone numbers, addresses, ages, and even known associates. He doubted many mortals thought twice about the information freely obtainable these days, but he counted himself lucky he didn't have to deal with it. Death was sure that by now his own name had been rubbed from the history annals, as had that of his elder sister and long beleaguered mother. After all, history is written by the victors.

He scribbled down the address and tipped his head to the librarian on his way out. It couldn't be far. In fact, in just a few short minutes Death found himself watching through tinted windows as a little yellow car pulled up outside 264 East McKinley Avenue. He clutched the scarab tightly in his hand as she sat her purse on the roof to stoop in and fill her arms with grocery bags. With a kick, she shut the door behind her, making her way towards the front door. Zooming in on her abandoned purse, he surreptitiously got out of his own vehicle and jogged over to the forgotten bag.

From his pocket he pulled out the scarab and grasped it in his fist.

"Kheper-i kheper kheperu, kheper-kuy. M kheper n khepri kheperu m sep tepy."

A white glow emmanated through the cracks in his fingers. Death focused all his intent on making the lump of stone cursed, praying it would work. Edgar hadn't exactly been explicit with details. Within seconds the glow shifted to a more menacing color and he uncurled his fingers to watch the silver veining turn crimson.

With a smirk he slipped the stone inside the abandoned bag, planning to hide and wait for her to come back for it. Then another idea overtook him. Grabbing the purse by its top, he strode up the path to the door and rang the bell. Inside there was a brief scuttle as someone hurried to the door. He took care to keep out of sight of the peep hole and, when she opened the door to look, he didn't give her time to recognize him.

"Excuse me, you forgot this on top of your car." He pushed the satchel into her arms, drawing her focus down instead of up at his face. With a snap, her luck aura ceased to shimmer. Now an ordinary yellow, he could easily and quickly flip through her file. The scythe clearly wouldn't work and he couldn't imagine doing the job with his bare hands.

"Oh, thank you. I hadn't realized."

He found it: An ethanol allergy. Over her shoulder he spotted a half-drunk water bottle sitting on a table. With a little bit of concentration he turned it to Everclear. The liquid bubbled for a moment before resettling. If the reaction didn't kill her, the alcohol poisoning would.

Down the lane, a transformer blew with a sizzling POP. She strained to see around him, distracted from looking at her good Samaritan once more. He smiled, ignoring the noise on the street. Suddenly, the hydrant on the corner exploded in a three-pronged geyser, which in turn set off a car alarm. Every dog in the neighborhood began howling. Her face flourished with confusion and fear. Curious, he turned to look, as well.

Without warning, the Yugo erupted into flames. They both stared as orange tongues licked the yellow paint off it's frame. With no time to do more than put two and two together, he shoved her into the house and locked the door behind them. Jacquelyn dropped her purse as she backed into the kitchen, probably thinking of escape out the other door.

"I wouldn't do that if I were you."

She froze in her tracks.

"Who are you?" She recognized him now, of course, though it was clear she still hadn't worked it all out.

He stepped back a pace and swept her a grand bow. "I am death incarnate. The Grim Reaper, if you will. Head of Human Demise. And you, madam, have escaped for the last time. For someone as old as myself, this last week has seemed surprisingly like an eternity. Exhilarating, infuriating, but an eternity no less. I congratulate you on that."

"Why are you doing all this? Why not just kill me and be done with it?"

He laughed mirthlessly. After all this to find out he'd been focusing on the wrong thing was beyond maddening. He'd been so intent on finding her and killing her that he'd let all the other signs, questions, and doubts fall to the side.

"As much as it pains me after all of our drama, it's now come to my attention that some things are more important than ushering you into the great Beyond."

Outside sirens approached, but over the noise he heard another, higher shriek that rang of disappointment. It felt like nails dragging up his spine and, combined with the insistent pressure of being locked in a house enshrouded by bamboo, it set his nerves on edge. If he wasn't mistaken, someone else was after her too. Or perhaps, given the circumstances of his leave, they were both in the line of fire. The wheels in his head were spinning with calculations.

He grabbed the water bottle and downed its contents. It certainly wasn't his preferred bourbon, but it would do. With a sigh he pinched the bridge of his nose. These new developments would need to be sorted before he could finish the job. The complications were mounting. Without a word he picked up her dropped purse and took possession of the scarab once more.

She'd done it. She'd been there. Not just as a wispy, incorporeal thing, but as a solid being fully capable of wreaking havoc. It had been as if the barrier between them had finally fallen. Her powers had been hard to direct at first. Still, watching the sparks fly and the water gush had been exhilarating. And when that damnable Yugo exploded into a fiery mass, she'd actually smiled.

Mallory had glimpsed the pair just as the old Grim Reaper had shoved her sister into the house. Her smile grew even wider as she concentrated on the building. How she hated that house, and now it could be destroyed while caging both little birds. A bead of sweat gathered at her hairline as she focused.

Nothing happened.

The wind didn't howl. The shingles didn't shudder. The beams didn't implode, nor did the foundation crumble. Flames that had so easily engulfed the car now shied from the wooden siding.

She turned her eyes toward an approaching vehicle with ridiculous abstract roses painted down the side. With a single thought, one of the tires blew and brought the van to a swerving halt in the middle of the road. Satisfied, she tried the house again.

Nothing. It was as if it didn't exist, like there was an invisible forcefield keeping her at bay. She stalked up to the door from her position down the block and tugged on the handle. It burned in her hand, causing a new and surprising pain. She yelped and snatched her fingers back.

Sirens blared in the distance. Mallory stepped off the porch and threw her whole being into disposing of those trapped in the bungalow. Another car burst into flames next door and every transformer on East McKinley exploded in a shower of gold and white sparks. Her desperate wail of frustration echoed down the now filling street as she returned to the Beyond once more.

Chapter Sixteen

FEW people remained outside, now. There had been a flurry of activity after the explosions: Several firetrucks, the water board, a few police. When the latter began knocking on doors, Jack and her captor went in the other room and pretended no one was home. The Yugo had turned to a smoldering heap long before anyone arrived, thanks to its supernatural firestarter. The only thing left to associate it with house number 264 was where it happened to be parked on the fairly crowded street.

Now, they sat in the living room not looking at each other. Jack picked at the molting fabric of a fleece blanket as Death reached inside his suit coat and withdrew a small flask. There had been utter silence between them for the better part of an hour. At first, Jack had been quiet and subservient out of fear. She'd used the time to pray in silence, but after half an hour she began chasing an idea as it spun through her brain. It was obvious he wasn't going to kill her just yet. Now, what she wanted more than anything else was to get to the bottom of this insanity.

"I've seen you before, you know."

"Yes. We've run into each other, what? Five times, now," he replied as he unscrewed the cap from the silver canteen.

"No, I mean, before."

"Being perched on the cusp of death, it's only natural that you can see me when others can't. You've probably glimpsed me carrying out my duties without realizing it."

Frustration tinged her voice.

"No. Before. Before New York. Here in California when I was just a kid. I think you were trying to kill me then, too."

Death made a small scoffing noise. "Trust me, I've never tried to kill you before. I've never even seen you before last week."

She considered for a moment before continuing. "Has anyone ever gotten hurt when you were trying to kill someone else?"

He looked at her sharply and for a moment she imagined he was offended. "Very rarely. I'm not omniscient. If someone is in such a position that I can't calculate around them or if they're well hidden and the trajectory of the tragedy is just right, then yes. But, I never take an unscheduled soul."

"Besides me, have you ever failed to kill someone?"

"No."

"Never?"

A look of pain flickered across his face and then was gone.

"Never."

"But, just suppose that you were confident someone had died. That your plan for them was inescapable. Have you ever just walked away before making sure the person was dead?"

He jammed the flask back in his coat. "Why are you so fixated on this? I would most certainly know if I had been sent to kill you in the past. Not only because I would have seen your aura and our precious little escapade would have begun much sooner, but also because of your name."

"You remember the names of everyone you've ever been sent to kill?"

"Just the one." His lips thinned and his blue eyes smoldered with pain. They sat in relapsed silence. The rays of sun streaming through the bamboo blinds angled ever steeper and lit the room in rosy orange. After several long minutes she spoke up again, quieter than before.

"My sister and I were raised by our grandfather. One summer, he built us a treehouse high in the arms of a South California Pine. We played in it for years, probably well past the age we should've. The walls were partially open to the breezes and there was a big hammock strung up inside. It was perfect.

"When we were ten, Mal and I had an argument in it. Over something stupid, probably, I don't remember. Mallory shoved me and as my head snapped back I saw across the yard. And there you were. You stood on the sidewalk watching us with your face screwed up in concentration. You wore a sweater vest and a long sleeve shirt, dark gray over blue, and I remember thinking you were nuts because it must've been a hundred degrees outside.

"There was a loud popping noise and the floor shook beneath us. Mal and I looked at each other and she was so scared. So many times we'd been through accident after accident, all freak occurrences and all barely escaped by the skin of our teeth. She usually received the brunt of the injuries in any given incident, and this was no exception. One of the biggest branches broke away from the trunk, tearing the tree house out from under us.

"She tried to grab my hand, but we fell in separate directions. A broken limb gave me a nasty scratch along my ribcage as I landed on the ground beside it. I was half-purple with bruises and had a mild concussion. I've still got the scar." She motioned down her left side. "Mal was laid up in the hospital for weeks. The school almost held her back because of it. When I asked about the man I'd seen, no one else had seen him. Not even Mal. So, I forgot about you. But, when I saw you in New York, it began to nag at me. Then, after the fair, I knew."

"Knew what, exactly?" She had his attention, now.

"That you'd always been after us. Mal and I were too accident-prone. Too many bad things, injurious things, happened to us to be coincidence."

"I see," he said in an even voice. "Where's your sister, now?"

She looked at him in disbelief. Her face and tone took a sudden, bitter turn.

"She's dead. Don't you know that? Or do the murders just become a blur after a while?"

He gave her an infuriating shrug, totally unphased by her accusation. "I'm not the only reaper, I'm just in charge. How did she die?"

Jack's eyes filled, but her jaw stiffened. "An antifreeze cocktail."

"Ah. Suicide. Why'd she do it? Depression, debt, disease? Suicides usually fall under one or more of those categories."

"Because she was crazy!" Jack yelled, her gaze hot on his. "Because she blamed me for being perfect. Because she couldn't face her own demons. But mostly because she didn't see the point in living if nothing ever worked out in her favor."

Instead of being taken aback, Death looked thoughtful. "She was probably a weeping rose."

"A what?"

"A weeping rose. Everyone has two auras that surround them from birth: A life aura and a luck aura. Depending on how close to death you are, your life aura can range from white to black. Sometimes there are things called locks where the aura is so white or black that it locks in place and never changes. Someone with a pure white aura – practically silver – would for all intents and purposes be invincible whereas a person with a deepest black aura would be marked for death. If your sister was a white lock, the only way she could die would be through self-infliction. No matter what else happened to her, she would always pull through."

"So why did you call her a weeping rose?"

"While there's always the element of free will, the luck aura is a big determining factor in how life plays out. The spectrum runs backward from red to gold with blue right in the middle. The color of it is set the moment you're born and it not only affects your life, but the lives of those around you. Red is unlucky, obviously, while gold is extremely lucky. Most people are teals or indigos, neutral with a dash of one side or the other. Blues are fantastic because they make all their own luck. But, reds... Reds can bring down the whole ship.

"The effect isn't as noticeable the closer to red your own aura is, but the farther away the harder you feel it. For example, you are a gold. If your sister was a red then every time you were around her, it damaged your luck. You never would have been in that tree house if it weren't for her. Somehow, your luck would have gotten you out of it."

"So, you're saying she was cursed with infinite bad luck to go with her infinite life?"

"Think of it as nature looking out for itself. Can you imagine what would happen if someone couldn't die? The consequences are more far ranging than you could imagine."

"Well, if I'm a gold, why didn't I affect her for the better? Why didn't my good luck balance her bad luck?"

"Honestly, I've seen so few golds over the centuries that I'm not sure. Maybe red is stronger than gold. Maybe you did have a positive effect, but it just wasn't enough. Did she seem worse once you moved to New York, or did she stay the same?"

"Worse. Much worse. I never should have left. If I hadn't left, maybe I could have helped her."

He made another noise of impatience and waved her off. "Haven't you been listening? She would've dragged you down with her. The only way for her suffering to end was by doing exactly what she did. Otherwise, she would have just kept being hurt both physically and mentally and so would everyone around her."

"But, suicide is wrong!" Jack felt the tears she'd been fighting free themselves, her mascara running in tracks down her face. "Even now her soul is probably wandering lost in Purgatory if it isn't already suffering in Hell."

He made a strangled noise, as if he was trying very hard not to laugh at her distress. "You're joking, right? You're sitting in a circa 1930s bungalow having a chat about luck and magic with the Grim Reaper himself, and you still think you're sister is endangered by a lake of flaming petrol?"

"The catechism says, 'We are obliged to accept life gratefully and preserve it for His honor and the salvation of our souls. We are stewards, not owners, of the life God has entrusted to us. It is not ours to dispose of.'"

"Do you want the truth? I mean, the truth about God and death and Heaven and Hell and all of it. Would you believe me if I told you?" She scrubbed at her cheeks and glared ferociously, as if she dared him to contradict the existence of God.

"The truth is, if there is a God, I've never met him. I've heard many things in the last eight hundred years and many of the immortals I know do believe in him, which is good enough for me. To be frank, considering how highly organized the Beyond is, I'd be surprised if there wasn't a God.

"The Beyond is vast—practically unending—much larger than this pale human condition. It's structured better than any corporation could dream and it runs in a very compartmentalized fashion. I work for the Department of Death and Demise. As Grim Reaper, I'm in charge of the Charonites who deal with those scheduled to shuffle the mortal coil. There are other divisions in the DoDD, naturally, and each one has a singular person in charge. Each of us then report to the department head, who is in turn a member of the Powers That Be.

"The PTB make overarching decisions about how the Beyond is run and how the antemortem is micromanaged. However, there are checks and balances. The Director of the DoDD, for example cannot simply make unilateral choices for the entire department on a whim. Either he needs the agreement of a majority of the PTB or the unanimous backing of the division heads within his own department. I'm afraid I make that last a bit difficult, but he's an overweight ponce who's too busy working his way up the food chain to give the Department the attention it deserves. Santana Nickleby's dearest ambition is to make the leap from senator to emperor, if you catch my meaning. If there were a God, Old Nick's goal would be to usurp him.

"When you die—whether by suicide, murder, or old age—there are a few things that can happen.

Souls who just can't move on stick it out for decades or even centuries on the mortal plane. They're the ones you think of as ghosts. The rest find themselves queued up in Purgatory.

"In death, talents and attributes you had in life are amplified because you are no longer constrained by your mortality. Sometimes these are particularly useful to the various departments and divisions and the dearly departed are given the choice of a job or an afterlife. You may always quit your job and retire into the afterlife, but you may not return from it. Not everyone is offered a position because, as I'm sure you can imagine, openings are few and far between."

She spoke up then, her horror at his stamping upon her religion receding into curiosity. "And what was your talent?"

His eyes flattened, as did his voice. "I have a rather unique combination of heartlessness, creativity, and tenacity. All traits I come by honestly enough and only one of which needed a bolster from death."

Death stood up, striding to the window and peeking through the blinds. The street outside was empty. He didn't know what he'd expected. Neither of them had seen their attacker. It was obvious enough that it had been someone from his side of the tracks, but who?

Of course, he supposed, the more important question was why? He'd never bothered to endear himself to his higher-ups, but she had never done anything to piss anyone off that he was aware of. Death looked back over his shoulder at her. She was hunched once more in a little knot on the couch. It took a lot of imagination to figure why someone would be after her. Then he saw the irony of the idea and amended it in his head to add "other than himself."

Nothing made sense.

Taking the five steps back to her, he reached out a hand. She gave him a cautious look before accepting it and hauling herself up. They stood in awkward silence for a moment more before he broke it.

"Right, well, I've been thinking that whoever is after one or both of us hasn't struck before. This means that somehow they can't track us properly. Since I was originally sent to kill you and was put on administrative leave when I failed, we're going to operate under the assumption that you're the target. It was hard enough for me to find you and I could really only do so once you'd been pointed out to me. Your luck must be acting as a very basic shield."

Her face wrinkled as she tried to follow along his logic.

"It would be easy enough for certain immortals

to track me, especially since someone obviously knows I'm with you. The fact that no one has attacked again is significant. I would wager that somehow your luck is now protecting both of us. As if it senses you need me in order to keep you alive." He waved his hand in a motion of dismissal. "Ironic, I know."

"So, what do we do, now?"

"The coast appears to be clear, but I don't know for how long. Eventually, someone is going to find us."

He contemplated their next move. It would be impossible for them to stay holed up for very long. On the other hand, he couldn't make a move unless he had more information. Death wondered if there was a way he could contact someone: Someone discrete, informed, and trustworthy. The trouble was, he could only think of one such person in the entire DoDD and he wasn't sure that any way to reach her wouldn't be intercepted.

Of course, he mused, he could always declare his vacation over and storm back into the department demanding to know what the hell was going on. But, then, there were worse things than death waiting if they were after him as well.

After a moment, Jack excused herself to go clean up the tear-tracks in her makeup that made her look like a horror movie victim. While she was gone, Death investigated the little room. The quilts and old-fashioned furniture definitely did not suit his fellow captive, but he reminded himself that it wasn't really her house. On a little side table he noticed a stack of mismatched journals. Picking one up, he idly thumbed through it. A few pages in he stopped, then turned back to the beginning, then returned to his place. Finally, he flipped through the whole thing, analyzing the script. The handwriting changed frequently, though the narrative was obviously by the same person, but he'd seen some of it before.

Three times I've tried! Every time a failure. How is she doing it? How is she keeping me down, keeping me away, keeping our lives unfinished. I have to confront her. Ms. Careby is always saying I need to confront my demons. SHE is my demon. She's always been the one holding me back. Today I went to the airport again. I made it farther this time. I bought the ticket, I boarded the plane. But Jackie had other plans. The plane wouldn't even take off. No one could tell us why, it just wouldn't go. I'm sure she's responsible. I don't know how. I don't know why. What happened? Ever since that stupid treehouse she's been this way. Vengeful and greedy. I just want a life of my own. I want to stop being hurt. I want the things she's stolen from me with her perfect life.

"What do you think you're doing? Those are private!" Jack emerged from the back, clearly incensed to see him with the book. Marching over without a second thought, she snatched it from his long, bony fingers. He looked at her with mocking disbelief.

"Are they yours?"

"They're my sister's and none of your concern. Have you no respect for the dead?" She stuffed the books onto a shelf with ferocity. Death gave her a measured look before unexpectedly softening his tone.

"Jacquelyn, listen to me. She's gone. The dead are dead. They have neither need nor concern for your respect. I promise you that she has no more worry for mortal thoughts than a raincloud cares if it floods. When people say to respect the dead, what they really mean is to respect the living. In your memory your sister is still alive, and for your own sake you wish some semblance of respect and decorum to be maintained."

She stared at him gape-mouthed. Obviously his argument, though tender and well thought out, did nothing to pall her outrage. Instead, she appeared flustered and unsure of what to say. Finally, she spit a single word out with as much venom behind it as she could muster.

"Jack."

"I've been called worse, but I was only trying to ease your mind."

"No, my name. My grandmother's the only one who called me Jacquelyn. Everyone else calls me Jack. Or Jackie. Or occasionally Jacks, though I don't like that one either."

"Jack, then."

They fell back into an uneasy silence. He rested his chin on his hands and continued to weave through the possible scenarios of their situation. For her part, she rummaged around the room looking in search of something to do. Finally finding nothing, she settled against the couch back with her knees drawn up to her chest. Jack turned her head toward him and considered a moment before speaking.

"So, what does happen when you die?"

It took a moment for her question to break his reverie.

"I told you, your soul goes to Purgatory to be evaluated for its usefulness."

"But, after that. What happens? You made it seem like there is no Hell. Is there a Heaven?"

He shifted in discomfort.

"I don't know. The truth is, there could be a Hell. I don't personally believe in one because I've never heard anyone else in the Beyond mention it. That doesn't mean it's not real, though. It's the same with Heaven. I know that something exists beyond Purgatory, but having never moved on myself I couldn't tell you what it is."

Jack considered his words for a moment. "Earlier, you said you'd only been around for eight hundred years. How is that possible? The world is much older than that." The corner of his mouth lifted.

"Observant, you are. Yes, the world is much older than that. And before you ask, don't. I've only worked for the DoDD for," he made a show of looking at his watch, "Seven hundred ninty years this September."

Her brows creased. "So, you haven't always been the Grim Reaper?"

"Certainly not. And I'm sure I won't be the last, either. No, I was a man once. A lot of the details become blurry with time, but some things stay with you. I remember my name, I remember my mother's face, I remember the day that I died. Those are the important things."

"How did you become the Grim Reaper?"

"I began as a Charonite, the official term for reapers. I worked my way through the ranks, biding my time. Then, when the job came open, I took it."

"But, I don't understand. If you're dead, if everyone in the Beyond is dead, how can there be a job opening?"

"The same as any other company. Immortals retire, souls move on, ranks get shuffled. It happens more frequently than you'd think. Of course, new positions are created as needed to deal with the burgeoning work load. Mortals are nothing if not both prolific and deadly. My first real assignment as a Charonite was on the battlefields of Genghis Khan. After his death, I was shuffled around various other Asian territories until the plague broke out.

"Strictly speaking, my division doesn't handle viral outbreaks, that's Leukippos' job. However, this one got a little out of control, in spite of all the careful planning. A large number of Charonites were reassigned to Pestilence for the duration. We were there to clean up the mess while the others attempted to contain the plague from growing larger. Not that it did any good, if you know anything at all about the Black Death."

"So, you were sent to England or France or wherever because of the plague?"

"No, I stayed in China. Most people think of Europe when talking of the Black Death, but it began in Asia. Two of us were assigned the prefecture of Yangzhou. It was an important post. Being assigned to a city as large as Yangzhou meant they trusted my thoroughness and they didn't doubt I could pull off such a grandiose assignment without more specific direction. They didn't doubt," he echoed his previous words, but it was a hollow sound, "that I could be dispassionate and exhaustive in carrying out my job."

He knew his voice sounded wrong, but he'd be damned if he could control it. She was bringing out memories he'd diligently repressed for centuries. He tried to tell himself that he could ignore her, that they had bigger problems to deal with than chatting about ancient history. But her hair, her eyes, even the point of her chin and the color of her skin were so familiar. Being this close to her, talking to her as if they were equals, it was hard to keep the past buried.

Death could practically see the wheels turning behind those hazel eyes as she watched him. It was the face of a woman searching for a particular piece of a jigsaw puzzle, both evaluating and determined. Finally, she spoke.

"Was her name Jacquelyn?"

"What?" His tone was sharper, more surprised than he'd intended. He cleared his throat, reached for the flask again, and tried once more in a calmer tone. "What?"

"Her name. My name. You said the only name you remembered was mine. Was her name Jacquelyn?"

"No." There was a long pause. What business was it of hers? It was his own personal demon that, truthfully, he should have exorcised long ago. What he needed to be doing now was march directly to either Celestial Intelligence or Immortal Resources and get to the bottom of all this. Instead, he found his mouth opening once more without his permission.

"Her name was Katerina."

Chapter Seventeen

JACK opened her mouth, but the words to ask about Katerina wouldn't come out. She could see he was in pain, but the story seemed somehow tied to her own and the curiosity tugged at her. Instead she let out a sigh and decided to focus on what would come next. Was he going to kill her? Had the game changed? Seconds ticked by, punctuated only by the sounds of the mantle clock.

Suddenly, for the third time since the attack, there was a knock at the front door.

Death rolled his eyes and held a finger to his lips. He tried to peer through the blinds without being detected, but from his posture Jack could tell he was having a hard time.

"Hello?" an unfamiliar voice called out. "Sir, are you in there?"

With stunning speed, Death threw off the locks

and opened the door. A neatly dressed woman stood on the threshold holding a large vase of tulips and looking just as confused as Jack.

"Gina!" he exclaimed, pulling her into the semi-dark room and closing the door behind her. The woman blinked as her eyes adjusted to the low light. Then she gasped.

The flowers slipped from her arms and plummeted to the floor. A splintering crash rang out as porcelain made contact with wood. Water rushed in every direction while the pretty blooms fell into a soggy heap. Jack rushed forward to assess the damage, stooping low to hurriedly gather the blossoms and throw her blanket down to keep the water from spreading.

"What are you doing here?" Gina demanded of Jack.

Her outrage and sense of betrayal was deafening. Gina stared at Jack with an almost comical look of horror. Death gave her a shrewd glance, but Jack remained wide-eyed and confused, crouched in the middle of the room.

"Gina, this is Jacquelyn Devlin," the older man cut in patiently. "Jacquelyn *Katerina* Devlin. I'm sure you remember."

The woman's eyes grew even larger. "She's Jacquelyn Devlin?" The disbelief in Gina's voice was palpable. Jack finally let out a noise of exasperation.

"Yes, I'm Jacquelyn Devlin. Does the entire

underworld know about me? Do they all think I'm some kind of freak just because of my luck? If I were really so lucky, wouldn't I be able to avoid situations like this?"

"What is she talking about?" The newcomer asked Death. He directed her attention back to Jack with a nod of his head.

"Focus, Gina."

The older woman squinted at Jack for a moment before snapping her gaze back to his. "My God. Her aura. All these years, all those notebooks, and you were right. But why is she still alive? And if she's here with you, then who is the new Head of Human Demise?"

Jack watched as Death's politeness utterly dissolved.

"What do you mean 'the new Head of Human Demise?'" he demanded.

"Nickleby didn't put you on administrative leave, sir. He replaced you. He wants you gone permanently, if you get my meaning." She dug a sheaf of papers out of her purse and handed them to him. While he read over them, Jack took the flowers to the kitchen and quickly returned with a towel and dust bin. Gina continued talking as she worked, but Jack could feel her eyes locked onto her face.

"The new Head is a terror. She's manipulative and hot-tempered and vindictive. She's been trying to have you tracked since you left, but everyone is either unwilling of is too far outranked by you. The only reason I could do it is because of how long we've worked together."

Death took their visitor by the bicep with surprising gentleness and steered her over to the couch. The delicate tinker of glass filled the background as Jack collected pieces of the shattered vase.

"My dear Ms. Valenka, I think you had better start from the beginning."

Gina took a deep breath. "After you left, I began sorting the names remaining on your list off onto other lists. As you can imagine, this took some time. I remember thinking how odd a week it had been, what with the light load on Wednesday and the other days bursting at the seams."

"Gina," he redirected her angling thoughts. "What happened?"

"Well, right before I left for the day, Mr. Nickleby came by my desk. He said he'd found a replacement for you and that she would start the next day. I didn't like his tone, it was a bit too gleeful; however, I knew we would need a temporary Head, so at the time I shrugged it off.

"She was already in the office when I came in the Friday morning. I could tell from the start that it wasn't going to work out between us. She was a bit too slinky, if you know what I mean. Like a cat in tight clothes. Very unprofessional. She tried to impress me at first, but she learned pretty quick that I don't brook nonsense. Her saccharine sweetness dissolved within the first few days."

Alarm bells clanged in Jack's head. Things that didn't make sense were beginning to fall into place. Gina's tone became excitable and her face flushed. Even her hands, previously calm and steady, began jumping around to emphasize her story.

"She's so inept, sir! I was at a loss how someone with so little experience had been placed in charge. My suspicions were raised from the moment she told me to continue farming out her share of the names. She told me she had more important things to work on than harvesting souls. As if that's all we do! I don't think she even knows why your list is different from the others—how even the most ordinary people can have extraordinary deaths.

"If that weren't bad enough, several times a day she would lock herself in your office or run down to Nickleby's. After a few days, I caught wind that she was trying to coerce other immortals into tracking you. She was becoming unbearable and her demeanor began to slip. I've seen her kind before. Obsessed to the point of madness in life, the soul gains clarity and unending drive in death. They'll stop at nothing to meet their objective, and with control of your office I feared what she could do. Then, when she brought me those forms to be filed, I knew I had to find you."

"First I went to Nickleby, distasteful as it was. I had hoped I could get some more information out of him first." She shook her head. "He really is the most pompous, self-absorbed, condescending, small-minded, over-reaching, Janus-faced, scheming..."

"We get it, Gina."

"... jackal of a man that ever had the pleasure of having an immortal soul." She was huffing and even in the dim lighting she was beginning to develop a rosy pink glow.

"What did he have to say?"

"Oh, he was delighted with the new Reaper! She was so much more agreeable. She didn't stand in his way just to spite him. She knew where her priorities lay. It was the best deal he'd ever made."

"Deal?"

"Precisely. From what I've put together, it looks like they made a deal. She convinced Nickleby she could find a way to take you out of the game permanently. She would then take over the mantle of Death and acquiesce to his whims and greater machinations. The only thing she asked for was to be able to fix some problem she'd had in the antemortem. I never found out what it was, though."

Silence reigned for several minutes. When it broke, a very small voice spoke from the corner of the room.

"Me."

Two pairs of eyes swiveled to the sound. Jack stood in the doorway to the kitchen, a new vase filled with drowsy tulips in one hand and a small note clutched in the other. She stared at Death and saw the lack of denial on his face.

"It's taken me a while to put everything together," Jack continued, "because I thought the answer was too self-centered to be true. But, you knew. I think you've suspected for a while. You were sent to kill me—pointed out even though you said my luck had kept me almost invisible. You were fired after you failed to do so, which would send anyone into a frenzy to correct their mistake. You've been overly curious about Mal and, now, your secretary flips out because she recognizes me as someone else. It's Mal, isn't it?"

Jack gave a short, bitter laugh that ended on a sob. "Mallory Isabelle Devlin, Grim Reaper Extraordinaire."

The two others exchanged glances.

"How long do you think we have?" Death asked Gina in a quiet tone.

"Maybe a day, at the longest. She knows where you are, her powers are growing, and it's only a matter of time before she finds a way around her shield," she replied, pointing at Jack with the last.

He nodded, jamming his hands in his pockets. "I have an idea, but we'll have to hurry. There's one last favor I can call in, if she's still talking to me."

"You do have that effect on people," Gina said curtly. He didn't bother to cut her a look.

"Look after her," he said, taking a deep breath and slipping out the door without a look back. As the lock clicked back into place behind him, Jack broke her silence.

"Where is he going? My sister is out there trying to kill us and he's just going to leave?" Gina stood from the couch and peeked through the blinds, watching him climb into his miraculously unscathed car and zoom off down the street.

"He knows what he's doing," she replied faintly. "I hope."

After leaving Jack in Gina's care, Death began a winding road north. The hour drive flew by as he ran over what to do in his mind. He'd needed this time apart from the two women to formulate a plan. Finding his intended would be the easy part. Convincing her would be another. Of course, a genius-level demigod should be able to pick up on the importance of the situation, but they had a tendency toward narcissism.

Berkeley was a typical California college town. The streets were busy, but the campus itself seemed quiet for a Saturday. He drove around for a bit, hoping what he was looking for would jump out at him. Soon, though, he gave up and began beating the pavement. For the better part of another hour he asked complete strangers variants on the same question:

"Do you have a philosophy club, or an especially artsy bar?"

Almost everyone he encountered gave him quizzical looks. A few looked at their watches and shook their heads. It was, after all, much earlier than most people went in search of a bar. At last, what must have been the one student awake nodded his head. He wore a neat button-up shirt with khaki shorts and weather-worn sandals, and his bushy beard was groomed with care.

"Yes, sir. It's over on the corner of Newton and Waddell, just off campus. A little place called the Athenaeum. It's a little unexpected, but you can't miss it. My group'll be playing there tonight if you want to stick around."

He thanked the young man, sidestepped the invitation, and headed in the suggested direction. When he found it, Death understood why it had been called unexpected. On the outside it looked like a squat antebellum plantation house. The building had only one story, but the wrap-around porch sported thick, ornate columns and a few friezes. The architect had tried very hard to imitate classic Southern design, which in itself was an imitation of Grecian style. In the end, while the goal was obvious, the execution was lacking and just a touch comical.

Death walked up the front steps and knocked on one of the large wooden doors. Through the glass panels, he saw a woman sweeping and straightening mismatched chairs. Her dirty blonde hair fell in tumbling waves down her back and her olive skin shone in the natural light from the plethora of windows. She looked up at the noise and stared at him a moment, hazel green connecting with pale blue, before walking over. Her gait was easy, but a small frown creased her lovely face.

"We're closed, Arthur," she called through the still locked door. "Come back at lunch."

"We need to talk."

She pressed her full, coral lips together so tightly they almost disappeared. After a few beats and without taking her eyes off his, she slid open the bolt. "This had better be important. I have a business to run." She propped her broom against a wall and sat down in a squashy chair. Crossing her ankles, she waited.

"It's nice to see you, too, Athena. There's trouble brewing. I think Santana is making another play for power."

Her face transformed from consternation to amusement. She laughed like a scattering of silver bells. "And what could possibly make you think that? He's tried and failed before, hasn't he? That's what you're there for. That's why, no matter how much he complains about you, you've stayed in power. You temper him. He hasn't made a single successful play since you've been Grim Reaper."

"I've been fired." The smile fell from her face. He could practically hear it break like a teacup on the hardwood floor.

"What do you mean you've been fired?"

"Canned, dumped, replaced, sent home, let go, put on notice, divested of power, revoked of pension, I could go on."

"Well," she sat back in her chair, deflated. "That's certainly unprecedented."

"There's more."

For twenty minutes he poured out his tale, including all his own suspicions and observations. When Death had done, she appraised him with a thoughtful look.

"What would you like me to do about it? I'm retired, as they say. An up and coming local act is supposed to play here tonight and I plan to give them a little boost. Plus, the university's philosophy department is having a lunch meeting here as they do every second Saturday. I can't just close up and go back with you to God-knows-where."

"For more than two thousand years you were one of the top beings in Celestial Intervention. You've been around for longer than that. Everyone who was and is anyone in the Beyond respects you as a beacon of wisdom and justice.

Even mortals remember your name."

"I retired because no one listened anymore. Maybe it was a selfish reason, but it's true. Yes, I'm famous, but people only like the idea of me. They like the idea of some fabled goddess of courage, knowledge, and inspiration. The follow through is lacking on their part. I'm nearly three thousand years old. I've spent most of that time trying to help mortals and all I got for my trouble was a fancy reputation. No, it's time to do something for me."

"So, you're going to sit here and tell me old men discussing life and teenagers waving lighters are of more value to you than keeping a power-hungry immortal at bay?"

She sighed. Standing with a svelte stretch, she took a turn around the room without looking at him. After a moment, resigned, she faced him with her hands on her hips. "She's no good to you alive, but she'll be no good to you dead, either."

"That's precisely what I was thinking. I've never brought someone over before without killing them. We have a history. I thought if anyone could do it, it would be you."

The Immortal brushed her fingers over the high gloss of the bar top before replying. "Tell me your plan and I'll see what I can do."

Aftermath

Yangzhou Prefecture, China — June 1342 AD

"ARTHUR!"

He stopped dead, momentarily forgetting about the young mother and child he had been about to visit. Yesterday their auras had clearly been a dusky charcoal, and today he'd yet to see them leave their house. He was sure it was time, but they could wait a few moments longer.

He turned to see Katerina sailing toward him in an elaborate Chinese gown patterned with plum blossoms. She smiled at him as she came to a stop.

"What do you think of my new hanfu? Papa had a woman from the city measure me and make it in the traditional style. Isn't it grand?"

Secretly, he thought to himself that she'd never looked more beautiful; the colors of the bright silks served to enhance the rose and olive of her skin, and the golden trimmings made her eyes sparkle.

"Where will you go in such a magnificent dress, Katerina?"

She pulled herself up into the most matron-like demeanor she could muster, her smile evaporating into a thin line of seriousness.

"I had thought to take a stroll through the marketplace and then perhaps down to the river. Of course, for a lady such as myself it wouldn't do to be unchaperoned."

"No, indeed."

He looked around to make sure no one was watching, then corporealized. Katerina couldn't tell the difference by looking at him, but he held out his arm for her to hold on to, reveling in his new trick as he did every time. They walked leisurely though the stalls of spices and silks, listening to the white noise of the merchants haggling with their customers.

The plague had only recently taken off across Asia with the gusto that had been predicted. In Yangzhou, however, it remained mostly within the walls of the poorer districts. There had not been a single case among the merchants or the Franciscan community up the hill. The wealthier citizens carried on with their business still, assuming that God was merely punishing the lower castes for the way they lived.

After half an hour, as they neared the end of the market, Arthur saw something he'd been dreading for months. The other Charonite had spotted him. Not just him, but Katerina. He raised an eyebrow at their companionable pose, but then his eyes grew wide as he took in the fact that she was marked. Marked and alive and wrapped around the arm of death.

He disappeared and Katerina turned her smiling face up to look at Arthur. So this is the end, he thought. For half a year he'd been stalling. At first he'd tried to kill her, but every time she evaded by the skin of her teeth. Day after day she avoided her fate, and he grew ever more amused and then captivated. Picking up their pace, he led her to a small pavilion just outside the market's line of sight. She laughed and picked up her skirt with her free arm to keep it from dragging on the moist grass.

"Katerina, I have to ask you something."

She blushed crimson, then straightened resolutely. "Did you ask my father first?"

"What? No. That is, I—"

Suddenly, she leaned up on her tiptoes and kissed him. It was a light kiss, barely enough to be called such, and it broke his heart. But he wouldn't, couldn't, let another take her first. She was his, and he'd do it himself.

"Have you led a fulfilling life?"

The light drained from her eyes and she frowned.

"I suppose so," she stuttered. "I mean, I've accomplished more than most women twice my age. I've seen the world, I've learned new things, I've met you."

"If you were to die right now, what do you think would happen?"

"I suppose I would go to Heaven. I fancy myself having lived a virtuous life. Why, Arthur! Whatever's wrong?"

She lifted a hand to his face and he could feel the kid-glove softness of her palm on his cheek. A thumb stroked under his eye and, though he couldn't feel it, he supposed a tear must have snuck out. He hadn't known that you could cry after death.

Throwing propriety to the winds, he pulled her close and kissed her, and as he did so he finally killed her. When they separated, it took her a moment to realize something was different. Then, she looked down.

"What in Heaven's name?!"

"Katerina, I can explain. I had to do it."

"You? You did this? You— You killed me?"

"If you'd only let me explain. There was no other way."

"How?"

"I'm a reaper, a Charonite. I have to take the souls of those destined to die. It's my job."

"Undo it!"

"I can't. Once you've been severed there is no going back. You've been marked for death since the New Year. It was only a matter of time."

"So you've been toying with me?"

"No, I—"

"Hasn't this meant anything at all to you? You string me along, you act as if you were about to propose to me, then you kill me?"

"I was never going to propose to you."

The pale translucency of her cheeks flamed brighter than the flowers of her hanfu. Without another word, she gathered up the ghostly trails of her gown and dashed away toward the enclosure of her Italian community.

"Katerina, wait!"

Then she was gone. Without a second look at the body lying motionless on the ground, he ran after her. For hours he searched the town for her spirit before projecting back into the Beyond to search for her in Purgatory.

In the end, she had vanished and no one could tell him where. Did she make it through to an afterlife? Was she still wandering the streets of Yangzhou?

Arthur shored up his senses and returned to the prefecture. With unerring efficiency, he took all the marked souls he could find. By the next day, the bells of the little cloister behind the mudbrick walls rang out to signify a funeral. Katerina's funeral. His jaw clenched as he carried on with his work.

Eternity was far too long to let emotions enter into the business of death.

Chapter Eighteen

THE breaks on the taxi squeaked as it came to a halt outside the Metropolitan Museum of Art. Jack stepped out of the car onto the glistening pavement and leaned back through the window to pay the cabbie. Footsteps echoed behind her and, turning, she saw Nate approaching. A grin broke across her face for the first time in days.

"You have no idea how much I've missed you. So much has happened! I don't even know where to begin."

He wrapped his arms loosely around her waist, his smile matching her own. Jack slid her arms across his chest, her fingers toying with the collar of his shirt, as she stood on her tip-toes to invite him in for a kiss. It was tender and sweet, with passion boiling just below the surface. She poured her soul into it, willing the comfort he brought to erase the chaotic memories from California.

Nate pulled back slightly, his lips still hovering only a breath away from her own.

"I lo—"

Shrill, staccato beeps interrupted what he was about to say, and Jack's eyes popped open. Scrambling off the couch where she'd fallen asleep, she rushed into the smoke filled kitchen to find Gina waving a magazine at the fire alarm.

"What the hell?"

"I was going to make breakfast. It didn't look like it would be that hard. Isn't the point of all your modern appliances to make things easier than they were in my day?"

Coughing, Jack turned off the stove and dumped the curling, black eggs into the garbage. She tossed the pan into the sink with a sigh, and struggled to maintain the good mood the dream had left her in. Shaking her head, Jack walked back to the master bedroom and busied herself getting ready for the day.

The clothes she'd worn yesterday had been the last of her clean ones, so she hunted though the remainder for the second best options. She had intended to do laundry, but her evening had been a little too occupied. When she was done, she plopped back down on the couch and stared off into space, her mind wandering to thoughts of Nate. A smile played at the corner of her lips, threatening to dispel the absurdity of her present circumstances.

"Is that the note that was on the flowers?"

Started at the sound, Jack looked up at Gina and then down at her hands, which had been absentmindedly fiddling with a little white card she'd found among the tulips. The small curve of before blossomed into a full-blown grin. He'd quoted Tennyson, albeit badly. If I had a flower for every time I thought of you today, you could walk through my garden forever. That was the Nate she had met at the gallery. Over the top with his wooing, not filled with the tender gravity he'd shown the morning after. Not that she preferred one over the other. Both sides intrigued and captivated her.

She nodded absently. Thinking of her own love life reminded her of a question she'd meant to ask the night before. She hadn't at first because it felt like intruding. Now, however, her curiosity was getting the better of her.

"Who's Katerina?"

Gina scrutinized Jack for the first time, taking in the dark hair and deep brown eyes. Even the light tan on her skin and the point of her chin, while all Italian in the most generic sense, must've caused her boss great pain when coupled with the name. Looking uncomfortable, she sat down on the edge of a chair and considered where to start.

"Katerina Vilioni was the scion of Italian traders. When her mother died, she along with her brother Antonio and her father Domenici moved east to China. A flourishing Italian community had sprung up there, which is sadly lost today. Unfortunately, shortly after they arrived and set up shop, the plague broke out."

"This was in Yangzhou, I take it?"

"Well, Y-pestis broke out across a large swath of Asia at roughly the same time, but yes. Yangzhou is where he met her."

"What happened?"

"You have to understand, he hadn't been on the job long. I think it was about a hundred years. His antemortem had been filled with such strife and loneliness it was only natural something like this came up. She'd seen him around the town while he carried out his duties. The thing you also have to remember is he likes to perform his job from a distance. It's rare for him to interact with those he's scheduled to collect.

"Katerina didn't realize what he was, only that he was a foreigner like herself. She struck up a friendship with him and he soon reciprocated. After a while, I believe he even came to love her. Unfortunately, if he did so it was at a detriment to his job."

"He stopped reaping souls?" Jack interjected, eyes wide.

"Oh, he continued to end others' suffering while she wasn't around, but he ignored something very important. Katerina herself was marked for death. According to stories I've heard, she was also extremely lucky, though not gold like you. The brightest of sunny yellows. For a time, that luck kept them both off the radar of the higher-ups. But, all good things must come to an end.

"When she was discovered by the other Charonite assigned to the city, he stepped in. He knew their time was at an end and, rather than let someone else do it, he took on the responsibility himself. I'm not sure what he did, but from that moment on he was on the fast track to be the next Head of Human Demise. No one knows what happened to Katerina's soul." Gina paused and looked thoughtful. In a measured voice she added, "I guess we'll never know."

"As soon as I was hired he laid down a few simple ground rules. The first was that he required decency of dress, stoicism, and a demanding work ethic—all things with which I was happy to comply. The other was that under no circumstances should the name Katerina appear on his list. Ever. When he saw your name, well..."

Gina trailed off and they sat in silence for a while. Jack felt like she was back in school, being bombarded with too much information in too few days. She felt sorry for Death in a way she had not expected. He'd been a political pawn as a boy, an outcast warrior as a man, and even the peace he'd found in death had been taken from him by the wayward chance of a mortal. Two mortals, she corrected as she remembered herself. The thought brought her back around to their present circumstances.

"What is he doing, now?"

"Honestly, I'm not sure. He knows people. I'm sure he's thought of something clever and unexpected. That's how he works. It's never the obvious answer with him."

"You seem to know him very well."

"I won't lie, a lot of his history I picked up through rumors and hearsay. There's nothing the dead love more than to gossip. However, we've been together for centuries. Sometimes I think I'm the only soul he trusts in the Beyond. The only person he confides in. I worry what will happen to him when I'm gone."

"Gone?" Jack asked, surprised.

"Of course. One day I'll retire and move on."

"What will happen then?"

"Well, if I have enough service or I've made a large enough contribution there's always the chance I'll get offered permanent immortal status. Old division heads, so-called gods and sometimes saints, those types of beings are routinely allowed to keep their powers even though they've vacated their job. They usually wander back to Earth and set up some kind of life for themselves. I could always refuse and be rewarded with an afterlife instead, but those are so uncertain."

"Uncertain?"

"No one really knows, now do they? Heaven, hell, reincarnation, dissolution. There's not a single soul that can tell us the truth behind the veil because once you move on you don't come back. All that's left is your famé, your immortal memory."

Jack recalled her earlier conversation with Death. "You mean where the dead live on in the memories of the living?"

"Yes, exactly. In ancient times it was thought you had to be a hero to achieve famé. Scandinavian mythology is full of examples. Ordinary people couldn't live on forever because they weren't brave or exciting enough. It's where you get the modern concept of fame from. Celebrity, if you will. But, over time, people realized that as long as they made an impact for ill or good on someone else, it was its own kind of famé. As long as one person remembered you, you were never truly gone."

Jack considered this. It was a type of legacy, she supposed. Sometimes it was small things like remembering how your grandfather made pancakes every Saturday morning. Other times it was bigger things like a movie role or a bestselling novel. She wondered what she would leave behind. There were her pictures, of course, but would anybody really remember her now that all her family was gone?

There were her roommates. They had their own problems, though. If she never came back they would move on with their lives and she'd be just a footnote at the back of their minds. Her boss might remember her, she thought, reflecting on Louis with kindness. He'd taken her under his wing and had done more for her career than four years of college. Still, he had a family and friends of his own.

Nate would remember her. A warm fluttering feeling filled her chest as she thought back to the night before last. She'd given him what no other man had been allowed near. He'd been a little surprised at first when she cried out against his shoulder, but she'd urged him on. It was a decision she'd made for herself, to finally let someone else in. Surely he wouldn't forget her.

Gina must have understood the inward look on her face. She reached out a tentative hand and placed it on the younger girl's arm.

"It's alright, you know. You're young. You have plenty of time to leave your mark on the world. He'll get us out of this and afterward I'm sure he'll want to stay as far away from you as possible. You've heard the old stories of people making deals with Death? Well, they're rare, but they're not wrong. Something will work out."

Jack tried to smile, but it felt more hopeless than hopeful. She considered her next question for a moment.

"How do you get a job in the Beyond? He said souls were evaluated in Purgatory, but is that all there is to it?"

"That's most of it. Occasionally those who interact with mortals will run across someone they feel is particularly suited for a position. That soul gets flagged for when it crosses over. Less often, a departed soul will make an argument for itself or, if cunning enough, will talk its way into a meeting with a department head."

"Is that what Mal did? Or was she flagged because she was a weeping rose?"

"Only those that work in Purgatory can answer that. Did she have any particular talents in life that death might've amplified?"

Jack made a bitter noise, no longer suppressing the unpleasant memories of the past. "Are seduction, manipulation, and insanity generally sought after traits?" As soon as the words left her mouth she regretted them, true or not. Gina seemed to take no notice, however.

"She could have used those to gain an audience. Maybe that's how she convinced Nickleby to let her try her hand in exchange for you. He's an immortal who tends toward indulgence as shown off by his expensive taste and over-large figure."

"I don't understand what you need me for, though. Your boss clearly doesn't need my luck if he's run off without us and I fail to see how I can be of any other help. Why not just let me go?"

Another voice answered.

"Because you can be of help. More than you know."

Both women nearly leapt out of their skins at the sound. It was earthy but musical, like a sparkling brook. The clock read a quarter to midnight and out of the deep shadows around the door emerged a woman neither had ever seen. She appraised them for a moment before continuing as if she'd always been there.

"Is he back, yet?" The two shook their heads in silent no. She walked farther into the room and took a seat on the edge of an end table, crossing her knees. "Well, it's not really my place to explain. I'm just here to assist."

"Excuse me, but how did you get in here, and who are you?" Jack asked, wary.

"Me? I'm nobody. Just a retired old goddess here to provide a little insight on your precarious situation."

"Goddess?" Jack's voice took a sharper pitch. She'd done her best to roll with everything thus far, but her faith could not stretch to include additional deities.

"Well, of a sort. It turns out if you mix a white gold aura with an above average IQ and a pretty face, ancient civilizations will revere you for all posterity." She gave them a bright smile before crinkling her nose. "They always got my nose wrong, though, which is a bit irksome."

Gina and Jack started at the sound of the door's locks clicking. A moment later, Death walked in, looking a tad rumpled but no worse the wear for his absence. He raised an eyebrow at their visitor.

"So much for retirement. You could have ridden back with me."

She shrugged. "I detest cars. I do wish chariots would come back in fashion."

"So, get a motorcycle."

She pursed her lips in a mischievous grin. "I have three. However, if you'd asked I would have brought you along with me instead."

The corners of his lips twitched. "I detest side-along projection."

She shrugged again, her upturned mouth unwavering. Jack looked back and forth between the two of them, unsure what to say. This bantering side of Death was new and unexpected. An explanation of their current position and what he planned to do about it did seem to take precedence, though. Opening her mouth, she blurted out just that, manners be damned.

"Can someone please tell me what exactly is going on?" Everyone turned to look at her and for a moment she was reminded with an echoing horror of her role as a heralding angel in her sixth-grade Christmas cantata. She opened and closed her mouth a bit like a fish on land. Then she sunk back onto the edge of her chair.

"I mean, I just want to put this whole ugly mess behind me. Can't we please get on with whatever needs to be done so I can go home?" As Jack's eyes fluttered shut she missed the ominous look exchanged between Death and the lovely Athena.

Death looked at each of them in turn, as if deciding whom to address first. Athena sat with a half amused look, her legs tucked demurely beneath herself on the settee. Gina had folded her hands in her lap, but a crumpled cigarette lay behind her ear and another stuck out of her chignon. Jack, by contrast, sat cross-legged with her elbows propped on her knees and her chin in her hands. She took a deep breath to steel herself. There was no way things could get worse.

Death cleared his throat and began.

"When a mortal is effectively immortal, one of two things happens. If they're unlucky enough, they take themselves out of the picture, we wash our hands and move on. The closer to gold they get, though, the trickier the situation becomes. If they don't clean up their own mess, there has to be what we term Celestial Intervention. There's an entire department, the largest in the Beyond, dedicated to this sort of thing and Immortal Mortality is only a small division.

"Those who don't realize what they have, what they are, are generally left in peace for a time. Tabs are kept on them, though, in case they figure it out or get too cocky. A lot of the immortal blues go into military service. Patton, for example, is considered one of America's greatest generals, but when the opportunity arose Immortal Mortality intervened. Oh, they don't cause accidents to happen like I do. The agents of Celestial Intervention have their own ways of doing things."

Athena spoke up, jumping in to add detail and form to Death's outline.

"When it's time to take a mortal who can't die by conventional means, an agent is dispatched to talk with them. They take their time and explain everything as clearly as possible. Once the mortal understands what is going on, they must make a conscious and honest decision to cross over. If they don't wish to go, they are allowed to remain on Earth as long as they don't cause too big of a mess. Once they start interfering in the Grand Design, it's out of our department. Eventually, they all come around. They begin to see not only the physical ravages of old age but the social ones as well, and they quickly change their minds.

"The important thing to remember, though, is much like suicides the cross over of unkillable mortals is completely voluntary. They must make the decision for themselves because their aura dictates they cannot die by ordinary means. No accidents, no spells, no old age. However, there are perks. This particular path to postmortem allows your soul to keep a bit more than just a jumble of fuzzy memories. You retain your luck, as well."

Athena's long-winded lesson was interrupted by the scrape of metal and a spark jumping to life. Gina dragged on the cigarette that had been previously cradled by her ear. Six eyes turned to bear on her as she let out a slow and foggy breath.

"I'm sorry. I didn't know I had to pay attention to this part. It's all for her benefit, right?" she asked, waving the smoldering end toward Jack. Athena rolled her eyes and Jack wrinkled her nose at the smell of burning carcinogens.

"Could you not smoke in my house, please?"

Gina shrugged and crumpled the cigarette in her hand. She uncurled her fingers to reveal a pristine specimen in its place, then tucked it back where it came from. Athena sighed and began again.

"The illustration I always liked to use with new recruits was to think of life as a womb. While here the placenta—your auras—makes vague definitions on who you are. You can only grow so big, you can only develop so much. However, when it breaks you are free to move on into the next grand adventure where you are essentially unfettered. When you die your auras, for all intents and purposes, snap. You are then unconstrained in your abilities. Any talents or traits you had before are amplified and you have the ability to use them for good or ill as you so wish.

"The major difference for people like me is, as I said before, we get to keep our luck. It's a technicality; we don't die so the band doesn't break. The conscientious decision is made to cross over with the help of the otherworldly, and you're taken as you are. This puts such souls at much greater advantage than most. With very few exceptions, the Beyond is your oyster. Departments will argue over who gets you because luck, even the middling kind, is a powerful asset in the afterlife."

Jack interrupted, then. Something the so-called-goddess said didn't quite sit right.

"But, Patton died. I visited his grave when I was spending a semester abroad at the Université du Luxembourg."

"Of course his body died. You don't take your remains with you into the Beyond. It's an all together different plane of existence. But the official cause of death is wrong. They couldn't very well say his spirit flew away amidst a symphony of angels' wings. I suppose what I should have said is your soul does not escape due to your body dying. Rather, your body dies because of your soul escaping."

Jack was somewhat mollified by the explanation, but she was beginning to grow wary. The conversation was not so much explaining a plan as using the word "you" more often than she thought appropriate. Jack looked straight at Death, staring him down over the tops of her glasses.

"What does any of this have to do with getting your job back?"

"As Athena said, luck is a powerful asset in the Beyond. Because most souls have no luck, in death we are only separated by the powers bestowed upon us. For example, as the new Head of Human demise, Mallory is technically more powerful than me. I have more experience with the powers and can probably fend her off, but hers are stronger because she's properly vested with them. Gina here does not have the same abilities as either of us because she was never meant to need them."

"What about her?" Jack asked, jerking her head at Athena.

"I'm retired. I still have most of my powers, and they are quite, well, powerful. However, I'm also limited in how I can interact with the Beyond. It's a sacrifice you make when you come back to this world. I could wreak some havoc, bring a soul over, but I couldn't cause any lasting damage."

"You see," Death continued, "when Mallory took her own life her soul still crossed over in the traditional way. Her bad luck was broken and she was freed. If someone with perfect luck were to come over retaining that luck, they would have a better chance of taking her down."

A fist clenched in Jack's stomach and her wariness ratcheted to alarm bells. "So, why don't you just get one of these unkillables to do your dirty work for you? It seems that would be a lot simpler than holing up in my house, swapping office stories."

The other three exchanged glances again and she knew what was coming before Athena spoke the words. "The best case scenario would involve another soul intimate with the situation. Someone who would be able see her for what she is and act accordingly."

"Someone like me?" When no one spoke she got to her feet and walked to the doorway of the kitchen. Jack stood there in silence, letting her mind spin and her heart race. After several seconds, Death spoke from behind her.

"Don't you want to confront her? Don't you want answers? Did you think by selling her house and reading her diaries you'd learn to live and let die? She's the only one who can give you any sort of peace. Knowing what she's become will continue to haunt you if you don't take this opportunity."

"Take the opportunity to what, die?" she yelled at him, whirling around. "Excuse me for not leaping on the chance! I'm twenty-five-years-old. I have a good job, a nice apartment, friends and responsibilities. I've been told I'm only scratching the surface of my career, but I've already won an award for one of my photography essays. Unlike my sister, I'm not exactly ready to forfeit my life!"

"You are capable of so much more," he replied. "You are both passionate and compassionate, rational and faithful, detailed and broadminded. You didn't just let your luck whisk you away, you worked for everything as if you were as unlucky as your sister. That's why you've gotten so far in so little time. And, those traits would be doubled were you to come with us. You could make an eternal name for yourself in the Beyond with ease."

"And what if I refuse?"

He looked a little deflated. "Then I'll let you go and never darken your days again. If we succeed, I'll leave you the scarab. Keep it somewhere safe. All you'll have to do is take hold of it when you're ready and your name should appear on my list again. I'll come for you, then, but it'll be on your terms. Of course, if we're not successful, Mallory will eventually find you. Even if she can't kill you straight away, she'll keep trying. Stubborn repetition is part and parcel of her madness, as I think you've come to realize."

Jack felt the weight of her necklace, normally unnoticeable, heavy against her chest. The air in the room felt even heavier. It was like drowning and suffocating and claustrophobia all at the same time. Her mind spun so fast she found herself grasping for something to hold onto.

Unbidden, the life that could have been flashed before her eyes. She'd had so many plans. He was right when he'd said she'd worked hard. Never in her life had she allowed herself to coast along. At twenty-four she'd beaten out thousands of other photographers for an award by the Photographic Society of America. Her freelance work was featured by several magazines around New York City, which meant national distribution, and she had a steady job with one of them.

She had even planned to begin teaching a seminar. Not a lot of people knew yet, but she'd been in contact with the faculty at Tisch School of the Arts at NYU. They'd offered her an adjunct position for the fall. It was only for one class, but it was new and exciting.

Jack's mind wandered to Nate. Even that had had potential for the future. When you met a fellow New Yorker three thousand miles away, you knew not to challenge fate. He had been funny and attractive and interested in much the same things as her. They might have gone their entire lives without meeting if it hadn't been for all this unpleasantness.

Her mind wandered ever farther into the future. She looked at the tulips, coral-pink against the shadowed white of the walls. How long would they have continued to date, she wondered? Perhaps they would have gotten married. Maybe there would have even been children; they both liked kids. Or, maybe someone else would have come along. Would they have lived happily-ever-after? She'd always planned to leave the Big Apple someday and move to Connecticut where there was access to the city without sacrificing the suburbs. There was so much left to life and now she would never know. A sadness crept over her, different from all the other emotions she'd been faced with of late.

And just like that, she realized she was thinking in finalities. Jack took a deep, steadying breath before speaking. "What could I possibly do? I don't have any supernatural abilities."

Gina spoke up. "I have a contact in Immortal Resources. We'll have you flagged for a position and, once you cross over all you have to do is accept it. You'll be immediately saddled with whatever powers the job entails and that, combined with your luck, should be enough."

"Enough to do what, exactly?"

All three faces before her became grave, Death's perhaps the most.

"There are worse things than dying," he replied simply.

Chapter Nineteen

"YOU want me to do what?" Jack yelled at Death. Gina tried to lay a soothing hand on her arm, but she shook her off. Death spoke slowly, as if explaining something to a child.

"She can't just be allowed to run free in the Beyond."

"There's a big difference between subduing my sister and sending her to Hell."

Death made an impatient noise. "You aren't listening. It's not Hell. It's Sheol."

Out of the corner of her eye, Jack saw Gina shudder at the name like it was a forbidden word. She rounded on the secretary. "Why is that worse than Hell? I saw your reaction. What makes this Sheol so especially bad?"

"Hell is said to be a place of tortures, of everlasting punishment. But Sheol is a place of darkness and isolation. The Great Nothingness. If Hell is prison for wayward souls, Sheol is solitary confinement. It doesn't sound so bad at first, but have you even been completely alone, utterly in the dark? I've heard it eats away at your soul until there's nothing left."

"And you people want me to send my sister there?"

"She tried to kill you," Death pointed out.

"She's my sister!"

Death opened his mouth to argue. Athena, who had taken a back seat during their disagreement, lodged herself between them. Turning to face him, she gave a brittle smile. "Arthur, can I talk to you for a minute?"

Jack crossed her arms and fumed while the retired goddess dragged the former Grim Reaper a few feet away. She rolled her eyes and pressed her lips tightly together, easily able to hear everything that was said as if she weren't even there.

"This isn't something you can bully her into, Arthur. She isn't one of your generals. This is her sister we're talking about. Do you remember how hard it was for you to take your own sister?"

Death grimaced at the wash of memories. "I did what I had to do."

"And what would you have done if you were told to send her to Sheol?" When he wouldn't reply, Athena continued. "Let me talk to her." With a grunt he stepped to the side and motioned for her to do as she liked. She closed the distance between herself and the other two women and draped an arm around Jack.

"I just don't understand why this is necessary," Jack protested. "Surely someone from the Beyond can deal with Mallory. Can't they just take her into custody and force her to take an afterlife?"

"Jack," Athena began, her voice softer than silk, "if Celestial Intelligence or Immortal Resources get involved, she will be sent to either Hell or Sheol regardless. There are no other options for justice in the Beyond. There's no jail or social workers or psychiatric wards. Everything is very black and white because death is the end of the line. Think of all the chances she's had to reform over the years. If she's made it as far as death and hasn't improved, she'll only continue to get worse. She's willing to manipulate the afterlife to kill her own twin. What else could she be capable of?

"There are two options if you choose to help us. You can assist in subduing her until she can be processed into the appropriate sphere of Hell, or you can send her soul to Sheol. That's it."

"That's horrible."

"That's death."

"If someone from Celestial Intelligence or Immortal Resources can handle this, why am I being asked to do it?"

Jack, whose attention had been focused on Athena, jumped when Death answered from over her shoulder. "For a number of reasons. One, you're already marked for death. Two, you could make cleaner work of it since you are an intimate of hers. Three, the Beyond is notorious for letting things stay the same as long as possible. If you don't take care of her now, who knows how long it will be before something happens."

Gina spoke up as well. "If she's not gone soon, I can't go back. I won't work like that anymore. I'd rather take the uncertainty of an afterlife. And you can't go back either, sir," she said, looking pointedly at Death. "You've been fired. If you try to go back and someone catches you, you might be the one that ends up in Sheol. Immortal Resources did give her the power to send you off."

"Alright," Jack said in a small voice. She was tired. She was tired of being afraid and she was tired of running from her problems and she was tired of pretending that there was something in her sister worth saving. It only made the heartache worse. "Alright," she repeated, "I'll do it."

Unlike Mallory, Jack spent a while considering how she would be found. They couldn't wait for her to go back to New York, and she didn't want it to look like suicide. In the end, she changed into her pajamas and climbed into the musty, old bed. Better to look like she died in her sleep, she thought.

Jack emptied out her mind as best she could and focused on her acceptance of crossing over.

Athena slid her cold hand into Jack's warm one and tugged gently. It wasn't a physical pull, but something else entirely, like something from deep inside being nudged outward. They worked at it for a quarter-hour, Jack slowing her breathing in an almost meditative state and Athena trying to coax out her soul.

Finally, it happened. Jack could only describe the sensation as sliding through herself—like walking out of a giant cube of Jell-O. She'd read accounts of people who claimed a ghost had walked through them. This, she thought, must be what the ghost feels. Jack climbed out of the bed and looked down at her empty body with a grim face. She found herself worrying about so many things that didn't matter now, like what her friends would go through. It was too late, of course, to do anything about it. Physically she was the picture of health with the exception of now being deceased, and she was sure her demise would baffle the authorities.

Sighing, Jack turned toward Death and Athena. Gina was long gone; she had left for the Beyond before they began the procedure in order to set things up. With a final look around and a sting of regret in her heart, Jack allowed the encroaching light to wash out the colors of the world around her.

When her eyes adjusted to her new surroundings, shock coursed through her system.

She didn't know what she had expected, but it hadn't been this. To say Purgatory looked like a bad day at the DMV was putting it lightly. In every direction stretched queues and velour stanchions. Some souls, having already been through the lines, sat on various pieces of furniture clutching little paper tabs with numbers on them. Many, though, never came back out of the doors through which they were called.

A large hand spread on the small of her back and she looked around to see Death nudging her forward toward a nondescript doorway at the back of the expansive, white room. Jack supposed Athena had left them to return to her retirement. Nervous but resolved, Jack reached out a hand for the little, brass knob and twisted it to the right. The door swung open with numb silence to reveal complete darkness beyond. Jack swallowed hard and Death inclined his head to murmur instructions in her ear.

"Take a deep breath and, as you walk through, acknowledge that you accept the mantle of your new position. Keep walking and in a moment you'll emerge in the general vicinity of the correct office. If Immortal Resources did their job, you should come out somewhere in the DoDD. Are you ready?" She nodded and took a step forward. Then another, and another, focusing on her intent to accept her new job whatever it might be. And suddenly, she was out of the darkness and in a brightly lit office. But the hand was no longer at her back.

Jack whirled around looking for her compatriot, but Death was nowhere to be seen. A moment of panic gripped her. What if Mallory came along before he found her? She had no real idea what her newfound powers were, nor how to effectively use them. Of course, she tried to comfort herself, neither did Mal. Not really, anyway. If Mal had had a grip on her own abilities, she would have disposed of Jack long before now.

An older man interrupted her thoughts as he walked into the office from an adjoining room. His advanced age was plain from the lines on his face, but his curly hair and energetic demeanor belied it. The immaculate white suit he wore seemed to almost radiate light and his golden tie practically sparkled against his starched shirt. He spotted her and stopped in his tracks. Furrowing his brow, he turned to approach her.

"May I help you?"

"Erm, yes, which department am I in, please?"

He quirked his eyebrows at her. "Celestial Intervention, of course."

"Celestial Intervention?!"

"That's right. Where did you think you were?" He looked her up and down for the first time, taking in her casual dress. "Or, rather, where were you told you were headed? Sometimes mix-ups do happen."

"I thought I was going to Death and Demise."

He titled his head with a frown. "Why would a gold be sent to Death and Demise? One does not need luck for such a position. No, I'm sure you were supposed to come here. Let me see..." he walked to a large desk and picked up a scroll of paper. Unrolling it he scanned the contents. "What is your name, my dear?"

She was beginning to panic, now. Time was wasting and she felt so alone. Glancing from the door to her inquisitor, she realized she'd never find her way without help. "Jacquelyn Devlin, but I really do—"

"Devlin?" he repeated, his voice taking on a sharp edge as he closed the scroll with a snap. "And you're trying to get to Death and Demise? Yes, I thought you looked familiar. Did you get lost, or are you here to make a play for more power? Well, I'm a busy man and I don't have time for people like you. Oh, yes, I've heard all about you. How you act sweet and innocent until you don't get your way. How you try to manipulate other departments into doing things your own refuses to comply with. Get out of Celestial Intervention, Miss Devlin. You have no power here."

Jack's breath caught in her chest. His eyes, once shining and bright, had become burning and power radiated off of him like light. She opened her mouth to speak and had to force the sounds out.

"I'm not my sister." The words sounded very small, even to her, and for several moments she was afraid he hadn't heard at all. Then he took a step forward.

"What did you say?"

"I said," she repeated with a voice growing stronger by each stilted syllable, "I am not my sister."

"Sister?" She nodded and he picked the scroll back up. Suddenly, he sat it down on the nearest desk and ran his finger over it, his face showing at first disbelief then curiosity. Jack tentatively leaned over to look as well. Sure enough, there was "Jacquelyn Katerina Devlin" inscripted in flowing, gold ink. Beside her name was a title that made no sense to her, but obviously impressed him. She snapped back as he picked up the roll and closed it slowly, examining her as he did so.

"So, Immortal Resources sent you here to balance her? I'm assuming that's why you were vested with this position. I confess I've never seen someone jump ranks like this before, but then, that's exactly what your sister did." He looked thoughtful for a moment before continuing. "Well, come along. I'll show you around and explain your part as deus ex machina."

Jack, however, stayed rooted to the spot. Straightening her shoulders and stiffening her spine, she faced him squarely. Reserves of confidence that had remained untapped in life welled up inside of her.

"I have to get to the DoDD. Now. It's about more than just balance. It's about stopping her before it's too late."

He stared thoughtfully at her for a moment before consenting. "Very well."

Death walked through the doorway with Jack and emerged to find himself alone at the end of the Human Demise hallway. Hoping she'd simply projected into an office, he began a quick search. Almost everyone was either on assignment or gone for the day. The few that remained brightened visibly upon catching sight of him. The Department had never been the most cheerful place in the Beyond, but now he found it positively morose. He hadn't been a bad boss, but he'd never expected so many souls to be happy to see him.

He reached the door to Gina's reception area, the gateway to his own office. Immediately he noted the brand new door. No longer a long pane of glass in a walnut frame, now it was a sturdy fireproof door with a peephole. What might have once been dread began to unfurl in his stomach. He felt no need to reach for the little chrome flask inside his jacket, though. Instead, his thoughts were solely of Jack. Was she trapped in there right now with her sister, unsure how to proceed and locked in a deadly struggle?

Death took a deep breath and swung open the door, prepared to do an uncharacteristic and unformulated heroic deed. Instead, he came face to face with the mirror image of Jack. It seemed to take her a second to recognize the significance of a strange man bursting into her office. Then, like a flash of lightning, she realized who he was.

Without a second thought, Mallory grabbed a fist full of pencils from Gina's desk. Her touch set them alight as she pulled back her hand and flung them like knives. Death barely had time to dodge. As it was, a wayward spark burned a smoldering hole. Things weren't off to an auspicious start. In the last few days, Mallory had apparently embraced her powers. While his grasp on the abilities was far superior, the strength behind hers was much greater.

Without batting an eye, he mentally pulled the room's lone bookcase down in her direction. With a satisfying crash it dragged Mallory to the ground with it. She screamed and he smiled, walking over to the heap. In his hands appeared the seven-foot scythe. As he approached the cracked wood and scattered manuscripts, it shifted.

Suddenly, pieces of the shelves splintered and exploded in every direction. He ducked and rolled behind the desk, dropping the weapon. Something sliced into his upper arm as he moved, and he seethed between his teeth. Looking down, a sliver had cut through his sleeve and now stuck out of his arm. Thank God he didn't bleed, Death thought. Grimacing, he pulled out the wooden shard and threw it to the floor.

"You won't get rid of me that easily!" Mallory crowed. "I am the Head of Human Demise, now. I have the power to put you away forever!"

That, more than anything else, made him angry. He had done nothing but dedicate his afterlife to ensuring the integrity of this department, and now she was authorized to send him into the Great Nothingness. He peeked around the corner of the desk to see her out from under the rubble and picking up his blade. Why hadn't it disappeared?

"This is very pretty, but it looks a bit too dangerous for you. I think I'll keep it. What's the Grim Reaper without her scythe?"

Leaping from his crouched position, he locked eyes with the handle and threw his entire being into ripping it from her hands. It flew across the room and embedded itself in the far wall with almost as much noise as the bookshelf falling. He wondered if the new door had made the room soundproof. Surely, no one could avoid hearing the commotion they were making.

In the moment he was distracted, she struck

again. Mallory kicked a book at him and while he batted it away, she picked up the desk chair and swung it at him. It was a small chair, but the unexpected force of it knocked him backward into the wall. He grit his teeth and tried to make the chair explode apart in her hands, but she dropped it and grabbed him by the shirt.

"I'm stronger than you, now," she growled at him. Her nails lengthened and sharpened, ripping his shirt and digging into his chest. "I. Win."

Mallory's other hand glowed as she reached for Death's face.

"Stop."

The single word of command held power, clarity, and most of all confidence. Both combatants turned toward the sound and found Jack standing in the now open doorway. She glided into the room with more grace of motion than he'd ever seen her use. Stopping mere feet from her sister, she spoke again. "Is this your plan then, Mal? You're going to pick us off one by one?"

The room seemed brighter now, as if the light radiated from Jack herself, and Mallory looked both afraid and infuriated. The glow around her hand dulled, and she retracted her claws from Death's chest. Jack continued speaking in soft, but commanding tones.

"What happened, Mal? We were so close, almost like we were the same person. And now

I've had to forfeit my own life to straighten out your afterlife. How could you let bad luck contort your soul into such a veil of hatred?"

Mal's nostrils flared and her fingers flexed. Without warning, she launched herself off of Death and onto her twin. Unflinching, Jack raised her hands and caught those coming toward her. They locked in a physical struggle, each trying to overpower the other.

Now that they were together, Death could see the subtle physical differences between them. Mallory was lean and wiry, with darker skin and lighter hair. Jack, on the other hand, was slender but toned. The former looked older, too, though he wasn't sure why.

"You're the one that did this! You've always been the one holding me back," screamed Mallory, gaining a little footing over her sister. Jack ducked as Mal took a swing at her. Quickly, she swung around behind her assailant and attempted to pin her arms down.

"No, you never tried to rise above your circumstances. You never once felt anything but pity for yourself. In your pursuit of martyrdom you became a spiteful, raving, old woman!"

"Old woman?" The insult seemed to give Mal new strength in outrage. She broke free of her sister's grasp and Jack stumbled backward and landed on her ass.

"You are the reason I'm here!" Mallory

screeched. Slowly, like a ghost in a horror movie, she approached her sister. "You and your perfect little life. Even when we were kids you stole the show. Every time I was laid up in the hospital, do you know what I always heard? 'Oh, Jackie's so lucky! Oh, I'm so glad you're okay, Jackie! Sweet little Jackie!' But, I figured it out. You were stealing my luck. You stole all the light so I was left in shadow. I couldn't get good grades because you had them. I couldn't have the best boyfriend because he was yours. I couldn't follow my dreams because you did.

"Did you know I had dreams, Jackie? Instead I was stuck moldering away in that musty, old house with a batty, old lady who couldn't remember my name. You, who had the perfect job and people who loved you. You stole all that from me. You ran off and lived my life and left me to die. So, I did. And now I'm more powerful than you'll ever be!"

Mal towered over her intended victim, the piranha-like glower spreading across her triumphant face. Her shadow began to eclipse the light around Jack as her features distorted into something far less than human. She seemed to be larger in presence than before, and her breathing was ragged with vengeance and satisfaction. Suddenly, she launched herself at Jack, who simply held up a hand with the palm facing out. It slammed into Mal's fast-approaching chest, stopping her in her tracks. A single tear slid down Jack's cheek.

"I'm so sorry, Mal. For this. For everything."

Mallory's eyes grew wide and all her features rippled back into normalcy. Light exploded around the edges of Jack's hand and more tears fell as Jack concentrated on what she had to do.

"Jackie?" came a voice from childhood, free of malice and madness and grief. Turning a deaf ear, Jack took a deep breath and pushed the punishment through to its end. The light turned dark and, like a black hole, suddenly seemed to be sucking Mal in. Within a moment she had disappeared and Jack was left staring at the empty space.

Chapter Twenty

"SO, that's it, then?"

Jack sat in the ruins of Gina's office, gazing emptily at the place where her sister had stood. Death approached her and helped her to her feet. "She was too far gone, Jack. There's nothing you could have done."

She nodded in silent agreement, but it didn't stem the ache. With a grimace, he pressed a hand against his chest and slowly pulled it across the ripped flesh and fabric. Fast as a blink, the frayed threads whipped out and rebound themselves into smooth silk. He ran the same hand down the arm of his jacket, then across a charred hole, to the same effect.

Straightening his tie, Death made his way to the far side of the room and with some difficulty removed a large stick from the wall. Jack's eyes flew wide when she realized it was the scythe from Hakone Gardens, buried almost to the hilt in the plaster-covered brick. He examined the blade, blew off some dust, then allowed it to vanish in a ribbon of smoke.

Together, they picked their way out of the wrecked office and started down the long hallway toward Santana's office. From behind them, the faint ding of an elevator echoed and heels clacked on the hard floor. Jack turned her face to see who was approaching and was surprised to see Gina followed closely by a young girl with golden ringlets.

"Sir. Sir!" Gina called out, hurrying forward while her companion strolled casually behind. Death turned to look, as well, allowing for them to catch up. His pensive eyes narrowed at the teen, but he said nothing. "Sir, forgive me, but I don't think the two of you should face Nickleby alone. He's much older and more powerful than either of you. Just because he works through proxies like her sister doesn't mean he can't do a job himself. Who knows what he could do."

Jack felt the tension sizzling in the air. She knew he wanted this confrontation with his erstwhile boss almost as much as she'd needed to face Mallory. Still, Gina had a point. The thought of ending up in Sheol alongside Mal had her skin breaking out in chills. If they weren't to confront him, though, what were they to do? And what was teenager, immortal or not, going to bring to the table?

As if reading her mind, the girl spoke up.

"I am authorized by the remaining PTB to deal with Mr. Nickleby." The gleeful look on her face was not lost on Jack. "If you will follow me, please." She strode forward with long, graceful steps and passed them.

Death leaned down as they fell into place behind her. "That's Iris, messenger of the Powers that Be and the most powerful being outside of them. Never cross her. She isn't as sweet as she looks."

"Thank you," Iris called back over her shoulder with genuine pleasure at his description. Death straightened and silence fell as they wound their way through the labyrinthine halls. Soon the threesome entered Luneil's domain just as Iris breezed past her and into the next office without so much as a nod. Ms. Fezwick's eyes were wide and her lips were so thinset in a frown that they were nearly invisible. Gina crossed her arms and stared down at the pixie-like secretary as if standing guard.

"Why, hello, Iris," Santana Nickleby's oily voice greeted his guest cordially. "To what do I owe the pleasure of your beautiful company?"

Jack and Death walked in behind the celestial agent and all pretense fell from the accused's face. In fact, it became quite terrible, contorting in an almost inhuman mask of indignation.

"What is the meaning of this?!" he cried. The lights flickered with his uncaged acrimony, but his visitors remained calm.

"It's over, Nick," Death said simply.

"Santana Nickleby, I have been authorized by the Powers that Be to terminate your employment with the Beyond. However, due to service rendered, you will be offered a choice between two severance packages. The first is you go quietly into the afterlife, leaving behind your cares and powers in the hope of grace and peace. The second is that you retire into the mortal world where you can cause no more irreparable harm and can no longer instigate, shall we say, revolution."

"What?" Death shouted. "After everything he's done over the centuries, the millennia? After you threatened me for something far more trivial?"

Iris held up a hand, ending his rant before it had a chance to snowball. She continued addressing Nickleby in an even tone. "Those are your options. Choose wisely. And remember, if you attempt to escape or otherwise deviate from these paths, I swear by all that is holy I will unmake you."

Nickleby's puffy lips twisted into a malign sense of triumph. "I'll take the retirement. Mortals were always more fun when dealt with directly. You'll be—" he was cut off as, upon his acceptance, he faded out of the office.

Jack looked to the two remaining in the room. "Where did he go?" she asked. Death took her by the arm and turned to escort her back into the reception area with a sigh. Iris answered pertly, though the question had not been directed at her.

"To the mortal realm, where I'm sure he'll attempt to wreck havoc amongst the humans. Fortunately, I diminished his powers beyond all recognition. If he's able to cause any serious trouble, I'd be very surprised."

"Why didn't you just send him to Sheol?"

"He has been around too long and done too much for the Beyond. Some, like myself, were in favor of it; however, the majority felt it was a slippery slope sending one of their own into such a place. Unfortunately in this case, the majority rules."

They stopped next to Gina, who was now having a staring contest with a distinctly terrified Luneil Fezwick. In all their years in the same department, Death had never seen the latter so confidence-less.

"What's going to happen to me?" she quaked out.

"You will be reassigned," replied Iris matter-of-factly. "Preferably somewhere where a proper eye can be kept on you. You're a faithful worker and you've never had a bad report, so take this as a warning to keep it that way. Report to Immortal Resources and they will get you sorted." She turned to Death and held out her petite hand.

"As for you, the Powers that Be would like to formally offer you Santana's position, should you choose to take it. Or, you may remain as the Head of Human Demise. The choice is yours."

Death thought about it for a moment. On the one side, he enjoyed his job as Grim Reaper. On the other, he wished nothing more than to be rid of the potential for another Katerina. Taking her proffered hand, he accepted the new position.

"Very well, then. I'll leave you to sort out your staff. Oh, and Miss Devlin?" Iris turned her large, brown eyes on Jack. "You have an appointment to appear before the PTB in exactly twenty minutes. Please be prompt." With that, she walked out of the doorway and disappeared down the hall with Luneil in her wake.

Silence reigned, each sorting their own thoughts. Jack drew her brows together, a single question worming its way through her brain.

"I don't understand."

"What don't you understand," Death asked, his voice still disgruntled.

"If she could do that, if she's that powerful, why did I have to die? Why couldn't she just take care of it?"

"Who, Iris?"

"Yes!" Jack cried. She could feel tears gathering at her lashes, but she refused to let them fall this time. "If that little girl could take out the man in charge of your entire department, why couldn't she do something about my sister?"

"Jack," Gina put in gently. "Few but the Fates have the power of prognostication. I didn't fetch her, I ran into her on my way down. Neither of us had any way of knowing she would get involved."

"So if we'd just waited two hours, none of this would have happened."

"In two hours we still wouldn't have known because we were with you. In two hours she could have come after you again and done to you what you did to her. In two hours you would still be marked for death on a celestial scale."

Jack took a deep, shaky breath and clenched her jaw. Then she gave her head a quick jerk of understanding.

"Well," Gina spoke up, casting a sad glance at her former boss. "Now that that's taken care of, I suppose this is goodbye."

"And just where do you think you're going? I need you."

"But, I've quit. I walked out on my post and willfully worked against my superiors. All I have now is the hope for a happy afterlife."

He considered her earnestness for a moment before replying. "My dear Ms. Valenka, did you tender a letter of resignation?"

"Not as such, no."

"Did I, as your immediate supervisor, accept your verbal resignation?"

"No." A twitch was beginning to play at the corners of Gina's mouth in anticipation of his response.

"Then, as Henry Robert once said, your responsibilities do not cease merely because you resign. Only once your resignation has been formally accepted can you step down. And, Ms. Valenka, I do not accept your resignation."

Jack had never seen Gina so happy. For a moment she looked as though she was going to throw herself at him, but he pointedly straightened his tie and she thought the better of it. Death glanced at his watch. "Please allow me to escort you to your meeting, Miss Devlin," he said with a small bow and an offered arm.

If Jack had thought the Beyond was large before, now she felt infinitesimal by comparison. They wound their way through passage after passage, sometimes taking stairs, other times taking elevators. Souls shuffled back and forth with coffee and folders and clipboards. Few bothered to glance their way after they left the Department of Death and Demise. Everyone seemed far too focused on their own work to stick their nose in someone else's wanderings.

Finally, eighteen minutes later, Jack and Death stood outside the massive, handsomely carved entrance. They heard a faint murmuring from behind it and she gave her companion a nervous look. He seemed distracted by his own thoughts and raised a reluctant hand to open one of the two wooden doors. As they stepped inside, all conversation ceased and every eye swung to the duo.

Jack found herself standing at the head of a large conference room. A gigantic, highly polished table dominated the space and around it sat six men and women of all ages and nationalities. Most were dressed in variations on formal business wear, though a few were considerably more eccentric. All, however, had a demeanor of grim purpose. The air was rife with power and intimidation descended like a hand from above.

Death took up the only empty chair, which sat closest to where she stood. A man in a bright purple agbada and matching aso-oke hat exchanged an askance look with another in brocade waistcoat and a pair of pince-nez, but no one objected. Besides, Jack thought to herself, it was his rightful seat now, since he'd taken over Nickleby's job.

Despite the incredibly antagonistic beginning to their relationship, she was very glad he was with her now. A woman several chairs away, almost at the head of the table, cleared her throat. Jack turned her attention to the sound, sharply aware of her position of scrutiny. The woman, of Middle Eastern descent with a warm and open—almost motherly—face, held her head high and leveled her clear gaze on Jack.

"Jacquelyn Katerina Devlin?"

"Yes, ma'am."

"You are currently invested with the powers of the Celestial Intervention Agency, am I correct?"

"I believe so."

"And you recently used those powers in conjunction with your antemortem experiences to aid against internal destruction within the Department of Death and Demise?"

"Yes, ma'am," Jack repeated, feeling a bit like a third-grader kept after class. The woman glanced down at a sheaf of papers before her, and the motion caused light to catch for one brilliant moment on the golden star at her lapel. A young man leaned in close to whisper something, and Jack thought she heard him use the name Madonna. Her breath caught in her throat.

"In your antemortem, I am taken to understand, you chose to die that others might be saved. I find this quite remarkable for someone in your position, as I am assured you were given the chance to evade death for as long as you wished. My question for you is, why?"

"It was the right thing to do. It was the only thing to do," Jack replied simply. The woman looked satisfied.

"Miss Devlin, based upon our observations, we would like to offer you a more permanent position in the Beyond. Or, if you so choose, as a reward we would be willing to let you return to the mortal plane."

"Would I be returned to life? Or would I be like Athena and Mr. Nickleby?"

"The latter. I'm afraid that once dead, you may not resume true mortality. Your soul is free and will not allow itself to be constrained again."

Jack remained silent for a few minutes. She thought of everything she'd been through. She thought of the use she could be in the Beyond, but she also thought of Nate. If she returned to Earth then she could find him, or someone else, and continue on with her life right where she left off. She would have her friends and her job and a whole new perspective on life.

Mentally, she shook her head. Her life would be hollow. Not only had she seen too much, but she would be stuck in perpetuity. She would be forced to watch all her loved ones pass on forever, the only constant in a constantly aging and changing world. And then there was her faith. Could she really continue to believe after all of this? Especially if she chose immortality. Would the unanswered questions from all she'd seen wear at her over the centuries until there was nothing left? Jack swallowed.

"If you don't mind, ma'am, I think an afterlife would be reward enough." All eyes turned, shocked, toward her. Even Death looked for a moment like he was going to say something to intervene. She continued quickly before anyone spoke. "I've experienced a lot over the last two weeks that has challenged everything I've ever believed in. I want to hold onto something, even as small as my faith in God and Heaven, because to me it's not small. I have to stay true to that. In the end, we're all only made up of our beliefs."

A wide smile broke across the other woman's face. She stood from her chair and approached Jack with unerring grace. Leaning in so close her lips grazed Jack's ear, she whispered a single answer to all of Jack's unspoken questions. Peace curved the corners of Jack's mouth.

"Thank you for everything," she said to the woman, though she looked directly at Death. A pained look creased his brow for a moment before it eased at her smile. Jack took a deep, steadying breath, letting the sense of freedom and serenity fill her. Then, gently, she faded away into the unknown.

Acknowledgments

FIRST and foremost I'd like to thank my husband, without whom I never could have made it this far. Thank you for all the plothole patches and late-night consolation.

Also, no acknowledgment would be complete without a million-watt shoutout to my critique partner and fellow author Sunniva Dee. This book has changed so much because of you (remember when it was a two week roadtrip?), but I don't regret a thing! You. Are. Amazing.

To my beta readers Veva, Ann, Nichole, Tessa, Jennifer, Suzanne, and Matt: I appreciate all your feedback! I hope you enjoyed being along for the crazy ride that was the evolution of this book.

And finally, I couldn't have done it without my amazing editor Michelle, who sent me back pages upon pages of bloodied margins. It was worth it.

About the Author

LEIGH has been writing stories since before she could spell, drawing pamphlets of illustrations and then reading them aloud to anyone who would pay attention.

In addition to degrees in both journalism and history, she's been the editor-in-chief of a city newspaper, a manager at a 14-screen movie theater, the baker at an award-winning Italian restaurant, and a nanny. Her work has appeared around the internet, as well as in newspapers, magazines, and poetry anthologies.

She lives with her husband in the Deep South, where she co-runs a family business and is hard at work plotting her next big literary adventure.

Visit

LeighTeale.com

For More Information About
Upcoming Releases,
The Latest News, and Events!

Become A Fan On Facebook:

"improbable, beautiful, and afraid of nothing"

Starlings have no particular religion or ethos. Instead, they have wonder, tempered by instinct and rounded by passion. They can learn from Mozart or Schubert, but ultimately their song is their own trilling masterpiece. They sing of the world around them and of the world within themselves. Experience is their hymnal and the universe is their accompaniment. So too must authors and publishers take wonder and passion and combine it with knowledge to create new life —literary art that can cross the ages and touch every soul. That is our mission at Midnight Starling Press: To cultivate works across multiple genres that strike a chord. Quirky, edgy, young, old. We represent books that speak to the heart of what it means to be both of and in the world—no matter the place, time, or person.

Visit

MidnightStarling.com

For More Information About
Our Authors, Books,
Events, and Much More!

Become A Fan On Facebook: